THE COLONEL AND MADAME GIN SLING

By

Jay Alt

KCM PUBLISHING

A DIVISION OF KCM DIGITAL MEDIA, LLC

Credits

The Colonel and Madame Gin Sling by Jay Alt

ISBN-13: 978-1-939961-32-7
ISBN-10: 1939961327

First Edition

Publisher: Michael Fabiano
KCM Publishing
www.kcmpublishing.com

For Easy

Acknowledgements

This book would not have been possible without the help and suggestions of several people. First of course, I must thank my wife Polly, who is a great editor and proof-reader. My agent Lois De La Haba, whose encouragement and sage guidance proved invaluable. Michael Fabiano, the publisher whose vision made this book a reality. And finally, Easy my cat, whose contented purring on my lap during the writing of this book helped me to persevere.

The Colonel
and
Madame Gin Sling

Jay Alt

Contents

1

Macau, exotic Macau, started to come into focus. From the distant blur, individual buildings were starting to emerge as the ferry from Hong Kong approached its landing. As they neared land, Pete Smith—the Colonel—saw randomly placed high-rises without a clear focal point of activity. But a clear picture of what made Macau tick had yet to become apparent. Macau was supposed to be a city of "anything goes." But, from his vantage point at the rail the city still looked like a cubist painting.

After serving exactly twenty years in the army, most of it in Special Forces, he had retired. Not having devised a plan for life after the military, and knowing he would be at loose ends upon separation from the army, he decided to take a tour of Asia. He had already seen most of Europe, the Middle East, and some of South America while in the service. Still, he would eventually need to find a job, and he doubted that he would have months off at any time in the near future.

The Colonel had already been approached by two private security firms inquiring about his availability after separation from the service. But, he decided this would be the perfect time to do a "grand tour" of Asia. Macau was the third stop on his Asian odyssey.

A cab took him from the ferry dock to the Sun Place Macau Resort and Casino. The entrance was typical of most casinos—about sixty feet wide with multiple sets of automatic doors. As he entered through the doors on the far right, he noticed a row of slot machines that curved around to the front desk. It had intermittent gaps to allow passage into the main casino area. Evidently, it was possible to start losing your money while checking into your room.

When he was halfway across the entry area and starting to turn toward the front desk, a man who had been leaning against the wall on the left side of the entry started to run across the area with a knife in his hand. The man never looked at him, his focus clearly elsewhere. Twenty years of Special Forces training kicked in reflexively, and Pete reacted. He dropped the handle of the suitcase he was pulling, which made a loud clattering noise. He took three steps and tripped the man. The man went down, landing flat on his stomach. Pete immediately pinned the man to the floor by placing his left knee on the man's right shoulder blade. His other knee he placed on the man's right forearm. Pete pried the knife from the man's right hand as a large Chinese man appeared from between the slot machines.

"I got him," said the large Chinese man. He reached down and grabbed the front of the man's shirt, lifting him so his feet barely touched the ground. Two uniformed security guards arrived from the casino area as Pete finished dusting off his trousers.

"What are you going to do with him?" he asked the large Chinese guy as he handed the would-be assassin to the security guards.

"Probably break one of his legs and put him on the Hong Kong ferry."

Pete chuckled at that remark.

The noise of the suitcase dropping, which had attracted the attention of the large Chinese man, caused the woman he had been escorting to look as well. She looked at the Colonel carefully. He had a deep tan, apparently from spending a lot of time outdoors. Large arms, a thick chest, and a very interesting face were all she could see. The rest of him was blocked by the slot machines. As the large Chinese man returned to her side, she asked, "Who was that guy? The one who stopped my uncle from killing me? He seemed pretty capable."

"Just some guest about to check in, I think."

"Well my uncle obviously wants to kill me. I'm glad the guy stopped him."

"I would have stopped your uncle if that guy hadn't."

"I'm sure you would have. Oh, by the way, break both of uncle's legs and put him on the Hong Kong ferry." Violence was no stranger to this lady. She had built a fortune on houses of prostitution and gambling. Indeed, she stood in her flagship gambling house, the Sun Palace. Madame Gin Sling continued toward her destination still curious about the man. Perhaps, she thought, he would like to join her staff. But, somehow she doubted that. As she continued on, her thoughts turned again to the man. He had reacted quickly and used only enough force to end the situation, she thought.

The man resumed his journey to the front desk as the noise of the slot machines continued to assault his senses with their bells, whistles, and blinking lights. The coins tumbling into catch pans and the other sound effects were designed to create the illusion that everyone wins in this casino. He shrugged his shoulders, thinking to himself perhaps it did generate enthusiasm in some people that was apparently lost on him.

As he waited in line, he reflected on the events that had just transpired. Twenty years of training in Delta Force, the army's elite Special Forces unit, had not deserted him when he had left the army and taken off his uniform. It also occurred to him that Macau did indeed appear to be a town where "anything goes." He had been in town less than thirty minutes and had already interceded one attempted stabbing. He was also semi curious to know if they were really going to break the guy's leg and put him on the Hong Kong ferry.

After a short wait in line, it was his turn. The receptionist found his reservation, and a few minutes later he was on his way to room 818. The receptionist had given him a plastic room key the size of a credit card. He hated those plastic things. They never worked very well. But, after reaching his room, to his surprise this one worked on the first swipe. The lock's green light started blinking immediately. He entered his digs for the next four days.

Typical hotel room, he thought, idly wondering where hotels went to buy such awful art. The furniture was also early Flatbush Avenue Renaissance.

He felt grungy after the ferry ride from Hong Kong and decided to take a shower. A quick investigation of the bathroom revealed that the hotel provided the necessary toiletries: soap, shampoo, and conditioner. The hot water came almost instantaneously, and five minutes later he was drying himself with the fluffiest hotel towel he had ever experienced.

He lay down on the bed and dozed off. Awakening, he looked at the hotel clock, which read six fifty-five. He could not believe it! He had slept for more than three hours. He arose and went over to the dresser where he had left his watch. It verified the time, although the hotel clock might have been just a few minutes fast.

He dressed in khaki pants and a dark blue Lacoste shirt. Topsiders completed his garb for the evening. He checked his pockets to be sure he had everything, especially the key card, and he headed for the elevators. He pushed the down button, a bell chimed subtlety, and the doors opened. An Asian couple was already in the elevator, each with a suitcase on wheels. The stop at his floor apparently had interrupted their conversation because as soon as the doors closed the wife or girlfriend verbally lit into the man. They, or she rather, spoke in Chinese, but from the contrite expression on his face there was no doubt he had lost more than she thought they could afford.

When the doors opened at the casino level, he indicated the couple should exit first. The woman's diatribe continued unabated. A confirmed bachelor, he thought, God, what a pain in the ass women can be, and without really trying.

He did look forward to playing blackjack and set off in search of the tables. By following the noise he arrived on the main floor of the casino. Typical of casinos in general there were two rows of about forty tables with a pit in between. The pit contained two podiums where the pit bosses kept spare cards. A telephone occupied the top of each podium. He walked idly down the tables looking for a seat at a table with, he hoped, a cold dealer. It was then that he saw her for the first time. The most beautiful woman he had ever seen. She was clearly Eurasian; her dark eyes were mildly almond shaped but not to the same extent as the local Chinese. He could see only the top half of her body, the lower half being blocked by the pit bosses' podium. She stood about five eight or nine, black hair piled on the top of her head except for a lock about one inch wide that curled down her back, ending just under her shoulder blades. High cheekbones and alabaster skin set her apart from other woman. She was reasonably well endowed in the chest but not overly so. The sleeveless electric blue mandarin-style dress would have looked gaudy and overdone on anyone else. He wistfully envisioned it slit up to her hip on one side. Her arms revealed an excellent muscular tone. She had double pierced ears and wore gold hoops in the lower holes and diamond studs, of at least a carat, above them. There was not an ounce of fat on her anywhere that he could see. A seat opened at the table in front of him, and he took it immediately.

As he bought a hundred dollars' worth of chips from the dealer he asked, "Who is that woman in the pit?"

"Madame Gin Sling," replied the dealer after glancing over his shoulder.

Two other people had left the table during their brief exchange and because there were now fewer players, the pace of the game picked up. He did not have the opportunity to ask any follow-up questions about the lady standing in the pit. As he played he tried to watch her, but the speed of the dealer and remaining players forced him to pay more attention to the cards than he really wanted. Once while glancing up he noticed that the woman's gait seemed bizarre, but refocusing on the cards he could not determine why. He lost track of the woman as his attention shifted to the cards.

After losing fifty dollars in the blink of an eye, he decided to change tables. Evidently, this was not the cold dealer he had hoped to find. The woman was nowhere to be seen. He found another seat, recouped his losses, and won about fifty more when hunger struck him with a vengeance. The ham sandwich he had eaten around noon on the ferry from Hong Kong no longer holding his appetite in check, he left the table in search of a restaurant.

One of the casino walls had dark hardwood paneling on one section of it. A sign, incorporated into the paneling, advertised "The English Pub." He pushed through a set of double doors and entered a room also paneled in a dark hardwood. A rectangular bar stood to the front of the room. There was a six-foot passageway between the bar and a row of tables making a "u" around the rectangular back bar. Red leather booths, raised about a foot above the level of the floor, surrounded the room against the walls. Only a few people sat at the bar, leaving him his choice of seats. He wandered down the left side of the bar, finally settling on the last stool on that side. The bartender followed him down the bar and took his order for a Heineken immediately. Glancing around the room he saw her again. This time she was seated in a booth against the back wall reading. He wondered what she would find so fascinating to read in a bar. She looked up as she fitted a cigarette into an ebony cigarette holder. She saw him staring, and he glanced away quickly.

A large Chinese man approached her and leaned over and said something to her.

Food forgotten for the moment, he ordered a second beer, this time with a glass. For the next thirty minutes he could not take his eyes off the woman. She captivated him pure and simple. I am acting like a teenager, he thought, wryly. Maybe I should go in the men's room and check for zits. She answered the phone at least five times during the half hour he watched her. Each time she looked up she caught him staring.

Finally, he shifted his gaze to the front, but when he looked back the woman was approaching him. She was missing her left leg and rather than use the latest thing in artificial limbs, she had an old-fashioned peg leg, a la Captain Ahab. Her peg leg, which appeared made of carved ivory, solved the mystery of her gait. God, he wondered, how had he not noticed her peg leg before? His powers of observation were normally outstanding; he never missed the obvious. But, he sure had this time. She walked directly and purposely toward him. He revised his estimate of her height. She would probably stand about five three or four without the high heels.

His staring annoyed her. But as she approached him she realized his staring was not the reason she found herself walking toward him. This was a very good-looking man. Brown hair, blue eyes, and very well-developed arms and shoulders were all she could see. She assumed the rest of him to be as fit as the portion she could see. There appeared to be no fat on him at all. This was the man she wanted to know more about earlier in the day. He had piqued her curiosity. For some reason, which she wasn't able to explain to herself, she continued to approach him wondering why at the same time.

"You keep staring."

"I know. It is very rude and I apologize. But—like the moth to the flame, I am drawn to great beauty."

"Oh, brother," she groaned in perfect unaccented American English. "Actually, I work for the hotel. I wanted to thank you for stopping the man with the knife in the entrance today." A plausible reason for being aggressive she thought, as she made it up while standing in front of him.

He waved his hand. "It was nothing," he said. "What happened to the guy, anyway?"

"He is healing in Hong Kong," she said in a blasé manner.

They really did break his leg, he thought.

She started to turn away but stopped. Hesitating for just a second, she turned to face him again. "Would you like to join me?" She had no idea why she had asked him to join her. In fact, it was so out of character for her she startled herself as soon as the words left her mouth. She had sworn off men more than twenty years ago.

"It would be my pleasure," he answered without a moment's hesitation, his curiosity about the fate of the attacker forgotten. As she led him back to her table, he realized she was as beautiful from the back as the front. Perfect hourglass shape, he thought. The missing leg did not detract from her obvious appeal but somehow created an exotic aura. She entered the booth from the left side and slid around to the center. He sat to her right. "I'm Pete Smith," he said, by way of introduction, adding almost as an afterthought, "and you are?"

"I am Madame Gin Sling."

"No, I meant your real name."

"That is real name," she said, slipping into Chinese-accented English.

"Madame Gin Sling was a character in an old Gene Tierney movie who owned a gambling joint in Shanghai. Does that mean you own the joint?"

"You pretty good, but the character's name was Mother Gin Sling," she said, still in the Chinese accent.

"What should I call you for short? 'Madame' has a somewhat unpleasant connotation and 'Gin Sling' sounds like I'm ordering a cocktail."

"Ha, ha," she said as the phone on the table rang. She answered it.

He realized that she had deflected his question again. He listened to the one-sided conversation in rapid-fire Chinese, or what he thought was Chinese. As she spoke on the phone, she realized that he did not know she owned the hotel.

When she hung up he asked, "What language were you speaking"?

"Chinese, or rather Cantonese."

"Are you Chinese? You don't look it," he said, at once realizing the social blunder he had made. "If you don't mind me asking," he tacked on, trying to make a graceful recovery although he doubted that was possible.

She smiled. "I was born in Vietnam." She liked his belated attempt to be polite. He seemed different from the other men she had met. He was not condescending, for one thing, or arrogant, and he was polite but not fawning. She decided to reserve judgment on him. He intrigued her and she knew it, although she did not know what to do about it. Then the thought passed through her brain that even if she did know what to do, she wouldn't do it. She reminisced for a moment. Most of the men she had met were intimated by her wealth. And the idea of having to take a bunch of guff off anyone, let alone some man, was just plain repugnant. She'd been running her own show for more than twenty years, and she liked it that way. But . . .

"Why did you come to Macau?" she inquired.

"Well, that's a long story," he said. She wiggled the fingers of her right hand, indicating to continue. He sighed, "Okay, but it is not a very interesting story. I retired from the army three weeks ago after twenty years. I saw a good deal of the Middle East, Europe, and some of South America, but I never saw any of Asia. So I decided to take a tour of Asia when I retired. This is probably the only time in my life I will have the opportunity to do it. I need to get a job when I get back to the States."

"Where have you been so far?" she queried.

"Tokyo and Hong Kong."

"When you leave here where are you going?"

"Beijing, Shanghai, Singapore, Bangkok, Jakarta, Sidney, Auckland, and Tahiti."

The just recited litany surprised her. "Wow! That is quite a trip. How long will you be gone?"

"About three months all told."

"And then, are you going home?" she asked.

"If you mean back to the States, yes. But I don't really have a home right at the moment. My last duty station was in Germany. So when I get off the plane in LA I've got a big decision to make." She smiled at that, and he said, "You should do that more often."

"What?"

"Smile."

"Oh, please."

"I doubt that I am the first person to tell you this but you become much more beautiful than you already are, when you smile."

"Stop with all the flattery," she said smiling. Still, he had the feeling that she was secretly pleased in spite of what she said.

"Changing the subject for a moment, if I may, why all the phone calls and reading in a bar?"

"I am sort of a troubleshooter for the hotel. The paperwork is shift cash reports. They often show problems developing while they are easy to solve," she replied.

"I cannot help but ask..." She looked at him expectantly. "Is your artificial leg made out of real ivory?"

"Yes."

"I feel compelled to say that I am not certain I agree with killing elephants to make artificial limbs for women, no matter how beautiful."

"Neither do I; this is zoo ivory."

"What is zoo ivory?"

"Have you ever noticed that when you see pictures of elephants in the wild, their tusks are six or seven feet long? Well, zoos and circuses prune their elephants' tusks for safety reasons, and that is where this ivory comes from."

The fact that he mentioned her leg surprised her. Most people tried to ignore it, some successfully, some not. But, this guy, Pete, not only mentioned it but his question implied a mild rebuke. She did not intimate him, she realized, smiling inwardly.

"One last little question before we get to the big question. How did you ever learn to speak English so well?"

She responded to that question with a bored look on her face, as if it had been asked many times before. "When I first came to Hong Kong I worked with two American girls and an English girl, and we spent a lot of time watching old movies together. They were kind enough to take the trouble to teach me. Now, what is the big question?"

"Will you take pity on a poor, homeless, wandering foreigner, who knows no one in Asia, except you, of course, and have dinner with me?"

A smile had broken out on her face before he finished the question. She did not know why but the question and the flattery implied completely surprised her. "Yes," she answered simply.

"Where would you like to eat?"

"Is here okay?"

"I thought this was only a bar," he said

"You can eat here as well."

"Then this is just fine unless you would prefer somewhere else. Being a stranger in town I place myself in your capable hands."

"This is just fine," she said with a smile. She couldn't seem to stop smiling.

He missed seeing Madame Gin Sling nod ever so slightly and said, "How do we find a waiter with a couple of menus?" No sooner were the words out of his mouth than a waiter appeared at the edge of the table.

"May I help you, sir?"

"Yes, we would like a couple of menus," he said.

The waiter immediately looked at Madame Gin Sling, unsure what to do. "Just order what you want. There are five restaurants in the hotel. Almost everything is available."

"Really?"

He chose the American male standard fare: steak and potatoes. She opted for a salad Niçoise. As the waiter started to turn away, he asked for a wine list. The waiter stopped, apparently expecting him to order. All right, he thought, we are going to give this a little test.

"I would like a bottle of Chateau Latour 2000 or 2001 and a bottle of a good Sancerre for the lady."

Without batting an eye, the waiter replied, "Very good, sir."

"I am not much of a drinker," she said

"The French say that if you get the wine right, the food tastes better. I think if you try a glass with your salad you will enjoy both more."

She leaned back in the booth pausing for a moment of introspection. She had sworn off men more than twenty years ago, after having been brutally abused for years. Her subsequent dealings on a personal level had done nothing but reinforced those feelings. Most men seemed to think that greater physical strength meant greater mental prowess, as well. She had not so much as kissed one on the cheek in all that time. But, now this man made her feel like a schoolgirl. The idea that he would order a special bottle of wine so she would enjoy her meal startled her, as did the consideration shown by that act. Most men expected a woman to like their choice of wine. Yet, he had picked something special to complement her meal.

"You must be fairly high up in the management to rate such service," he said.

She decided she did not want him to know who exactly she was at this point. She enjoyed his company immensely and did not want who she was to interfere with that.

"I suppose. I work in the accounting department," she replied, carefully considering her answer. "This hotel has five restaurants but only one kitchen so there really is no inconvenience in ordering as we did."

"How long have you worked here?" he asked.

"Since it opened ten years ago."

"You must like the work," he said.

"I do but sometimes the never-ending grind gets me down. How about you, what did you do in the army, and what will you do now that you are out?"

"Well, I was in Special Forces." A quizzical look appeared on her face so he followed up saying, "the Green Berets."

"You must have enjoyed that to stay twenty years," she said.

"It had its good times and bad times. The last few years were pretty boring. The more you advance in rank, the more desk time seems to be required of you. I enjoyed being in the field. The completion of a successful mission gives you a tremendous feeling of satisfaction."

"That's very dangerous, isn't it?"

"It can be. But the six P principle applies."

"What's that?" she wanted to know.

"Proper preparation prevents piss poor performance."

"Still people get killed don't they?"

"Yes, unfortunately. I remember the name of every man who was killed during a mission. What did Winston Churchill say about that, 'There is nothing as exhilarating as being shot at when they don't hit you,' or something like that. When you are in a firefight there is no time for deliberations. You must make instant decisions and they have to be right."

"Why didn't you leave when it got boring?"

"The pension benefits are great. Because of my pension all my basic living expenses are covered with enough left over for the occasional beer. But, if I want to live well, a job is mandatory."

"What rank were you when you retired?"

"I was a colonel, although my pension is based on a lieutenant colonel's pay."

"Why is that?"

"You have to have served three years in a grade to retire with that as the pay basis for your pension."

"Why didn't you serve the extra time? It's more money isn't it?" she asked.

"I made the decision that I would serve twenty years before I went into the military. When I got to twenty I was not doing one day extra."

The waiter arrived with their dinner.

"Open the Sancerre first," said the Colonel. The waiter did as instructed. "I'll taste for Madame," he said. She watched as he swirled the wine in the glass, then sniffed it, and finally took a small sip. She thought it a little much but politely said nothing. "It is fine," he said to the waiter. The waiter took a fresh glass, filled it, and put it in front of Madame Gin Sling. The waiter went to the bar and returned with another bottle and a clean glass. He showed the bottle to the Colonel. They had the 2000 Latour. That surprised him. He sampled the wine and declared it delicious. The waiter then filled his glass.

She did not normally drink but took a sip of the wine to be polite. She loved it. After a few bites of salad, she realized the salad was better than normal. Another sip of wine improved the taste of the salad even more. "I have new respect for the French. They are right. The right wine does improve the food."

He chuckled at that. The conversation stayed light over the rest of the meal. As soon as he finished, Gin Sling fitted a cigarette into her ebony holder. He lit the cigarette for her with her gold Dunhill lighter. Moments after clearing the table, the waiter reappeared and asked, "Dessert anyone?"

"I don't care for any," she said.

"Nor I," added the Colonel.

"Would you like to have a nightcap in my apartment?" she asked, crushing out her cigarette in an ashtray. She wondered where that came from. What was going on here? She could not understand it. Then she realized she was, for the first time in her life, going "gaga" over a man. She'd heard about it but always thought it complete nonsense.

"Love to," he replied. "Let me pay the bill and we are on our way."

"The hotel gives me a comp here," she said. "They just write it off on the high roller account, so please be my guest."

"You must thank the hotel for me."

As they left the restaurant, he immediately noticed that the two enormous Chinese men he had seen in the restaurant got up and followed them. He was pretty sure one of them had taken the knife-wielding gent off his hands earlier in the day. Again, she surprised him by turning left toward the elevators instead of right toward the entrance. There was a car waiting as luck would have it. The two very large Chinese gentlemen entered as well. He assessed them silently. One stood about six four and looked like Odd Job in *Goldfinger*, the old James Bond movie. The other stood about six two and was built like a walk-in freezer. Neither said anything. When the elevator doors opened, the two followed them out and they went down a short hall.

As they approached the last door, she still wondered what had possessed her to invite him up to her apartment, although she knew the answer to that question. What she did not know was why she wanted to make love to this guy so much. She had not had a man in her bed for more than twenty years, and she had never wanted to make love before. Oh well, she thought, everyone is allowed to do something stupid once in a while. But, then again, maybe it wasn't stupid.

She opened the door and he followed her into a foyer. Directly in front of him was a wall against which was a table with a bowl of alabaster fruit. To the left there was a dining room table, to the right was a living room, but his eye was caught by the picture hanging on the wall directly in front of him. It looked like a real Picasso. Madame Gin Sling had crossed the living room and started down a hall to the right. Before he could say anything, she said tantalizingly over her shoulder, "Are you coming?" She had unzipped the back of her dress, and it slowly slid to the floor. She wondered if she was doing this right.

The question of the Picasso forgotten, he raced to catch up with her as she entered what he guessed was her bedroom. On her back, she had a tattoo of a dragon. It started an inch or two below her neck and ended an inch or so above her derriere. The black lace bra hit the floor next. "What are you waiting for?" she asked. He striped to his underwear in fifteen seconds flat. Then she asked, "Leg on or off?"

"You decide," he said, crawling onto the far side of the king-size bed. That made her smile. If he wanted it on perhaps he was a voyeur of some sort. If he wanted it off, it repulsed him. His answer showed an indifference and acceptance at the same time. She left it on.

She sat down on the edge of the bed still debating the wisdom of what she was doing. He reached an arm across the bed and circled her stomach with it. He drew her close to him, and as she lay back he kissed her. That ended the debate.

"Be careful with me, it has been a very long time." They kissed again.

He said nothing but he cupped her left breast in his right hand and lightly rubbed the nipple with his thumb. The kiss seemed to be never ending, not that she minded. Finally, his hand left her breast and with the back of his fingers he started stroking her stomach ever so gently down to her pelvic bone. After a minute his hand continued to her clitoris. Slowly he brushed her clitoris, and finally his hand slide to her vagina. The wetness told him all he needed to know.

He entered her slowly. Her hips began to move involuntarily. He let her set the pace. After about fifteen minutes she was building to a crescendo. They climaxed together. As she did, she said something loudly in what he thought was Chinese. They were both breathing very deeply. As her breathing slowed down, she said. "That was first time for me."

"What, making love?"

"No, climaxing. I've heard about it, but never experienced it before."

He pulled her closer and rolled onto his left side. Her back was against his torso and he put his arm over her. The idea of leaving flashed through his mind, but before he could arrive at a final decision he fell asleep.

He awoke feeling great. Looking around a bit, the clock on the bedside table said seven fifty-four. Madame Gin Sling was gone. There was a note on the pillow next to him, however. It said, "I ordered croissants and orange juice for you. The croissants are on the table, the orange juice is in the refrigerator. If you want anything else, call room service." He found his clothes neatly folded on a chair. He didn't know why, but that surprised him a little.

Going toward the dining room, he noticed the art on the walls. He saw another Picasso, a Matisse, and perhaps a Monet. They sure looked real. Working in a casino must pay awfully well, he thought. As advertised, there were croissants, butter, and jam on the dining table. A place had been set at the head of the table with a newspaper beside it. He walked over to the kitchen phone and picked up the receiver. After being connected to room service, he ordered a double order of bacon and a pot of hot chocolate.

Warm bacon arrived along with a piping hot pot of hot chocolate five minutes later. He perused the Hong Kong paper as he ate. As he finished breakfast, he decided he needed a shower and returned to his room. He thought about the recent events as he stood under the hot water. He had missed something, and it was nagging at his subconscious. His powers of observation seemed to be impaired around the woman. It was not like him.

Madame Gin Sling had left her suite to go to her office. She was smitten, and she knew it. She asked her secretary to get Toy for her, the larger of her two bodyguards. Toy had been with her since day one. Over the years, she and Toy had become quite close. She used him as a sounding board from time to time. Toy came into her office and she said to him, "I want him followed. Use as many men as you need to be sure he does not know it. When he leaves the hotel I want someone to enter his room and take any paperwork he may have there and copy it. They are to be sure that he cannot detect that someone has been through his things. I also want a report every half hour when he is not in the hotel on what he is doing. Stop smiling and go, Toy."

"Yes, Madame Gin Sling." He did not need to ask who she was talking about; he knew. He also knew her well enough to say nothing further.

Pete left the hotel and walked to the sidewalk in front. He looked both ways and decided turning right looked the most promising. He wanted to just walk around and get the feel of the city. As he strolled along he went into any store that looked interesting. By happenstance his wandering took him to the Hilton, and he entered, looking for the concierge. On locating the concierge's desk, he asked for the name of the best restaurant in Macau. He thanked the concierge for the information and continued his stroll.

His travels took him past the Sheraton, and he did the same thing there. Continuing, he found the Intercontinental Hotel. When the concierge recommended the same restaurant as the concierge at the Hilton and the Sheraton, he asked for directions and filed the information away.

As the time for lunch approached, he found a small restaurant that looked promising. He went in and took a table.

"Well what is he doing now?" she asked when the phone on her desk rang.

"Eating lunch," came the reply.

"Keep me advised," she said, hanging up.

Later, the voice on the phone said, "He made diner reservations for two at the Golden Dragon," then added, "For eight o'clock."

She smiled, secretly delighted. She picked up the phone and told her secretary to call the Golden Dragon and tell them that she would be dining with Mr. Smith and to be sure the table was for four to accommodate her leg.

"He is back in the hotel," the voice advised again.

She called the voice mail on her apartment phone to check for messages. The first one, from earlier in the morning, asked if she would have dinner with him. She had already responded to this, agreeing of course. The second one, fifteen minutes old, said, "Take off your shoes if you are going to walk around in my mind." It was corny but she was so thrilled she could not believe it. What was the matter with her? Actually, she knew but did not want to admit it.

They met at the appointed hour of seven o'clock in the English Pub. Their conversation was light and airy. After a bit he looked at his watch and said, "It is time to go to dinner." She made a signal to Toy. When he arrived, she said something in Chinese. Looking at Pete she said, "Toy is bringing one of the hotel's cars around so we need to give him a couple of minutes." After a short pause, she asked innocently, "Where are we going by the way?" He told her.

The car turned out to be a stretch Mercedes limo with a ride that was like floating on a cloud.

Immediately upon entering the restaurant, the staff started fawning over Madame Gin Sling. When they were seated he asked, "Who are you really? Why are we getting such special treatment?"

"Well, I told you I'm the troubleshooter, but I am also the head of the accounting department. And I approve the credit lines in the casino. As such I am the person who can extend the repayment time. The owner here is a very big gambler."

The conversation shifted into other areas as the waiter brought the menus. Pete was not familiar with most of what was on the menu so he said, "You come here often, so why don't you order for both of us?" She did, all in Chinese, so he had no idea what was coming.

She had ordered duck, which was served with an orange sauce, a vegetable medley, and rice. The food was delicious, but neither ordered dessert. He called for the check and paid it.

As they returned to the hotel, she said, "Why don't we have a nightcap upstairs?"

"Good idea."

As they went through the door to her suite, history repeated itself.

When he awoke, she was still asleep with her back to his stomach. The clock said three minutes past eight. He lay there thinking about what a wonderful woman she was. After about fifteen minutes she awoke as well. Looking over her shoulder she saw he too was awake. She rolled onto her back and stretched. She felt great. "Three times last night."

"I was there remember? So what's the plan for today?"

"I have to work; what time is it away?"

"Eight twenty-two."

"Oh my God, I'm late!" she exclaimed. He reached down and put his hand between her legs. Any thoughts of leaving the bed vanished, and she said, "That's not fair."

"All's fair in love and war." He continued to massage her clitoris with the palm of his hand. "Let's spend the day together," he said.

"Okay, I think that can be arranged. But I have to call my secretary," she said, rolling onto him and starting to kiss him.

"Call later, please!"

They made love again slowly, lacking the fever pitch of the previous evening. She could not believe when she climaxed again thirty minutes later. She lay back exhausted. A few minutes later she asked, "Shall we have breakfast here in the room or would you like to do something else?"

"Your choice."

She rolled over and leaned out to pick up the phone. "What would you like?" she asked. "I need to call my secretary, too, and let her know I won't be in today."

"Double order of bacon, croissants, and hot chocolate. And I would like it in about thirty minutes, if that's okay."

As she hung up the phone, he said, "I want to run up to my room and take a quick shower. I'll be back before the food gets here. Can I take the key so I can let myself back in?"

"Yes. I am going to do the same thing."

He returned just as the waiter finished setting the food on the table. She entered the room moments later. She wore a white blouse, a dark blue skirt, and a dark brown leather sandal on her right foot. Her hair was done up in a ponytail. "You look great," he said. "So what's the deal with this suite? How come you get to use it?"

"This is really a suite for very high rollers. Management lets me use it until all the other similar suites fill up. They want me on the premises as much as possible to deal with problems as they arise.”

“This is a really nice perk.”

“Yes, occasionally I have to move out. All I do is put all my personal stuff in one of the closets and lock the door.”

“Is all this art real?” he asked.

“Yes. We get it when the big losers can’t pay off.” Changing the subject, she hoped subtly, she asked him, “What would you like to do?”

“Let’s just walk around and play tourist. Wait a minute, perhaps that is not such a good idea. I am sure it is difficult for you to walk any distance,” he said.

“I do better than you might think,” she replied.

“Well then, I tell you what, let’s just walk around. When you get tired, we’ll take a rickshaw to the restaurant of your choice, where I shall buy you lunch. How’s that sound?”

“Wonderful. Are you ready to go?” she asked.

“Born ready,” he replied stuffing the end of a croissant into his mouth.

“Then let’s go.”

This is the most wonderful man I have ever met, she thought. He’s willing to adjust his trip, or at least this day of it, to accommodate my handicap.

They left the hotel holding hands. The employees were shocked. No one had ever seen Madame Gin Sling with a man, let alone holding hands. She looked over her shoulder and saw Toy starting to follow them. She shook her head no.

“Which way shall we go?” she asked.

“Yesterday I went straight down this street before wandering around. So I would suggest that we go down to the corner, turn right, go up a block, and then turn left, parallel to this street.”

“Sounds good to me,” she said. They set off still holding hands, feeling like teenagers but loving it nonetheless. The weather cooperated with their mood: clear, cloudless, with bright sunshine. The temperature was about eighty-two degrees. It was just a beautiful day to be outside. They wandered into curio shops and antique stores.

"I love these places," he said

"Why is that?"

"Well, they show where we have come from." Pointing to an old butter churn, he continued, "This was the state of the art not all that long ago. Now if you want butter you go to the store and buy all you want, No need to milk the cow or pump the handle."

They left the shop, continuing to idly stroll along. Next they went into an art gallery that carried European Impressionists. "I like these," he said.

"Why is that?" she queried.

"I really don't know. It's a question of what you get used to, I guess."

"Who is your favorite painter?"

Without a moment of hesitation he replied, "Claude Monet."

"Why him?"

"I love his use of colors. At the Musée d'Orsay in Paris there is an entire floor dedicated to the Impressionists. I visit it every time I go to Paris." Then he added, "I would love to show it to you sometime."

Uncharacteristically, she said, "There is no one I would rather have for a guide." She realized she had started to reveal some of her feelings. Heretofore, she had always been guarded with her feelings, fearing the vulnerability of open emotions. "How about that rickshaw you promised?" she asked brightly.

He looked around for a rickshaw, but the best he could do was a sort of rickshaw pulled by a scooter. She gave the driver the name of a restaurant and away they went in a cloud of blue exhaust smoke and ear-shattering noise.

As they entered the restaurant he said, "That was an absolutely dreadful ride. I apologize." She nodded in response. As soon as the staff saw her they bent over backward to be accommodating. Seated at a lovely table overlooking the water and fawned over by the waiter he asked, "Another gambler?"

"Most Chinese are," she replied.

After lunch they strolled aimlessly and continued to browse through any shop that interested either of them. But after an hour, she suggested they return to the hotel, claiming work called. They found a cab and ten minutes later were deposited in front of the hotel. Agreeing to meet for dinner in the English Pub at seven o'clock, they parted in front of the reception desk.

Pete walked into the pub at the appointed hour and saw Madame Gin Sling already seated in "her" booth and on the phone, as usual. He ambled over and sat on her right. He did not understand a word of the conversation but knew she was unhappy and as a result someone else was very unhappy as well. When she hung up it was obvious that she was hopping mad. She took a deep breath and fitted a cigarette into her holder. She said, "There is always something." He lit her cigarette for her as she regrouped.

After she finished her Perrier and he finished two-thirds of a scotch and water, they decided to eat in the French restaurant in the hotel. They were walking between the bar and the row of tables. A drunk sitting somewhat sideways with two friends got off his stool. He bumped into Gin Sling hard enough to knock her over. As she started to fall Pete caught her and pulled her erect.

"Look out," the drunk said. He could not have said anything more foolish if he tried. Pete's temper flared. He stepped around Gin Sling and hit the guy with an open palm uppercut right on the bottom of the point of his jaw. Gin Sling tried to see what happened. By the time she maneuvered to see around Pete's broad back the drunk's eyes were rolling back into his head, his expression a blank, his knees buckling. Pete grabbed the man's lapels and with his right foot hooked a chair, spinning it ninety degrees. He put the drunk, now out cold, in the chair. He turned to the drunk's two friends and said, "Tell your friend, when he comes to, that if he ever touches this woman again, I will really hurt him." Turning to Madame Gin Sling he said, "Let's go darling." Toy and Chou rushed up, prepared to throw the drunk out of the hotel. Pete saw what they had in mind and said to Toy, "Let him come to here, Toy. You throw him out and it is the big bad hotel's fault. Leave him here and he must explain. He will lose much face." An enormous grin spread across Toy's face. Pete took Madame Gin Sling's hand as they left.

By the time they reached the door Madame Gin Sling knew without a doubt that she was in love. Not just in love, but rather, she had fallen head over heels for the first time in her life.

They went into the hotel's French restaurant. As usual the staff made a big fuss over Gin Sling. After they were seated, Pete said to her, "You ordered for us last night. How about I order for us tonight?"

"Okay."

When the waiter arrived he placed menus in front of them and then asked if they would care for something from the bar. The waiter spoke in English with a heavy French accent. She ordered a Perrier and he a scotch and water. While he scanned the menu she said, "Let's eat soon. I am starving."

The waiter returned with the drinks. Pete said to him, "I think we are ready to order."

"Very good, sir," responded the waiter

"Madame voudrait le filet de boeuf avec une sauce poivre vert et le gratin dauphinois avec a petite salade verte a cote. Et moi, je voudrai le beouf bouginon avec la patte."

"Vous parlez très bien français, monsieur," replied a surprised waiter.

"Et pour le vin une bouteille de Chateau Latour 2000 pour Madame et un Saint-Émilion pour moi," Pete continued.

"Excellente choix, monsieur." With that the waiter departed.

"What was that all about?" she asked.

"I ordered diner. You said you were hungry."

"I did not know you spoke French. Where did you learn?"

"I took four years in college just because languages have always been easy for me. Then I was stationed in Belgium for two years."

"What am I getting, by the way?"

"For you my dear, I ordered the good ol' American standby, meat and potatoes, but with a French flare."

They chatted as they waited for their meal. She asked him if he had any hobbies.

"I like to play golf and . . . well, I have a little business that is really more of a hobby than a business really.

"What's that?" she queried. Business always got her attention.

"I buy old British sports cars, restore them, drive them for a while, and then sell them."

"Do you make a lot of money doing that?" she asked.

"Not really, that's why I think of it more as a hobby than a business. But, I just really enjoy running around in an open roadster." Their meal arrived just then. He sampled both bottles of wine and declared them absolutely excellent. She declared the same for the steak and sauce, and after sampling the potatoes said, "I never knew we had such good food in this hotel. This is delicious."

"The chef is outstanding," he agreed.

The conversation over dinner was sparse as they each concentrated on their food.

After the table had been cleared, the waiter returned and asked in French if they would like dessert. Pete responded in French ordering fondant au chocolat.

She asked what had been said.

"I just ordered a little dessert for us."

"I could not eat another thing," she groaned!

"Just have a bite, and if you do not want the rest I'll eat it."

After the waiter served the dessert, she tried a very small piece. The warm liquid chocolate center oozed from the small chocolate cake onto her plate. After one taste she declared, "This is the best dessert I have ever eaten. I wonder why I never knew we had such good food in this hotel." She devoured the whole thing. When he finished she asked, "Night cap in my suite?"

"Sounds like a wonderful idea."

When they entered her bedroom they slowly undressed each other. As he looked at her standing he noticed, for the first time, that the upper portion of her artificial leg was covered in leather. A sheath was sewn into the upper portion on the outside which contained a knife. "Do you always carry a knife," he asked?

"Always," she answered. "Women are very vulnerable, and handicapped women even more so."

Forty minutes later after they had both climaxed she lay on her back and said in a very serious tone, "There is something I have to tell you." She felt compelled to tell him the depth of her feelings for him. She also hoped it might influence where he went when his tour ended. She hadn't quite decided how she was going to lure him back into her life, but she knew she wanted him to return to her.

"Oh," he said, dreading what was coming.

"I love you." After a couple of minutes passed, she said, "Aren't you going to say something?"

"If I let myself think about it I would probably find I feel the same way. But I am not going to do that. We are star crossed lovers, like two ships passing in the night. Your life is obviously here. It is apparent that you have a great job and a good life here. I don't even have a job at this point, but I am going to have to get one when I return to the States. It will most likely be in the Washington, D.C. area. I have seen many couples try long distance romances and they never work."

"So you don't think there is a future for us?"

"I don't see how there can be. You are the only woman I have ever met that I will never forget." With that he reached his arm behind her back and pulled her close.

He was right, of course, but that did not make it any easier to accept that he was about to walk out of her life. After a while they both dozed off knowing he would continue his tour in the morning.

When he awoke the next morning, she still slept. But as he buttoned his shirt, she sat up in bed, held out her arms and said, "Kiss me good-bye."

He came around the bed, and their embrace was long and passionate. "I shall never forget you," he said. "Perhaps I'll be back one day, you never know." He disentangled himself and went to his room to pack. But when it came time to select the elevator button for the lobby, he pushed the one for her floor.

He knocked on her door. After two minutes he was getting ready to knock again when she opened the door on crutches wearing a light pink night shirt.

"I couldn't leave without one last kiss." She jumped into his arm and kissed him even more passionately than before, if that was possible. The crutches clattered to the floor. "I will always remember you, and doubt I shall ever meet a woman as wonderful as you again." After picking up her crutches and handing them to her, he turned and walked toward the elevator.

She watched him until his suitcase disappeared into the elevator. Then she turned and went into her bedroom and did something else she had never done before. She lay on her bed and cried over a man. She had loved and lost and she knew it.

2.

Macau, Mid-September, two months later

"Well, Madame Gin Sling, are you here for a routine checkup or is there some specific problem?" asked Dr. DaSilva, her OB/GYN.

"A routine checkup, but I have not had my period recently and I think I am a little young for menopause," she responded. She hated the indignity of these exams. The nurse had to lift her peg leg for the doctor to be able see correctly.

After just a few seconds he nodded to the nurse, who released her leg. "Please get dressed and the nurse will show you to my office," he said.

As she sat in the doctor's office waiting, she could not help but wonder what was so wrong with her she had to receive the news in his office. The doctor entered his office and sat behind the desk.

"Well, what's wrong with me?" she blurted out, before he had said a thing.

"Nothing. Pregnancy is a very normal condition."

"I'm pregnant?"

"Yes," he replied simply.

"Doctor, many years ago you told me that it would be virtually impossible for me to get pregnant because of the scarring in my uterus caused by, as you put it, back alley abortions."

"I believe that what I said was, 'it would be a miracle if you got pregnant.' Well, that miracle has occurred."

Dazed, she left the doctor's office with a bunch of pamphlets on pregnancy, a prescription for vitamins, and a due date of April 1. As she approached the car Toy opened the door for her. He realized something was wrong immediately. Her demeanor gave him no clue as to what it might be, however. He had been with her for more than twenty years and thought he knew all her moods. This was a new one. She gave no hint as to what had transpired in the doctor's office.

She was still in a daze twenty minutes later when she entered her office. "No calls, no interruptions of any kind," she said to her secretary. She sat in the chair behind her desk for about twenty minutes then moved to lie on the couch. She reached a decision. She picked up her phone and asked her secretary to bring her Pete Smith's travel itinerary. It certainly is a good thing her staff retained his itinerary after he left, she thought. After a quick review, she called her secretary and told her, "Call the airport and tell the pilots that they are going to pick someone up in Tahiti. Tell them to take all four pilots. This trip is to be done as fast as possible. Then ask Toy to come here."

"Toy, I want you to go to Club Med in Tahiti, find Pete Smith, and bring him back here. You are taking the jet. The pilots have already been called and should be making preparations to leave now. Take Chou and two other men with you. You will probably need to use drugs on him. I doubt he will go quietly, and I don't want him bruised."

"Yes, Madame Gin Sling."

Club Med, Tahiti

Pete Smith entered his room slightly the worse for wear. He knew he had had too much to drink, but, oh well, those things happen. He flicked the light switch but nothing happened. Great, he thought, continuing into the room. Suddenly both of his arms were grabbed and he felt a prick at the base of his neck. "What the he . . ," he said, fading into unconsciousness.

Macau

It was four in the morning when the phone rang in Madame Gin Sling's room. She answered simply saying, "Yes."

"He is in room 818, as you ordered."

Recognizing Toy's voice she said, "Well done." She hung up and went back to sleep.

When Pete Smith came around the next morning he felt as if a thousand Russian soldiers had marched over his tongue wearing sweaty, wool gym socks. The clock said eleven o'clock but his stomach was saying, "Feed me." It was a few seconds before he realized he was in his old room in Macau. "Impossible," he thought. He got up, not without a minor throb in his head, and went to the window. "Yep, Macau." He knew who must have brought him here but not how or why. Looking around a little further he discovered all his luggage was there as well.

He went into the bathroom, turned on the shower, and stood under the scalding water for what seemed an eternity. He felt about two-thirds human as he dressed a few minutes later.

Deciding he had to eat something, he went to the door and opened it. In front of him stood two Chinese men each about the size of a delivery truck. "I am going to get something to eat," he said, taking the positive approach.

"You stay here," one said, adding, "Madame Gin Sling send for you when she ready."

The other grunted, "Room servee." He took the outside of the door knob in his hand and jerked the door shut.

Pete stood there looking at the now closed door, stunned. He shrugged his shoulders and headed for the telephone.

He realized he had become a prisoner, and he did not like that feeling. But until he spoke with that bitch who had brought him here he would not try to escape.

He spent most of the next five hours pacing in his room, his ire rising. A short nap did nothing to assuage his anger. At five minutes of seven, the door opened and Toy entered. "Madame Gin Sling will see you now," he said. As Pete followed the massive Toy out the door, he thought no one had ever been so misnamed. They were immediately surrounded by two other men. They rode the elevator to the casino level. Upon exiting, they went to the English Pub. Madame Gin Sling was seated in what he had come to think of as her booth. Still under escort, he walked to the booth. He slid into the booth beside her. Toy and the others withdrew to a respectable distance, but still close enough to react quickly if needed.

But, just the sight of her had started to defuse his anger. Damn, she was beautiful. He folded his arms and put them on the table. Without turning his torso he looked at her and said, "Well, you have gone to a great deal of effort to bring me here. Would you mind telling me why? And, by the way, I do not like being held prisoner."

"I am pregnant and you are the father," she blurted out, continuing, "We are being married on Saturday at one o'clock." If he was shocked finding himself in Macau, he was flabbergasted now.

"Whoa—just hold the phone here. Listen, I understand my responsibilities to aid you financially with raising the child and will do so, but I am not getting married. I am a confirmed bachelor who would make a lousy husband." His rage at being brought to Macau melted away now that he understood why she had gone to such trouble to bring him back to Macau.

"That is your final word?"

"Yes."

"Let me explain your options. You can change your mind and walk to the altar with a smile on your face. Or Toy, Chou, and their ah… associates are going to take you to the basement where they will 'persuade' you to change your mind."

"Let me be sure I understand the options. I can marry you with or without pain."

"I think you have captured the essence of your options perfectly," she said.

After a moment he said, "I guess I choose the altar pain free."

"Good, now I shall explain the rules of this marriage to you. We will at all times present the face of a loving couple to the public, and more importantly, to our son. That will not be necessary in private. We can have separate bedrooms if you want."

"My wife sleeps in my bed naked," he interrupted.

She raised an eyebrow at that edict but continued, "You will not cheat on me. First time I catch you at it I will have one of your nuts removed. Second time, remaining nut will be removed and that will be the end of that problem. If you try to run, I will find you, bring you back, and fix it so you will never run again. You may divorce me the fall our son enters the university. Do you have any questions? No? Good. The schedule is as follows, at nine tomorrow the tailor will measure you for a suit. We will be married at one o'clock on Saturday."

Suddenly it struck him. Who is this woman? She had an authority indicating she could back up her marital threats.

"Actually, I do have one question, if you don't mind. Why are you doing this?"

"I was raised in Saigon without a father by a mother who worked. Trust me, that is a miserable childhood. Our son is going to have the best of everything and that includes two loving parents. I want to apologize for having to press you so hard, but I do not have much time."

"Oh yeah? How do you know it is a boy?"

"Because I have decided to have a boy."

"My dear, you may be able to control a great many things but over that you have no control." She gave him a dismissive gesture with her right hand.

"You must have friends in high places to get me here and through customs drugged. But friends or no, there is one thing you should know before you make me go through with this," he said. She raised an eyebrow. "As I said earlier, I am a confirmed bachelor."

"What does that mean?" she queried.

"I like being alone and, now that I'm out of the army, I do not take well to direction," he responded. With that he got up and left. He had wanted to ask how she got so much power, for lack of a better word, but opted for the dramatic exit.

He was escorted back to his room.

The tailor arrived the next morning promptly at nine o'clock. Pete was impatient for him to leave because he hadn't had his breakfast and he was hungry. As soon as the tailor left, Pete slipped on his Topsiders and got ready to leave. Again the two large Asians stopped him. They told him "room servee" in response to his statement that he wanted to go to the restaurant.

He went back into his room and picked up the phone. When the operator answered, he asked to speak with Madame Gin Sling. The hotel operator transferred him to someone, probably a secretary, who answered, "Madame Gin Sling's office."

"This is her intended and I would like to speak to Madame."

"One moment please," responded the voice on the other end of the phone.

"Hello," Madame Gin Sling said brightly, "How are you this morning?"

He ignored her question, saying instead, "I refuse to be a prisoner. If you don't get rid of those goons in front of my door I am going to start World War 3 in the hall."

"Give me two minutes and I'll take care of it. Stay in the hotel," she said, hanging up. Reflecting on their short conversation she realized people hadn't talked to her in that tone of voice in a couple of decades. It became clear, too, that she was going to marry a very strong-willed man. Instinctively, she knew she could push him only so far.

As the second hand on Pete's watch hit the two-minute mark, he opened the door. The Asian guys were still there, but he had no trouble walking down the hall as they followed him.

That evening he decided to go to the English Pub at seven o'clock and see if his prospective bride was there. The same two large men followed closely behind him as soon as he left his room. She was indeed there. He sat down to her right again and said, "I need to do some shopping so I'll be going out tomorrow."

"Shop in the hotel, charge whatever you need to your room. I'll take care of it later."

"Unfortunately, that is not possible. I need to buy you a wedding present and a ring."

"I have already chosen the wedding rings."

He saw the opportunity for a mini rebellion. He did not like the idea that she had picked out a ring for him. He simply did not wear rings for one thing. He did not like the idea that anything might get snagged on something when he was working on car engines.

"May I see the rings?" he asked out of curiosity, plans for rebellion forming in his mind.

"I do not have them with me at the moment," she replied. "I will see that you get them in time for the ceremony."

"You should know that the tradition is that the man pays for the ring," Pete said.

The next morning as he left the hotel, he saw Toy following him. He stopped and waved Toy to come over to where he was standing. "I am sure you have orders to follow me," he said to a smiling Toy, "and that is fine, but you cannot come into any of the shops with me. I don't want you telling Madame Gin Sling everything I buy. If you want to you can call somebody else so they can cover the back door, okay?" Toy gave him what he had come to think of as his "Odd Job" smile but said nothing. Having wandered through Macau before, he had an idea of where he was going. Toy waited in front of each shop as he entered, watching him closely.

After about four hours, he hailed a cab for Toy and himself to return to the hotel.

That evening he returned to the English Pub and found his intended in the same booth, on the telephone as usual. He sat again to her right, waiting impatiently. When she hung up he said, "I am going to Hong Kong tomorrow."

"Why? Is that really necessary?"

"I was unable to find what I wanted here today."

"What is it you want? Perhaps I can help?"

"Your wedding present, and if you helped it wouldn't be a surprise, would it?"

"Very well, I will send Toy with you to make sure you have no problems."

"It's really not necessary, I'm a big boy now," he said getting up.

"I will feel better knowing that nothing can happen to you. Hong Kong can be a very dangerous place."

He shrugged and left.

Watching him go, she began to get the feeling of exactly how mad he was about this upcoming marriage.

His day in Hong Kong proved to be productive. He found the gold Rolex watch he had been looking for and a plain gold wedding band that was fairly wide. American Express required a phone call to approve such a large amount, but they accommodated him. He and Toy rode the evening ferry back to Macau. On reaching the hotel, he went directly to the English Pub and as usual Madame Gin Sling was seated in "her" booth. He asked her, "What am I supposed to do tomorrow?"

"All you have to do is be ready at twelve thirty. Toy will show you where to go. First, we will be married by a minister from the Church of England and then the mayor of Macau."

Promptly at twelve thirty Toy knocked on his door. He simply walked out and said to Toy, "What now?"

"Follow me," Toy replied. He led Pete down to a small room somewhere on the main floor. "The religious ceremony will be first and in English," Toy said, "but the civil ceremony conducted by the mayor will be in Portuguese. Macau is no longer Portuguese but we still do it that way. Portuguese law only recognizes civil marriages. There is a table to the left of the altar and on it is the marriage book. You will have to sign it. The mayor will tell you when and where… Oh yeah, remember when the mayor looks at you, say 'si.'"

"Where did you learn to speak English so well, Toy?" he asked.

"I was raised by American missionaries in the Northwest territories," he answered.

"That explains it," he said. He looked at the wall clock. Still fifteen minutes to go. Time seemed to stand still. The second hand on the clock appeared to take five times as long to complete one revolution. At two minutes to one, Toy cracked the door and peaked through the narrow slit he had created. "The minister is there, time for you to go. Here are the rings," he said. Pete put them in his left pocket.

Pete walked over to the minister and said, "There's been a slight change of plans. We want a single ring ceremony." With that Pete pressed five hundred dollars into the minister's hand. Pete then took his place to the right of the altar. A minute later the wedding march started and Madame Gin Sling came down the aisle unescorted. My God, he thought, he had never seen a more beautiful woman. She wore an off-white high-collar mandarin dress. Her makeup was perfect, her black hair was glistening. She looked stunning. As he glanced past her, he saw one wife give her husband an elbow to the ribs for ogling.

He said his "I do's." When the minister turned toward her he said, "Do you Sophie Marie Nguyen take this...," the rest was lost on him as he realized he had just learned the real name of the woman he was marrying.

When it was time to place the ring on her finger he reached into his right pocket and pulled out the ring he had bought in Hong Kong. He hid the ring from her view under his forefinger and middle finger. Then he slid it on her finger. She looked down at the ring and rage momentarily flashed across her face.

When the minister said, "You may kiss the bride," she leaned just past the side of his face away from the crowd and hissed, "You rat!"

Next they moved over to the mayor's table, where he intoned away in Portuguese. Evidently, he had mumbled "Si" at the right time because the mayor finally handed him a pen and showed him where to sign. She then signed the book, and with that, in the eyes of God and the law, they were married.

As they walked back up the aisle, the rear wall of the chapel slid open to reveal a large reception area. Along two walls there were forty-foot tables loaded with all manner of hors d'oeuvre. There were three bars in various locations around the room and an army of waiters with trays of champagne. They stopped by the entrance and greeted the entering guests.

Sophie introduced Pete to at least a hundred people. After two hours she threw the bouquet and they left.

As soon as the elevator door closed, she said, "You rat."

"Me?"

"Yes, you. Look at that ring. Now I have to wear this thing for the rest of my life."

Sounding like a schoolteacher he said, "It is elegant in its simplicity and tasteful. It is not gaudy like that diamond-encrusted thing you bought. It makes its own quiet statement. Besides which, the man always buys the ring."

She was somewhat mollified as she left the elevator, but he knew that he had not heard the last of this.

When they entered the suite his voice took on a hard edge saying, "Come over here and sit down," pointing to a couch. She complied rather docilely. She knew what was coming. She had decided that she had to be completely open and honest with him to have any chance of success in this marriage. "Now Madame Gin Sling Sophie Marie Nguyen Smith, I want to know who the hell you are."

"I am not sure I understand the question."

"I just attended my wedding reception, which by the way I didn't even know we were having, and was introduced to the American counsel, the mayor, half the city council, the presidents of at least three banks, and assorted other dignitaries. Those people don't go to the wedding of some girl who works in the accounting department. So, I ask again, who are you?"

She took her cigarette case and holder from the small purse she had been carrying and fitted a cigarette into the holder. Then she looked into her purse for her lighter. Finding it, she lit the cigarette. She stood up with her left forearm underneath her breasts and the fingers of her left hand in the crook of her erect right arm. She took two strides toward him, looked him straight in the eye and said, "I own the joint." The truth was now on the table.

"What joint?" he asked. The full impact of what she had said had not yet registered.

"This hotel," she answered.

"You own this hotel?"

"Yes," she simply.

"You and who else?" he asked, the truth and full impact of what she had just said dawning on him. Of course, how could he have missed all the signs, everyone jumping when she spoke?

"No one."

"How much do you owe on your hotel?"

"Nothing."

"Let me be sure I understand you correctly," he said. "You own this hotel and casino outright, free and clear."

She pursed her lips together and nodded rapidly with a little girl grin on her face.

"What is this hotel worth?"

"I am asking five hundred million."

"What else do you own?" he asked tentatively, not really sure he wanted to hear the answer.

"I own a couple of businesses that I agreed to sell last week but have not yet been paid."

"So you own them today?" She nodded. "What are those businesses?" he asked.

"I own some whorehouses and machine rooms," she replied.

"How many whorehouses do you own?" he asked, somewhat intrigued.

"Two hundred forty-seven."

"Two hundred forty-seven!" he howled. "So you really are a Madame."

She nodded again.

"How much did you get for your whorehouses?"

"Twenty-five million."

"Good god," he said.

"Very good business," she observed.

"And the machine rooms, what are they and how much?"

"You know when you walk around Macau you see rooms with gambling machines and usually a mahjong parlor in back? Well, that is a machine room. I got thirty million for mine."

A thought occurred to him just then so he asked, "How much cash do you have on hand?"

"I am not exactly sure," she said.

"I don't believe that for a moment."

"Let me explain," she said. "When your current president was elected, I realized his economic policies would destroy the value of the dollar, so I converted all my dollars into Swiss francs."

"How many dollars did you convert?"

"Three hundred eighty million. This does not include the cash in the cage or the operating account."

"And did the dollar drop?" he queried.

"Yes, about twenty percent so far," she responded.

"So that means you have about four hundred fifty million in cash."

"Somewhat more than that," she agreed.

"If my math is correct, that totals to about a billion dollars." Then a thought occurred to him, and he asked if she owned anything else.

She walked over to the window. "I own that," she said pointing out the window. "I own those two blocks and half of the ones behind them," she said.

"How much is that worth?"

"I am asking two hundred million."

How dumb am I, he thought. I missed all the signs. Waiters kowtowing to her everywhere she went. The only way she could have brought him here from Tahiti was on a private jet. He had just accepted everything she told him to be true. He'd lied to enough women in his day and should have realized that being skeptical early in a relationship was mandatory. He was momentarily stunned as the full impact of whom he had just married sank into his consciousness.

"Well, you're a long way from a little girl who works in the accounting department, aren't you? You lied to me big time. And, that really pisses me off."

"No, I didn't."

"Oh, how do you figure that?" he queried.

"I own the accounting department, therefore I work there."

"You are splitting hairs now."

"Every man I meet is intimated by my wealth."

"Almost every one. Where's the scotch?" he asked.

"You'll have to call down for some, but your favorite wine is behind the bar."

"That will have to do," he groaned. She returned to the living room couch and watched as he opened a bottle of wine. What is coming next, he wondered as he opened the wine. It suddenly occurred to him that he was pissed because his new wife was a billionaire. How stupid was that. Beyond words! The realization calmed him down instantly. His ire dissipated, and he returned to the living room and sat down on the couch. He had had the nagging feeling he had been missing something. And now he knew what. She mesmerized him, and he had simply not been looking.

"Are you ready to hear the rest of the plan now, or would you rather wait?" she asked.

He sipped his wine and thought about it, finally deciding now or later wouldn't make any difference. Besides which, he didn't think he was going to like it anyway. He also sensed her impatience and knew she wanted to tell him. Finally, he said, "Go ahead." As an afterthought he added, "What happens if I don't like it?"

She chose to ignore the question. "Monday my application for a green card will be submitted to the American consulate in Hong Kong. We will have to go to an interview in Hong Kong about two weeks from now. As soon as that is finished you will go to America and buy us a mansion. I will join you there when I have my green card and have sold the hotel."

"Do I have to sign this application?" he asked.

"Yes."

"Where is it?"

"On the bar," she replied.

He went over to the bar, found a file neatly labeled "Green Card Application," and took it back to the couch. After he had perused the application for a few seconds he asked, "Where is there a pen?" Sophie walked over to him, opened a drawer in the end table, and took out a pen. He signed. Looking up he said, "I did not know you were a French citizen."

"My father was French, and when I was born he registered my birth with the French counsel in Saigon. That was the only thing he did for me before he split."

"Where do you want this mansion, anyway?"

"I don't care other than to say somewhere where it doesn't snow. I think I would have a lot of difficulty getting around on snow and ice."

"You know mansions are very expensive."

"I don't care. I decided that our miracle baby will have the best of everything. I made it and now I am going to spend it."

"Why do you call it a miracle baby?"

"When I was fourteen and fifteen, I had three, what you would call, back-alley abortions. When I finally saw a competent doctor he told me it would be a miracle if I ever got pregnant because of the scarring in my uterus."

"One more question if I may. Why did you decide to make such a dramatic change in your life, giving all this up and moving to a foreign country?"

"Well, I looked at the choices in front of me. I could turn eighty as a withered-up, one-legged, old half cast with five billion in the bank, or I could marry a man I love very much and whom I think loves me, although he won't say it, and raise a family in style. There really wasn't much of a choice when you think about it."

"Why not raise the child as a single mother? I am sure you considered that."

"Of course, but I was raised like that and always wanted a father. I always felt as if something was missing. I want our son to have a full life and not experience any of the things I went through. Thus far, however," she said walking toward him, "I feel like a single parent." Sitting in his lap, she put her arms around him and kissed him. He gently slid his arms under her, stood, and headed for the bedroom. "I think you are beginning to understand a part of the single parent problem," she said.

The pent-up frustration and desire of the last two months flooded into her being. He set her down standing next to the bed. She grabbed the front of his shirt and yanked. Some of the material tore and some of the buttons popped. He, meanwhile, had jerked down the zipper of her dress. Her dress and his pants hit the floor at the same time. He took her in his arms again and they fell across the bed together. Neither of them could wait. He fumbled with her underwear and she with his. Finally he was in her. He was unsure how long it took before they had a simultaneous explosion. The only thing he was really sure of was that they were both gasping for breath.

The next morning when he awoke, he realized this was the first day of being a married man. He was now responsible for another person and would soon be responsible for two! He did not know how he felt about that. He felt he had lost his independence, but on rethinking it, he recognized that he had traded his independence for sharing his life with someone else. Only time would tell if he had made a good bargain or not. More fully awake, his period of introspection over, he realized that he had slept on his right side with his left arm over his wife. Her back was against his chest. Tousled black hair seemed to be everywhere. This bargain looked better all the time. Nature was calling him to the bathroom. He tried, unsuccessfully, to get out of bed without waking his new bride. As he slid across the bed, she rolled onto her back and said, "Good morning."

"Good morning," he responded automatically, adding. "The potty is calling."

"Use the one over there," she said, pointing to a door close to the interior wall.

When he went into the bathroom, he noticed his shaving kit by the sink. Further inspection revealed his bottle of Head and Shoulders in the shower. As he got back into bed he said, "Whatever the plan for today is, I'm modifying it. Breakfast is looming large on the horizon. We did not eat dinner last night, and I am starved. What time is it anyway?"

"The clock is on your night table."

He looked at it. "This says seven forty-five. But that can't be right, can it?"

She smiled at him and said, "Breakfast will be here in fifteen minutes."

"I am going to take a quick shower. As he walked toward the bathroom he turned and asked, "What did I order for breakfast?"

"Steak, medium rare, hash browns, two eggs over easy, English muffins, orange juice, and hot chocolate," came the response.

How the hell did she know that was exactly what he felt like eating, he wondered.

When he left the bathroom after having showered and shaved, he heard the shower in the other bathroom. With a towel wrapped around him, he started to search for his clothes. He opened a door that looked logically like it should be a closet. It led into the biggest walk-in closet he had ever seen. Indeed, the biggest closet he had ever heard of. It was full of Sophie's things. It contained so many dresses she could open a department store. The next door he tried opened to a smaller walk-in closet. All his clothes hung on half of one rod. They had all been cleaned and pressed. The rest of the closet was also full of her things. After dressing in a pair of khaki pants and a dark blue T-shirt, he decided a little CNN would be in order. But as he reached for the remote, there was a knock on the door. He opened the door to find the room service waiter with the breakfast cart. He stepped back, allowing the waiter to enter.

"Where would you like me to set it up, sir?" asked the waiter?

He pointed to the dining table. The waiter had just put the last plates on the table when Sophie entered the room using her crutches. Her hair was in a ponytail, large, thick glasses perched on her nose, and she wore only an oversized T-shirt. She could not have looked sexier if she had tried. Maybe this marriage thing was going to work out after all. He pulled out a chair for her and helped her scoot it to the table. In between mouthfuls he asked, "What is the plan for today?"

"I don't have one"

"You're kidding."

"I know, I must be slipping."

"Yep, you must be. How did you miss today? The next three months are already programmed."

"Look, I know I have taken over a lot of the planning of our future. And I know that couples should make most of these decisions together. But you were not available for consultation, and there were decisions that needed to be made. Also, for the last few days there your mood could best be described as sour."

He decided to let her off the hook, his point already made. "You've done all right so far." She beamed. It was clear to him she was happy and wanted him to be as well—always a good start to a marriage. "Well let me rephrase the question then. What would you like to do for the rest of the day?" he asked, putting the last piece of steak into his mouth.

She got a funny little smirk on her face but said nothing.

"Oh, yeah," he said. "I don't think I can go all day long."

She stood up and started to pull the T-shirt over her head and said, "You'll never know if you don't try." Naked she started toward the bedroom.

"Well I'll give it the old Joe college."

"What's that?"

"An American expression, the old college try," he explained, following her into the bedroom.

Over her shoulder she said, "Well, make it a good Joe college.

An hour later, she was smoking a cigarette, without her holder, and his mind was wandering, when she asked him, "What are you thinking?"

"That a week ago I was in Tahiti without a care in the world . . ."

"With a French tart on your lap," she interrupted.

"Is that jealousy I hear?"

"Damn right! And, I do not expect a repeat performance."

"You mean to tell me I cannot go to Tahiti if I so choose."

"You know exactly what I mean," her voice taking on a harder edge. Then in a much softer tone she said, "I don't share very well."

"I think you have made that very clear."

"I may have been a bit harsh the other night, but it was not from jealousy. My concern then was that you not humiliate me. I had forgotten how much I love you. I confess to a shift in attitude."

"May have been a bit harsh?"

"Okay, was. Does that make you happy?"

"Happy, no, but mollified, yes."

She rolled over so the upper portion of her chest was on the upper portion of his chest. "I want to ask you a very serious question. Do you love me?"

"I keep thinking about that trip to the basement."

"Answer the question."

"I did."

"All right, so you needed a little prodding."

"What I did not need was to be threatened." With that he kissed her. Intuitively she knew to let the subject drop—for the moment.

"Do you know what time it is in New York?"

"No, why?"

"I need to call my parents and tell them I got married yesterday."

"I didn't know your parents were still alive."

"What did you think?"

"I don't know. I guess I never thought about it. What do they do?"

"My dad is a retired shipyard worker and my mother is a retired school teacher," he replied.

"Where do they live?"

"Mystic, Connecticut."

"Do you have any brothers or sisters?"

"I had a younger brother but he died six years ago of a drug overdose."

"How sad."

"I don't think my parents ever got over it."

"It must be terrible to lose a child. I cannot imagine anything worse," she said sincerely.

"So anyway, how do I pay for a phone since I have the very distinct feeling that you checked me out of my room?"

That got him an annoyed look as she said, "You pick up the phone, dial nine, wait for a dial tone, dial zero, one, one and the number."

"Prepare yourself, I am sure they will want to speak to you and welcome you to the family." He followed her instructions and thirty seconds later his mother answered the phone. "Hi Mom, it's Pete."

"My God, Pete, where in the world are you? We thought you had gotten lost or worse, since you were supposed to be home a while ago."

"I am in Macau, Mom. It's a city near Hong Kong."

"I know where Macau is. What's wrong? Why are you calling?"

"Mom, I am calling to share some happy news with you and Dad." In the back he could hear his father asking who was on the phone.

"It's Pete," she said to his dad. "Okay, what's the news?"

"I got married yesterday."

"Joe, he got married yesterday!" she said relaying the news to his dad. Then to him she asked, "When do we get to meet our new daughter-in-law?" Adding, "When are you going to make me a grandma?" The questions just seemed to keep coming.

"Well, Sophie needs to get a visa before she can come to the United States, and that will take about three months. So I would imagine sometime shortly after that."

"Is she there? Can I speak with her?"

"Here she is, Mom," he said, passing the phone to Sophie.

"Hello, Mrs. Smith," she said tentatively.

He could hear his mom's voice as she boomed out, "My name is Sally and my husband is Joe. You are part of the family now, and we're not very formal. But, I really just wanted to welcome you into our family and say how glad I am someone finally nailed down my wayward, shiftless son. I did not ever think he would marry. I also want to tell you that I can't wait to meet you. I know you must be a really special person if Pete married you. I am going to give the phone to Joe. He wants to talk to you, too."

"Hello, Sophie, I just wanted to add my welcome to the family as well and tell you that if there is anything you ever want or need, we will move heaven and earth to do it for you." Their welcome was so warm and heartfelt that the tears were streaming down her cheeks.

She managed to stammer out, "Thank you." She passed the phone to Pete, unable to say anything further. He chatted with his parents for a couple of minutes more before hanging up.

Sophie had regained her composure by then. She looked at him and said, "I never cry. I'm sorry." Then she added, "I hate women who cry all the time."

"There's nothing to be sorry for," he said.

"Their welcome was so heartfelt, so warm and open that it touched me."

He got out of bed at that point and said, "I am going to raid the breakfast leftovers. Would you like something?"

"No," she answered simply.

He ambled back into the bedroom gnawing on a croissant and climbed back into bed. "So tell me about your family."

"There's not much to tell, really. I have no idea where any of them are."

"Really?"

"About twenty years ago my uncle came to see me. He wanted money and had heard I was doing well. I threw him out and told him to never come back. Then about seven years ago, he showed up again begging for money. He told me my mother was dead. This time I had Toy throw him out and told him if he ever came back I would hurt him very badly. A couple of months ago he tried to knife me to death—the man you stopped. Now, I think, he is somewhere in Hong Kong healing. I guess he thought he would inherit something."

"What did he do to piss you off to that extent?"

"When I was fourteen, my family had a birthday party for me. The very next day my kindly uncle sold me into prostitution."

"I understand why you wouldn't much care for your family. How did you ever get out of that mess?"

"Well, first they put me, along with about twenty other girls, into the hold of an old junk. The thing stopped along the way and added more girls. We were fed rice and fish once a day. There was one bucket for use as a toilette that the crew emptied once a day. Finally, we got to Hong Kong. I was taken to a whorehouse and told I now belonged to the owner. He promptly raped me. At first I resisted, but he hit me in the mouth so hard he broke six of my teeth. He was really mad then because he had to pay to have my teeth fixed or I would be of no use to him. So it was off to the worst dentist in Hong Kong. All the crowns were a different color, and they were the type with the gold wire around the bottom, you've seen them. About two weeks after that, he took me into the kitchen and had me duct taped to the big eating table. That's when the dragon was tattooed on my back and my lips tattooed red. For the next year and a half, I was turning tricks like every other girl in the house.

"After what I went through, my uncle is lucky he is not drinking tea with his ancestors. Believe me, I thought about having him eliminated when he showed up the other day."

"Why didn't you just run away?" I asked.

"I considered it. But sooner or later you consider the realities. I was fourteen years old. I had no money. I was in a strange city. And I could not speak the language. After about a year and a half, I decided the only way out was to kill myself. So I stole a knife in the kitchen and was walking by the office when the pig who ran the place saw me and called me into the office. He intended to rape me again, but I stabbed him instead. He had several day's receipts on his desk and the safe was open. I took it all and walked out the front door.

"As soon as I walked out the front door, I realized what I had done. All I could think about was going to jail.

"I met Toy on his way to work about two blocks away. I was so scared by that time I told Toy what I had done. He took me into a small café, ordered me a pot of tea, and told me to wait until he came back. An hour or so later Toy came back and said everything was taken care of. I never found out what he meant by that. Then he asked what I was going to do next. At that point, I had no idea. But as I looked over Toy's shoulder I saw a vacant store. I said, 'I am going to rent that and turn it into a whorehouse.' It was the only business I knew anything about.

"But I decided to do it differently. The girls could come and go as they pleased, they got to keep a percentage of what they earned, and I insisted on regular doctor checkups.

"So there I was, fifteen and a half years old and the owner of a thriving whorehouse."

"You have really had to overcome some adversity in your life," Pete said solemnly.

"Not really," she said. "To live is to have problems. . . But, I must admit that two legs would have been nice."

"Tell me, how did you lose your leg?"

"Well I was born and raised in Saigon. When I was five years old, during the fall of Saigon, I was playing in the alley in front of my house. A bullet hit a wall and ricocheted into my leg. It hit me just above the kneecap. My mother rushed me to the hospital. The doctor said it would heal, and I would be fine. But it became infected. The communists had stolen all the drugs from the hospital. My leg was amputated to save my life."

"But why the peg leg? Why haven't you bought the latest thing in artificial legs?" he asked.

"When I first left the hospital they gave me a pair of crutches. I hated them with a purple passion. I could not play with my friends or anything because my hands were always busy with the crutches.

After about a year one of them broke and then I had to sort of hop everywhere. The old man who lived across the alley was a wood carver. You know, one of those men who carves elephants and other figures and sells them on the sidewalk. He called me over one day and measured my stump and the distance to the ground. About a week later he called me over to the house again. This time he fitted my stump into a peg leg that he had carved. He had nailed some leather around the top and with old shoelaces tied it together so that it would stay on. What an improvement. I could actually walk and use my hands at the same time.

"When I started making money I went to a guy who makes the latest thing in artificial limbs. He told me it sometimes takes about a year of using crutches before you feel comfortable enough to walk unassisted. Some people wind up using a cane forever. I did not want to use crutches again so I told him just to make me a good comfortable peg leg that would stay on without a lot of problems."

"Well, you seem to have improved on that simple peg leg by turning it into an art form."

"That was sort of an evolution. I was always envious of women wearing high heels because they looked so elegant. I thought I could wear shoes with low heels if I had a leg the right length. So I went back to the leg maker and asked him if he could make a leg where I could change the length. It worked and I could wear any heels I wanted. Then I thought, why not make the peg leg my trademark, if you will. I sure couldn't hide the fact that I wore a peg leg so why not make it special and something unique to me. That's when I started having carvings done on my various legs. It worked, made me famous, and was great publicity for my business. An ivory craver offered to settle a gambling debt with an ivory leg. And, the rest as they say is history."

"You've made the peg leg a trademark, so to speak and being a madame an art form. But, how did you get into the gambling business?"

"I came to Macau to look for new locations for whorehouses. Everywhere I went, I saw machine rooms. Well, it did not take much to figure out the economics of that business so I started buying machine rooms every chance I got. The profit is incredible. Then, for whatever reason, I went into a casino. That really opened my eyes. So I started buying land with the profits from the machine rooms."

"Your life has been absolutely amazing. Just out of curiosity what does this hotel make a year?"

"The best year it made one hundred twenty-one million, the worst year forty-seven million, it really depends on the whales.

"Okay, I'll bite. What's a whale?"

"A player who will play between a hundred thousand and a million a hand. When they win they can really hurt you. That is the reason you have to carry so much cash on hand in the cage. But enough about me, tell me where you were raised and went to school?"

"I grew up in Mystic, Connecticut. I did well in school and won a scholarship to a private school. From there I went to Yale University, also on a scholarship. I went into the army within a month of graduating from college. After basic training, I applied for Special Forces training. Then I applied to Delta Force, which is the elite of the elite."

"How did you become an officer?"

"I made it through that training and along came the first Iraq War, and off to war I went. When I got back, I applied to Officer Candidate School, went through the training, and became an officer. I was back in Iraq for the second war there. After that I did a tour in Belgium with NATO and then three tours in Afghanistan. Not much to tell really."

"Sounds to me as if you spent a lot of time in one war or another," she said.

"Not really because the actual time in combat is very limited. My last two tours in Afghanistan I was with intelligence and never went into the field once. It involved a lot of computer work."

"You don't seem to have lost the Special Forces edge."

"What makes you say that?" he asked.

"The way you took down my uncle in the lobby a couple months ago."

They passed the rest of the morning idly chatting about nothing special and everything in particular. Basically, it was a second date conversation.

Toward lunchtime, she said, "Pete, there is one thing I need to tell you because it is going to come up one of these days, and I don't know quite how to do it."

"Try straight out and we will go from there."

"In every whorehouse that I own there is a full-size picture of me to welcome the clients."

"Look, Madame Gin Sling met her demise at one o'clock yesterday afternoon. I see no reason to resurrect her now or in the future." But as he said it he had the feeling that they would have to deal with it again.

She rolled over and up on his chest and kissed him. "You really are a special man," she murmured. She, too, knew that this fact would come back to haunt her. The only question was how and when.

"All right as long as we are playing true confessions, I think I probably ought to tell you something. I may live to regret telling you this. But, here goes. I had made up my mind that when I reached Honolulu, I would come back to Macau and ask you to come to the States with me."

"You rat! You've spent the last week acting like you were about to be drawn and quartered. And, what's with this 'I'll help you financially with the baby' shit?"

"I had a feeling that I shouldn't mention that," he said, getting out of bed. He walked into the closet. Sophie marshalled her thoughts, preparing to lambast him again, when he said, "Here's your wedding present."

Her curiosity overcame her ire. She opened the box to find a beautiful gold lady's Rolex watch. She was touched and a little misty eyed for a moment.

"I ordered yours but it hasn't come yet," she said.

"What would you like to do for lunch?" he asked some minutes later.

"Room service."

So they ordered, ate in bed, and spent the rest of the afternoon in bed. Their conversation just rambled from subject to subject. They turned the television on for a while but were soon bored, and then shut it off.

"What's the sexiest thing you have ever seen a woman wear?" she asked him later that afternoon.

"Well, one time I saw a woman with a peg leg and a tattoo of a dragon on her back," he replied.

"No, I am being serious."

"I don't know."

"There must be something," she said pursuing the subject.

"I think what is sexy is really based on your mood that day. Sometimes a dress cut down the front turns you on. Sometimes a dress cut down the back turns you on. I like ladies that wear hats with big brims and big glasses sometimes."

"Oh, boy, are you a disappointment," she said. "You're telling me that there is nothing you find erotic or exotic? You just like plain vanilla?"

"Well I don't like ladies with a bone in their nose, if that's what you mean."

"There must be something."

"Okay, there is a tribe in Thailand where the women wear rings around their necks to protect them from tiger bites. That is certainly erotic," he said. As he looked at her he could see the wheels of her mind going. "But don't you do that."

"Why not?"

"Because the women damage themselves. The weight of the rings compresses their chest, making the neck look long. Their neck muscles atrophy so if they ever take the rings off, there is a very good chance they will break their neck and die. So don't do it."

Around seven o'clock, he asked about dinner.

"I don't really want to get dressed, and I definitely don't want to get out of bed," she responded.

"I guess its room service again," he answered. And, that was what they did. They made love again after taking the plates out of the bedroom.

Just after turning out the light she said, "I think it has been more than twenty years since I spent a day without wearing my leg and using only crutches." He did not respond.

Pete awoke about eight. Sophie had already left the bed, and he could hear her in the bathroom, although she was trying to be quiet. He stretched just as she came into the bedroom saying, "I have to go to work."

"You know we have not really talked about this mansion you want to buy. Will you come and sit down here for moment?" She came over and sat on the edge of the bed, letting her peg leg rest on the floor.

"Okay, what is it specifically you want to know?"

"Well, what I would like to know is exactly what you have in mind; how many square feet, how many rooms, that sort of thing?"

"What I want you to find is a very large house you would like to live in." She took a cigarette from her purse and put it into her cigarette holder. The conversation paused as she lit it.

"I do not consider that an acceptable task description," he said.

"Why not? If you like it, I'll like it. That's all you need to know."

"Be specific."

She stood and with her cigarette holder held between her index finger and middle finger waved her hand away from her body in a gesture of dismissal. She turned and started to leave the bedroom. Just as she reached the bedroom door, he said, "By the way, you have to quit smoking. It is bad for the baby."

"I've tried. I can't."

"Try again. I am going to need a computer," he added, as she left in a cloud of smoke.

Without turning she said, over her shoulder, "Buy whatever you need. Stop by my office and my secretary will have a credit card for you to use." And with that she was gone. Clearly she had slipped into the efficiency mode.

Just as he finished unpacking his new computer, someone knocked on the door. He opened it and found a young Chinese man of about twenty-five standing there. "Hello," he said, "I am John Chen. I am the information technology guy for the hotel. Madame Gin Sling, err I guess Mrs. Smith now, asked me to come and give you a hand setting up your computer."

"Come in. How did you learn to speak English so well?"

"I'm third generation American, born in San Francisco. I spoke Cantonese in the crib, and when I graduated from college with a degree in computer science, I was offered a job here. It paid better than anything I could find in the States, so here I am."

Fifteen minutes later he was on the Internet. He thanked John and promised to buy him a beer.

He had Google humming all afternoon. By six o'clock, he had found half a dozen possibilities. He had just called it a day when the phone rang. He picked it up. "How about a drink in the English Pub," she said without further introduction.

He decided to give a little zinger. "Carol, is that you? How did you know I was here?"

"This is not Carol," Sophie said in a very frosty tone.

"I know. I'm on my way."

When he entered the English Pub, he saw Sophie seated at her table, lit cigarette in the holder between her fingers. He sat down and gave her a quick kiss on the lips. "You have got to quit smoking. It is bad for the baby."

Changing the subject, she said, "I don't like jokes about other women. I find myself afflicted with a severe case of jealousy."

"Get over it."

"Get over it?"

"Yeah, get over it," he said.

"I can't and I don't want to. I thought I told you, I am not a very good sharer. And if I did not make it clear earlier let me do so now. And I don't want to learn."

"That hits me as a definite character flaw."

"Perhaps," she opined. "Listen, I have never been in love before nor felt so possessive. I never even had a boyfriend before, so this is all new to me."

"I am going to help you work on it."

"Don't bother," she said flatly.

"Oh, it's no bother," almost popped out of his mouth, but in the interest of domestic tranquility he changed the subject. "I've been looking for your mansion online and have about a half dozen possibilities."

"Oh, where are they?"

"They are all over the southern states; a couple in California, a couple in Texas, and three in Florida."

"What's the price range?"

"They are priced all over the map, between ten and forty million," he responded.

"What are you going to do next?" she asked.

"Make a few phone calls and decide which one to see first."

"Which one do you favor?"

"Santa Barbara, I think, although there is a very nice one in Beverly Hills as well."

"Beverly Hills sounds nice."

"It is nice, but it is in the LA area, and I don't like LA very much. There are too many people and too much congestion."

"What do you want to eat?" she asked, feeling her stomach growl.

"I don't know, let's walk around and see what strikes our fancy," he said. The fact that she had not even batted an eye at a price of forty million was not lost on him.

By the end of the week he was bored. When Sophie came to the apartment he asked her when the interview at the consulate was going to be.

"I just got the letter today," she said. "It is scheduled for a week from next Tuesday. I thought maybe we could go to Hong Kong for the weekend."

"That's pretty fast, isn't it?"

"Yes, but I called the counsel Monday when the papers were filed."

"I gather he moved things along rather quickly after that call. Well, I guess I might as well leave for the States as soon as the interview is over. What time is the interview?"

"Ten o'clock," Sophie answered, missing him already. She was having a great deal of trouble understanding her own emotions about her husband. It had started the moment she saw him and had continued ever since. There was no logic to it. She knew

it and wondered why. She could not figure out where her common sense had gone. "Have you decided where you are going
first?"

"No, but Beverly Hills is the logical choice. The plane is going to
land in LA, and Beverly Hills is just up the road."

3

As they walked into the consulate, he looked over at Sophie. "You look nervous," he said, voicing his observation.

"I am."

"No reason to be, just let me do most of the talking. As I told you, I understand these government types. And the other thing, of course, is to tell the truth. That makes things simpler," he said, trying to reassure her.

"I always worry about things I cannot control."

"No problem, I took charge the moment you said 'I do.'"

"Huh."

It surprised him that she did not react to that.

They passed through the security screening at the door and proceeded to the waiting room. They were to see a Mr. Kozloski, who would be conducting the interview. After fifteen minutes their names were called and they entered a small office painted in a light government green. Dreadful, Pete thought to himself, wondering how he had survived twenty years in the army. The only wall covering was the obligatory presidential picture.

"Good morning, Mr. and Mrs. Smith. I am Stan Kozloski and I will be conducting this interview for Mrs. Smith's permanent residence visa. The counsel has spoken to me about this already; apparently he attended your wedding. This is more a formality than anything else. But let me see here, I do have a few questions. You met and were married two months later. Is that correct?"

"Yes," Pete answered.

"Why so fast?"

"Sophie got pregnant. I would appreciate it if you not mention it to anyone else though. It is rather personal."

He could see the light turn on in Kozloski's mind. Now that he understood the motivation, things were going to go easy and fast.

After a couple more preliminary questions, Kozloski said, "I am required to split you up for a few questions, so Mrs. Smith, will you excuse us for a few minutes?"

After Sophie had left the room, the interviewer asked, "What brand of toothpaste do you and your wife use?"

"I use Crest. I don't know what kind my wife uses. We have separate bathrooms, and while I have been in hers, she leaves nothing out on the sink as I do."

"Does your wife have any scars or other distinguishing marks?"

"She has a dragon tattooed on her back."

"Do you have any scars that are not apparent when you are fully clothed?"

"Yes, I have bullet wounds, entry and exit on my right thigh and in the left quadrant of my abdomen."

"You've been shot twice?"

"Yes, I am retired Army Special Forces, Delta Force, if that means anything to you."

"It certainly does. And I would like to thank you for your service to the country. You can send your wife in now."

Sophie and Pete switched seats. "Does your husband have any scars not apparent when he is fully clothed?" Kozloski asked.

"Yes, he has bullet wound scars here," she said indicating her right thigh, "And here," indicating the left side of her abdomen.

"What kind of toothpaste does he use?" he asked next.

"Crest."

"Do you have any scars or distinguishing marks not apparent when you are fully clothed?"

"Yes," she answered, "A dragon tattooed on my back."

"Okay, that's enough," he said, getting up and opening the door. "Come in, Mr. Smith." After Pete entered, Kozloski said, "Everything is fine. I'll put the papers through today."

"How long will it take?" Pete asked Mr. Kozloski.

"Well, I have seen it take as little as forty days and as long as one hundred twenty, so it is really hard to say."

"I guess all we can do is wait," Pete said, holding out his hand. They shook and Pete said, "Thank you, sir." Sophie, likewise, shook his hand.

"See, that was easy," Pete said as they were leaving the building.

"You were right."

When they reached the limo Sophie had rented, Pete opened the door for Sophie and extended a hand to help her get into the car. Once they were both in the limo and the door closed, Pete said to the driver, "Airport."

"I miss you already," Sophie said.

"It's time to get on with the rest of our lives."

4

*H*e arrived in LA absolutely brain-dead. He had flown straight through from Hong Kong, stopping only in Honolulu to clear customs and change planes. His baggage finally came around on the carousel. He went outside, found a taxi, and went to the Airport Century Plaza Hotel. Pete checked in and went to his room. He lay down, thinking he would get up and take a shower in just a minute. But it was not to be. Next thing he knew it was five o'clock in the afternoon. He had slept eight hours, and he still needed a shower.

When he was showered and fully dressed, he went down to the bar. He had two beers and a cheeseburger while sitting there. Then he returned to his room around seven o'clock and fell asleep again. He awoke about six in the morning feeling like a new man.

He lay in bed finalizing the plans he had started making on the plane. First, rent a car and drive by the property in Beverly Hills. Then if he liked it he would get in touch with the real estate agent and go to see it.

After spending forty-five minutes stuck in traffic trying to get from the airport to Beverly Hills, a distance of about fifteen miles maximum, he felt certain LA was not for him. But he pressed on anyway. Finally, he found the address on the listing form. The house disappointed immensely. It looked much bigger in the pictures and most of the land lay between the street and the house, giving the place a huge front lawn, but probably a small backyard. It was not what he had in mind. The price tag was forty million, and he could not see what that kind of money bought except an address.

So he went back to Sunset Boulevard and headed toward the ocean. Turning north on the Pacific Coast Highway he left LA behind to corrode in its own private smog cloud. An hour and a half later he reached the outskirts of Santa Barbara, the second stop on his quest for Sophie's mansion. He filled the car with gas and bought a map at an Exxon station. After looking at the map, he headed for the address of the second possibility. He drove by the outside once, looked very carefully, but was unable to see much because of a high fence in front of the house. The fence was obviously there for privacy, and it worked very well. He turned around in a driveway a few hundred feet down the street. This time as he came up to the entry gate no one was behind him. He stopped in the street. This was a true mansion; Spanish-style architecture, cream-colored stucco walls with a red tile roof. What he could see was gorgeous. This was definitely worth seeing. His watch said noon as he left the neighborhood so he drove into the commercial district looking for a place for lunch. He saw a Wienerschnitzel on his side of the street, and he pulled into the parking lot. After waiting his turn in line, he ordered three chili cheese dogs, a large fry, and, as a concession to his bulging waistline, a Diet Coke.

He ruminated on what he had just seen. From the street, it appeared to be perfect. To see the entire thing meant contacting the real estate agent. Before that, however, he needed a good camera and a cell phone. He also realized he needed a motel with free Wi-Fi. The lunch rush had subsided so he went up to the window and asked the young girl where he could buy a camera. She gave him directions to a mall. In any mall worthy of the name, there would also be a store selling cell phones.

As he left the mall he reviewed his purchases: a new iPhone with a hundred prepaid minutes on it and a top-of-the-line Sony digital camera. He also bought new jogging shoes, shorts, and a tank top. The next step was to telephone the real estate agent. As soon as he reached the car, he retrieved from the passenger's seat the listing sheet he had downloaded in Macau.

The phone in the real estate office rang twice before it was answered by what sounded like a young woman. He asked to speak to Mary Schumann, the listing agent, but she was unavailable.

"I may be able to be of service to you," she said. "How may I help you?"

Pete told her the house he wanted to see. She told him that property was shown only by appointment, but she would see if she could make an appointment for him.

"That sounds wonderful," he said.

"Let me have your phone number," she said.

He gave her the number of his new cell phone. She said she would let him know when he could see the property. Apparently, when houses reached a certain size they became "property," not "houses." It was clearly a simple marketing ploy, as far as he was concerned.

He started to work on the next item on the agenda: a place to stay. He drove out of the parking lot heading toward the center of town. When he had traveled about six blocks, he came across a Motel Six. He pulled in, parked, and went into a typical nondescript, beige office. "Have you any rooms available?" he asked the young, pretty receptionist.

"Yes sir," the receptionist responded. Then she added, "For how many nights?"

"One for the moment, but that may stretch out considerably," he responded.

The receptionist looked at the computer, punching a few keys from time to time and finally said, "That should not be a problem, sir." She went on to ask, "Do you have any preference in rooms?"

"Nonsmoking and on the ground level if it is available," he responded.

"Certainly, sir. May I have your credit card, and would you fill out the registration card, please?"

A minute later she handed him his credit card and a key to room 108. As he was leaving, his cell phone rang. "Hello," he said while walking toward the rental car.

"This is Mary Schumann with Pacific Realty. I have tentatively arranged to show the property you inquired about at four o'clock this afternoon, if that meets with your approval."

"That's fine, the sooner the better. Where are you located?"

"Do you know Santa Barbara at all?" she asked.

"Not at all," he replied.

"It would probably be best if I pick you up then. Where are you staying?"

"At the Motel Six."

"Sir, forgive me for asking, but can you afford thirty million dollars?"

"Not only no, but hell no," he answered. He then went on to say, chuckling, "But my wife can."

"Oh, OK," she said somewhat dubiously. "I'll see you at about quarter of four then."

She arrived precisely on time. As they drove to the property, Mary gave him the house's history as she drove. The house had been finished, she explained, in the early forties. It had been built by one of Hollywood's major producers at that time and resold to another in the late sixties. The present owner was in his nineties and wanted to liquidate his assets to facilitate the distribution of his estate.

She went on to warn that there was a considerable amount of deferred maintenance. Largely cosmetic in nature, she explained, but it would lower the amount of bank financing available.

"I don't think that will be a problem," Pete said. "I believe my wife intends to pay cash." Ms. Schumann just nodded. He could see the wheels in her brain calculating her commission. He went on to ask her how long the property had been for sale.

"Just over two years," she answered.

When they drove through the gate, which he had glimpsed through earlier, he was stunned. The whole property far exceeded anything he had imagined. The three-hundred-foot driveway led to a circular turnaround in front of the house. The driveway forked, leading to a two-story, four-car garage. "Are there employee apartments over the garage?" he asked.

"Yes, there are two, but they are quite small and really only fit for one person," she answered. They parked in the circular drive and walked twenty feet to the front door. Mary rang the bell. A uniformed maid opened the door and Mary introduced herself.

"Mr. Pederson is on the back terrace," she said. "You may look at anything you like."

Pete got his camera out and started snapping pictures. The entry ceiling was at least twenty-five feet high. The real estate agent guided Pete to the left into the most enormous living room he had ever seen. There were two fireplaces in the living room and several conversational furniture groupings. It had to be a least eight hundred square feet. They walked through the living room into a library. The library looked like a movie set. It had wood paneling and floor-to-ceiling shelves completely full of books. The library also had a fireplace with a ten-foot hearth.

Pete kept taking pictures.

He lost count of the rooms. There was a billiard room with a poker table, an office, a formal dining room with a table that seated twenty-four, a smaller breakfast area, a ballroom, an office, an exercise room, and a den. The kitchen would have brought a smile to the face of any mess sergeant in the U.S. Army. Beyond the kitchen, there were servants' quarters. They went out onto the wraparound terrace. The owner was there in a wheelchair, looking every bit of his ninety years. A barbecue pit sat on the left side of the terrace. The Olympic-sized pool was about fifty feet from the house. Behind the house there was an outbuilding. "What's that?" he asked.

"That's the guesthouse. Let's take a look."

They walked around the pool to the guesthouse. It was almost the same size as the house where he had grown up. It had a living room, a bedroom, and a small kitchen with an eating area.

They went back into the main house and climbed the stairs to the second floor. The second floor had eight bedrooms, four of which had sitting rooms attached to them. They all had private baths.

He had to admit to himself that this house overwhelmed him. Pete was really not sure what constituted a mansion, but this had to be it. It had a great floor plan. The classic Spanish architecture of the outside continued inside with rounded doors and archways, but as he examined things closer, he saw the deferred maintenance the real estate agent had mentioned earlier. There were nicks in door frames and a lot of cracked and peeling paint. He was no expert but he thought a lot of exterior wood would need to be replaced.

"What, no wine cellar?" he asked jokingly.

"Oh did I forget to show you that? Follow me," Mary said.

The door to the wine cellar was off the kitchen. After descending about twenty steps, he saw what seemed to be about twenty-five wooden wine racks. They were mostly empty, and judging by the dust, had been for a while.

He and the real estate agent returned to the entry. Halfway to the car the agent asked him, "What did you think?"

"I love the building but I am really in doubt about how much it will cost to bring it back into top condition."

"Well, the good news is that you don't need to do it all at once," Mary responded.

"You don't know my wife. I need to email these photos to her and let her look at them. I don't suppose you have a floor plan do you?"

"Actually, I do," Mary answered.

"Do you have a computer and a scanner I could use to send them?" Pete asked.

"Of course," she responded.

"Hello, Sophie," he said into the telephone.

"Who is this?" a weary voice asked.

"Pete."

"Do you know what time it is?"

"Ah . . . no," he answered. Then he went on to say, "I found your mansion today. I emailed you about seventy photos and the floor plan."

"It's six in the morning. That's not too bad, I guess. I need to get up soon anyway."

"Well," he said, "after you have looked at them, give me a call, and we can discuss it."

"Okay, it will be a couple of hours before I have reviewed them."

"All right, talk to you later."

"I miss you and wish we were together," she said, hanging up.

"Me, too."

Three hours later the phone rang. He answered, sure of whom it would be. He had guessed correctly, it was his wife. Without so much as a hello, she said, "I love the house but you are right, it needs a lot of work."

"Hello to you, too," he replied.

"I really cannot talk right now but stay near a telephone until noon tomorrow."

"Okay," he said somewhat surprised.

"Talk to you tomorrow then, bye." Click. He held the receiver away from his ear and stared at it for a couple seconds before deciding she must be involved in something very important. Having reached that conclusion, he laced up his new jogging shoes. He set out with the intention of going five miles. He pulled up gasping at the three and a half mile mark. Not only had the fine food taken its toll on his waistline, but a three-and-a-half-month running layoff had done its damage as well.

At two o'clock the next afternoon, his cell phone started to chirp like a little birdy. He really needed to change the ring on the phone. He guessed it was Sophie and he was correct again.

"Hi," he responded. "How are you?"

"Busy, very busy," she said. "I think I sold the hotel yesterday, and I spent considerable time on our house project."

"Sounds like you have made up your mind to buy it," he said.

"Actually, no, I haven't. But I think it might be what I had in mind. Before we go any further, though, I want to know if you like it and would be happy there."

"Fully restored, the place would be a palace. And, yes, in that condition I would be delighted to live there," he responded truthfully.

"That makes me happy to hear. Tomorrow morning a contractor, an interior decorator, and an architect are going to meet you at your hotel. You need to arrange for them to get in to see the house. Is that going to be a problem?" she asked.

"I don't think so, but I'll call you back if it is. Will you email me the names of these people?"

"Good idea."

"How are you though?"

"I'm fine," she answered.

"Have you been to the doctor and is everything well with the baby?"

"Yes and yes."

"If there is nothing else, I am going jogging, I'll be gone about an hour," he said.

"One last thing," she said. "You better open a bank account locally. Email me the wire transfer instructions when you get them."

"Okay," he replied. Bank account, of course; that was something he had not thought of, even fleetingly.

The next morning he waited outside, in front of his room. It was a beautiful morning with a clear, blue, cloudless sky and temperatures in the low seventies. Sarah Godwin, the interior decorator, arrived first. She wore a dark blue skirt and a white sleeveless blouse. She was a stocky woman in her mid-forties.

Mike Johnson, the contractor, drove up in a battered pickup truck that looked as if it had seen one job site too many. He wore a faded light blue dress shirt with a frayed collar and Levis. He had a barrel chest with thick arms. It was apparent he had worked many years with his hands.

Mary Schumann arrived with Ben Pollack, the architect. He stood about six one but was very thin. He had on bone-colored slacks and a dark blue knit golf shirt with a St. Barth's logo over the left breast.

After the introductions and a brief discussion, they decided to take two cars.

A couple of minutes before nine o'clock Mary rang the doorbell. The same maid who had shown them in on their last visit opened the door. She invited them in with a large smile. Pete had the very distinct feeling she was angling for a job if the property sold.

As the group wandered from room to room, it seemed the decorator had taken charge, with the others advising as to what was possible. From time to time, someone would ask Pete a question and the response was the same each time, a Gallic shrug. Finally, he said, "You will have to give me the options for me to render an intelligent response." He started to feel like a fifth wheel and did not like that feeling at all. As they wandered on, he wondered what he could do about it. Complaining to Sophie would get him nowhere. He knew what she would say, that he had as much input as she did. Fine, he thought, but the fact remained it was still her thirty million dollars that would buy the thing and her money that would be used for the renovations. But for the moment, all he could do was to wander off by himself. He walked out to the guesthouse. On his last visit he had not realized there was a tennis court behind the guesthouse. He walked around the guesthouse to get a closer look at the tennis court. It was in terrible condition. There were weeds everywhere. It had been many years since anyone had played tennis on this court. He did not like the game, and he was reasonably confident Sophie would not be taking it up in the future.

He stood looking at the pool when Mary Schumann wandered over. She, too, apparently had become bored with all the technical talk.

He asked her, "How much is this place really worth?"

"How long is a piece of string?" she asked, but continued in a more serious tone. "It really depends on how much the buyer wants a place like this and the market conditions at the time. It has been on the market for two years and the seller has lowered the price twice. Originally he was asking forty million. In 2007 he probably could have gotten it, but now, who knows? You want to start low and see where the negotiations take you."

After about three hours they all assembled in the living room.

"Do you have anything special you want in the house or any requests?" Ben Pollack asked.

He thought for a moment. "Hardwood floors throughout," he said.

"That is going to cost a lot and will take time. Rug is easy and quicker," Mike Johnson said.

"That's okay."

He noticed each of the experts had about half a legal pad full of notes. "I need you all to put together a guesstimate of the remodel costs by about eleven tonight. I want to speak to my wife this evening with the idea of being able to make an offer tomorrow. Equally as important, however, is the time it will take to complete the renovation."

The group returned to the parking lot of the Motel Six. From there they left for their respective offices and calculators.

Pete, however, changed into his running clothes. He set off with the intention of jogging five miles. And this time he did.

At about seven o'clock the telephone rang. Mary Schumann spoke first, introducing herself and stating that it was a conference call with everyone on the line. The consensus was that it would cost about five million to put the house into first-class condition and furnish it. But the estimates came with plenty of caveats about damage that was not visible.

"How long will all this take?" he asked.

Mike Johnson answered, saying, "It is difficult to say."

"Can it be done in ninety days?" Pete asked, pressing the point.

"It is possible," Mike said, "But you would have to put on extra men and that would increase cost."

"One last question. When can you start?"

"I have a few projects to wrap up so in a week to ten days," Mike answered.

He thanked everyone for their efforts and lay back on the bed. He needed to wait about four hours before he could call Sophie and expect any kind of cohearent response from her. But that, he decided, was a blessing in disguise. He knew Sophie was going to ask for his opinion, and he didn't really have one. On the one hand was the price: thirty million. And that was just the opener. The place needed the extensive, expensive remodel. But on the other hand, it would be magnificent when completed.

At eleven o'clock Pete called Sophie. She did not answer, however, so he left a brief message. Fifteen minutes later she called back.

She skipped all the preliminaries. "Tell me, what is the consensus on the cost of the remodel?"

"I'm fine. At the moment it is five million but, but, but," he responded.

"What does that mean?"

"Well, first of all, it is an estimate and not a guaranteed price. Second, it does not include anything that either turns out to be greatly more extensive than is apparent at this time or anything that cannot be seen."

"What can't be seen?" she wanted to know.

"Any rotten wood inside the walls they may find once they start moving things around, for example."

"Oh. So this is what you Americans call a ball park estimate," she said.

"I think you understand exactly."

"But it is a very big ball park, isn't it?"

"It is enormous, practically without a fence," Pete said.

"Well, what do you think?"

"Sophie, that is a big question. In what regard: price, or the house itself, or the people?" he asked.

"All of that."

"Well, as to price, it is certainly a lot nicer than the place I saw in Beverly Hills for forty million. But, that is in Beverly Hills, and that fact alone makes it worth more. I asked the same thing of the real estate agent. She said it was very difficult to tell because of the depressed market. The price has been reduced twice from forty million. So who really knows. There is nothing comparable on the market. There may be nothing comparable in the area. The house itself is big, very big. I like most aspects of the floor plan. The people you found seem to be competent, I liked them as well."

"Do you like it?" Sophie asked.

"I was afraid you would ask me that."

"Why?"

"I don't want you to spend thirty million on my say-so," he replied.

"I trust your judgment completely, but let me ask you this. Would I like it?"

"I think so." He did not want to say that, but did it anyway. He didn't think he knew her tastes well enough to judge.

"When will you know?" she asked. And, then went on, "When can they start, and how long to finish?"

"I asked those questions as well. They can start in about a week to ten days. How long will it take? It depends on what they find once they start. If everything goes well, ninety days, but they will have to hire additional people. And that will most likely jack up the price."

"All right, let's make an offer."

"Okay"

"Offer twenty million, closing in ten days. You will need to give the real estate agent a check with the offer. Make it for a hundred thousand dollars but check with the bank to make sure the wire transfer has arrived."

"Is there that much money in the account?" Pete asked.

"I put two million in there yesterday," she answered.

"Two million dollars!" he hollered. "Are you crazy?"

"You never know how much money you will need for a deal like this and right now we have no financial credibility in the United States. So I wanted to be sure you had enough to finish this if that is what we decide."

"I'll make the offer tomorrow."

"Good. As soon as you hear what happened call me, any time of the day or night. I am starting to get excited about this."

"You got it."

"Well, I guess it's good night then," she said.

"Wait a minute, how's the baby?" he wanted to know.

"Just fine," she said.

"And you?" he asked.

"Tired, but other than that, I'm fine as well."

"Well don't overdo it," he said.

"Talk to you tomorrow then, bye-bye. Love you."

The next morning, after jogging six miles, Pete showered and shaved. He went to the bank. He had opened the account with one hundred dollars. This branch was small, only three teller windows, and at eight thirty only two were open. He waited patiently in line. When he reached the window, he showed the teller his checkbook. "Would you check the balance in this account?" he asked, handing her one of the temporary checks.

As she pushed numbers into her computer terminal, he studied her. Dark hair, brown eyes, and a slight olive tint to her complexion indicated a probable Spanish heritage. As he watched her, her eyes got bigger and she said, "Will you wait here for just a moment sir?"

"Of course," he replied.

Less than a minute later a man came out of a small office. He walked directly to Pete and said, "I'm Mike Fox, the manager here. May I speak with you for a moment?" Mike Fox was an overweight man of about thirty-eight, about five feet, ten inches tall, and soon to be bald. He wore an ill-fitting cheap tan suit. As they entered his office, he indicated Pete should be seated in one of the chairs in front of his desk. The office itself was about three times bigger than a phone booth. Pete wondered if the size of the office reflected what upper management thought of Mike Fox.

When they were both seated, Fox said to Pete, "A very large deposit was made into your account yesterday. It came from overseas, Switzerland to be precise."

"Yes," Pete replied, giving nothing away.

"Whenever we receive large deposits, we are required by law to make sure the funds were not illegally obtained. I am not suggesting you may have done something illegal by any manner or means, but I need to ask the source of these funds?"

A couple of smartass responses flashed through his mind but he instead replied, "My wife is one of the richest women in Asia. She wired me the funds because we are thinking of buying a house here."

"How did she earn the funds?"

"She owns, among other properties, the Sun Palace Resort and Casino in Macau," Pete responded. After a moment's thought he added, "Call the president of any bank in Macau and ask about Madame Gin Sling."

"That should be sufficient," he said. "When the compliance people in San Francisco call, I'll pass that information along."

"Good enough," Pete said, rising to leave.

Mike Fox stood and said, "It was a pleasure meeting you, and thank you for your time."

As Pete left the bank he called the real estate agent on his cell phone. He was surprised she was in her office. He said, "I want to make an offer on the property. I am prepared to pay twenty million, closing in ten days, and a hundred thousand in earnest money. Can you prepare the papers while I am en route to your office, and oh yea, where is your office?"

She gave him directions and said she would have to call him while he was en route if she had any questions so as to have the paperwork complete on his arrival. He told her that would be fine and pulled out of the bank's parking lot.

As he was parking in front of the real estate agency, his cell phone rang. He ignored it and walked inside the building.

"Good morning," Mary Schumann said. "I just tried to call you. The only thing I am missing is your full name, wife's name, and how you want to take title."

"I was just parking in front of the building when you called. Peter James Smith, Sophie Marie Smith, husband and wife as joint tenants, I think. I am sure there will be a counteroffer and we can change it then if we want. I will check with my wife."

"If you will give me the check, then sign here and sign here," she said, indicating a line at the bottom of the multipage form.

Pete signed both the check and the offer to purchase at the same time. Mary Schumann left to present the offer, while Pete went to his motel.

Pete was lying on his bed when the phone rang. He picked it up saying, "Hello."

Without acknowledging his greeting the real estate agent said, "We drew a counteroffer of twenty-eight million. He also wants the earnest money increased to a million."

"Was everything else okay with the offer?" he queried.

"Price and earnest money are the only issues at this point, remarkable really."

"No problem with the ten days?"

"Actually, he said he would like five days. But I told him it was impossible and that I had my doubts about ten days."

"I have to call my wife in Macau. I'll call you back as soon as we've spoken."

"Talk to you later, bye."

"Bye."

Pete dialed the number in Macau. The operator connected him to Sophie. "Well, what happened with the offer?" Sophie wanted to know without preliminaries.

"Where are you? In the English Pub as usual?" he asked.

"Yes. Now, get to the offer," she said impatiently.

He chuckled and then said, "Everything is fine except he wants twenty-eight million and the deposit increased to a million." She did not respond immediately, and he could picture her mental calculator whirring.

"Okay on the million and up the price to twenty-four million," she said.

"Sophie, are you sure about this?"

"No, but do it anyway."

"Sophie, there is one other thing we need to discuss. That is how we are going to take title."

"What's that mean?" she asked.

"Title is the statement of ownership. I told her we would take title as joint tenants, which means that if one of us dies the other automatically owns the whole property. The other option is put it in your name alone since you are paying for it."

"I like the first option better," Sophie said.

"Okay," he said. He went on, "I don't like these abrupt phone calls. You act as if you're talking to a pit boss or something. I need to know how my wife and son are doing."

"I'm sorry," she said contritely. "But right at the moment I am under an enormous amount of pressure trying to get this hotel sold."

"What are the problems?"

"A bunch of little ones, plus they think they are buying the cash in the cage."

"How's the baby?"

"The baby is doing just fine."

"Please don't overdo. I'll call you as soon as I hear something."

Upon hanging up, he called Mary Schumann. "My wife wants to raise the offer to twenty-four million, and she'll go for the million down payment. Everything else stays the same."

He could hear her wheels grinding as she worked out her commission. "Great, I'll prepare our counteroffer and bring it to your motel for your signature."

"I'll be waiting."

Three hours later the phone rang. Wasting no words, Mary Schumann said, "He has counter-offered at twenty-six million."

"Let me make a phone call. I'll get back to you."

Sophie had just lain down when the phone rang again. "Hello," she said, after flinging her hair away from her ear.

"Hi," Pete said.

'Oh, hello my husband. How are you?"

He wondered what had mellowed her so much. She had to know the reason for the call, and she was not wearing her business hat. "I am very well."

She casually asked, "Have you heard a response to our counteroffer?"

This was a game two could play. "Yes," he said.

After a pregnant pause, she asked, "Well?"

"Well what?"

"What was the goddammed counteroffer?" she said exploding into the phone! Evidently, her patience had expired.

"Oh that," he said with exaggerated disinterest. "Twenty-six million. Everything else is fine."

"Okay, counter-offer again at twenty-four million five hundred thousand, and we want access to the house during the escrow. You can be the world's most exasperating person when you want to be."

"Moi?"

"Yes, you!"

"Okay, I'll call you when I hear something."

"Talk to you later then," she said by way of signing off.

After a quick phone call to Mary Schumann, he lay back down on the bed. He had been watching CNN, but he shut off the television. His thoughts drifted to where all this was leading. He could not help but think the plan mapped out by Sophie was going to unravel somehow. But for the life of him he could not see how or why it was going to happen. A knock on the door interrupted his circular introspection.

"Hi," Mary Schumann said. "I need your signature and I'll be on my way."

He signed and Mary breezed out, saying over her shoulder, "I'll be in touch."

Two hours later the phone rang again. He picked it up, but before he could even say hello Mary Schumann said, "He countered at twenty-five million and says that's it. He is not moving another dime."

"I need to call Macau again. I'll let you know what happens." With that he hung up.

"Hello," Sophie answered in a just awakened voiced.

"Good evening, dear" Pete said.

"Okay, tell me where we are now with this deal."

"He made a counteroffer of twenty-five million and says it's his last counteroffer."

"I think it is time for me to get involved. Give me the number of the real estate agent." He did. "I'll call you back when I know something," she said, hanging up. He looked at the phone and shrugged as his stomach made a demand to be fed.

Mary Schumann answered on the third ring. After a few preliminaries Sophie got to the point. "We will accept the seller's final counteroffer if you reduce your commission by five hundred thousand dollars."

"I never reduce my commission," she lied. She had already agreed to a reduction in commission with the seller.

"Do you have a pencil," Sophie asked.

"Yes."

"Let me give you my phone number so you can call me back if you change your mind"

"Okay, go ahead," said Mary.

Sophie gave her the number and then added, "I have always found something is better than nothing," and with that she hung up.

Mary Schumann looked at the receiver in her hand, watching one point four million dollars flutter out the window. She got up and walked to the convenience store just down the street. "A package of Marlboro reds," she said to the clerk.

As she left the store, she did something she had not done in fifteen years. She lit a cigarette. She slowly walked back to her office, crushing out her cigarette on the sidewalk before entering. She became madder and madder. Who did that bitch think she was, chopping her by five hundred thousand dollars, for Christ sake! She went back outside and lit a second cigarette. Pacing slowly as she smoked it, she realized that the bitch was right. She had no choice and she knew it, too.

Mary made a Herculean effort to compose herself sufficiently to call Sophie back.

Mary agreed to Sophie's demands, and Sophie said that she would advise Pete to expect Mary with the paperwork for his signature.

Just as Pete returned from lunch, his cell phone rang. "Hello," he said.

"Well, we made a deal," Sophie said. "The real estate agent will be over with papers for your signature shortly."

"Good, I guess. Are you sure you want to spend twenty-five million on something you have not seen?"

"I trust you implicitly."

"I just hope it's not misplaced."

They exchanged good-byes and then hung up.

Fifteen minutes later Mary Schumann knocked on the door. She came in saying, "I think this will be the final time for this." He signed where indicated. She left, her anger under control. After all, he was not the one who had ground on her for the half million.

Two hours later Mary called him. "We have a deal," she told him.

"Great," he replied. "I need to tell my wife."

"How 'bout I buy you a celebratory diner tonight at the Chart House," she asked.

"Sure, what time?"

"Is eight o'clock all right?" she asked.

"I'll meet you there," he said. With that he hung up. He dialed Sophie's number.

When she answered, he said, "We bought a mansion."

"Oh, that's great. Well, what are you going to do to celebrate?"

"Mary Schumann is buying me a celebratory dinner this evening."

Sophie instantly realized that while Mary Schumann might be the world's best real estate agent she was also a world-class poacher. "I am going to send Toy to California to help with all the details that are going to arise as we go through the remodel."

"That's not necessary."

"He will be a big help, I assure you. Make him a reservation at the hotel where you are staying. He should be there tomorrow."

"Okay."

They exchanged good-byes and hung up.

Later that evening, just as the waiter at the Chart House was serving diner to Mary and Pete, his cell phone rang. "Hello," he said, somewhat surprised.

"Hi," Sophie said brightly.

He looked at Mary and as he rose he said, "It's my wife. Please eat, don't let your food get cold." As he was walking to the foyer he said to Sophie, "What's up?"

"I am not sure I like you having dinner with that woman."

"That woman?"

"Yes, she is trying to poach on my territory."

"Sophie, this conversation is nonsensical. You don't know what you are talking about. And maybe more importantly, you have not seen her."

"I still do not like it."

"Sophie, you have got to learn to control your jealousy. You're not a teenager anymore. I'll talk to you tomorrow. Bye." With that he hung up and went back to the table.

He was getting out of bed after having slept in until ten o'clock when there was a knock on the door. He grabbed his pants, went to the door, and opened it. Toy stood in front of him.

"How did you get here so fast? Sophie only told me you were coming last night."

"Madame . . .er . . .Mrs. Smith sent me in the jet."

"What jet?" he asked.

"Mrs. Smith owns a Gulfstream."

"Well, come on, let's go to the office and we'll get you a room." As they walked toward the office a thought suddenly occurred to him. He had no idea how much it cost to fly a jet like that across the Pacific, but it had to be a lot. Clearly, Sophie was upset. And clearly he needed to calm her down. He didn't know exactly how to do it long distance, however. A phone call would be a good start.

As they walked into the reception area, the manager appeared from a small office behind the reception desk. "I need a room for my friend," he said, realizing that he did not know Toy's real name. He continued, saying, "Put his room and all charges on my bill."

"Certainly, sir," responded the manager.

Pete looked at Toy and said, "I need to call Sophie. I'll be in my room."

Toy nodded in acknowledgement.

Back in his room, he dialed Sophie's number.

When she answered the phone Pete said, "I just wanted you to know that Toy arrived."

"Yes, I know, he called me from the airport."

"I didn't know you owned a jet," he said

"Normally, we just use it for bringing the high rollers to the casino."

"How are you?"

"I am fine."

He was getting nowhere with this conversation so he decided to go at things directly. "Are you still jealous?"

"What do you think?" she asked frostily.

"Well, you certainly don't sound like your usual cheerful self."

"I don't like you having dinner with single women."

"Sophie, she is business professional. And we deal with one another on that level. You have to get over this jealousy thing."

"I don't think that is possible. I think you must stop making me jealous."

"So your jealously is my fault?"

"Yes."

"Look, you can't expect me never to speak to another woman. And I certainly don't expect to be hidden away somewhere."

"I know you are right, but it is very hard for me. I have never been in love before, and I guess I am not handling it very well. I will try harder in the future."

"Good because I have a date with a beautiful blonde tonight."

"Ha, ha," she said and hung up.

Pete looked at the phone in his hand and started laughing. He had found her "hot" button but he knew instinctively that he had to be careful how he used it or he would have a volcanic eruption on his hands.

5

The next few days were intermittent flurries of activity punctuated by long periods of boredom. Escrow instructions had to be scanned and emailed to Sophie. Then she had to FedEx them back. She had the thirty million transferred to his bank account. This drew the manager's attention in a positive fashion. Every time he walked into the bank, the manager brought him a cup of coffee.

The people Sophie had hired for the remodel had wanted access on three different occasions. Finally, they had applied for all the remodel permits. The day before the closing, Pete had the bank transfer the necessary funds to the escrow company.

The closing was anticlimactic. The title company did it all without any input from anyone; the closing documents having already been signed. Pete spent the better part of the morning waiting for someone to call him. Finally, he called Mary Schumann. "What happens now," he asked her.

"Nothing. You and your wife now own the property. If you stop by the office, I will give you the keys."

"Okay. I'll see you soon."

He knocked on Toy's door, and when Toy opened the door he said, "Let's go see the house my wife bought."

After a quick stop at the real estate agency, they pulled up to the front of the house. Mary Schumann had given him a box with about thirty keys in it. Five minutes later, after much trial and error, they had the front door open.

There was trash everywhere, and the former owner had left most of the furniture. They stuck their noses into everything. They opened every door, closet, and cupboard. It took about an hour and a half. Pete looked at his watch and figured it was about eleven at night in Macau.

He found an abandoned easy chair in one of the living rooms. Sitting down, he pulled his cell phone from his right front pocket. The hotel operator tracked Sophie down in the English Pub. She answered, saying simply, "Yes." It did not sound as if she had had a very good day.

"Well, we own it. I am calling you from the living room while sitting in an easy chair the former owner left behind."

"That's wonderful. Will you call everyone and tell them to start the remodel as quickly as possible?" she asked

"Sure. You don't sound as if you've had a very good day."

"I spent the last ten hours negotiating with the Po brothers over the sale of the hotel. They want to haggle over everything. As soon as I eat, I am going upstairs to sleep ten hours. I am going to tell the operator no interruptions, so consider me incommunicado for the next ten hours."

"I'll let you go then. Don't forget to take good care of my son and get plenty of rest. Nothing is more important than that baby you are carrying."

"I know. I find I don't seem to have the stamina I used to have."

"Please don't overdo," he said before signing off.

She could not stop herself from smiling; his interest in the baby delighted her. She was always worried that he would resent the "shotgun" nature of their marriage. "I will, good night now."

For the next three mornings, he and Toy drove to the house. There was nothing happening. But on the morning of the fourth day, when they arrived, there were about ten guys working. They were ripping out walls. He saw the contractor and asked, "How do you know what walls to rip out?"

"These are the plans I was given," he said, handing Pete a stack of eleven by fourteen sheets. He leafed through the plans, finally finding a sheet representing the area in which they were working. The changes they were going to make actually looked like real good ideas, and he thought they would make the house better.

While he had been talking to the contractor, Toy had wandered off. Pete went looking for him. After a couple of minutes, he found him. Toy had his shirtsleeves rolled up and was in the process of using his tremendous strength to rip out some board that had evidently stymied a couple of the contractor's men.

"Toy, how did you get so strong?" Pete asked.

"I worked on a beer truck unloading kegs for ten years."

"Let's go," Pete said to Toy. They went back to the motel. By noon Pete was bored to tears. Then it hit him. He needed to renew his love/hate relationship with golf.

The yellow pages listed a couple of local golf shops. He wrote down the addresses and looked them up in his Thomas Bros. map book.

He was back at the motel an hour later, eighteen hundred dollars poorer but the proud owner of a set of Ping clubs, shoes, balls, tees, and a glove. The kind folks who lightened up his wallet had also given him directions to a driving range and municipal golf course.

For each of the next four days he went to the driving range every morning. Then he and Toy went to the house. There were a few more men working than there had been the day before. It seemed the contractor was adding three men a day. He asked Mike about it. He was told his wife had said she wanted things done fast, so he was hiring as fast as he could, but it was hard to find good men.

A few days later when he and Toy came back from their morning inspection of the house, he stopped the car in front of Toy's room. He said, "See you later, Toy."

"Where are you going?"

The way he said it confirmed that Toy's assignment included watching him as well as the house. "I am going to play golf." Toy got out of the car. He was really in doubt what to do. He finally decided that he would call Madame Gin Sling.

When Sophie heard Pete was off to play golf, her first reaction was concern. But after reflecting on it for a few seconds, she decided Pete's playing golf was a good thing. He would need something to keep himself occupied, and after all, what was the harm. She didn't think he would meet any women on a golf course, but she wasn't sure.

Pete drove to the course. When he got there, he changed shoes in the parking lot and went into the pro shop to sign up. They paired him up with a twosome at first that was starting in a half hour. But when he was called to the first tee, a fourth person had been added to the group. They introduced themselves to one another. Tom and Jeff apparently played together often. John, like Pete, was also a recent arrival.

Tom was an airline pilot who had retired early. Jeff owned a plumbing company, and John had just been hired as a professor at the local junior college. Pete explained he was retired army. It was a beautiful day and they all enjoyed the round.

As they were walking to the parking lot Tom asked Pete and John if they would like to join them for a beer. He explained that they always stopped at a little place on the outskirts of Santa Barbara called the Blue Fox. They both thought a beer sounded great. They exchanged phone numbers with the intention of playing together again.

For the next three weeks, they played golf a couple of times per week, but Pete was still bored. It had finally gotten to the point where he did not like going to the house. Every time he went there, someone asked him a question. He didn't really mind making all the decisions. He knew he was redoing this house to his taste, but he really didn't know his wife's taste. When he was not at the house or playing golf, he had absolutely nothing to do.

Finally, he realized there was no reason for him to hang around Santa Barbara. As soon as that light had illuminated, he jumped on the Internet and reserved a seat on a commuter to San Francisco and a seat on the red-eye to Paris. There remained only one thing to do; tell Sophie. The question was when? After pondering over the problem, he decided to call from the airport in San Francisco just before getting on the plane. Then he wondered if the yellow streak running up his back showed.

He slid out of Santa Barbara without saying anything to Toy. He turned in his rental car at the airport.

They were just about to call his Paris flight, and he could not put it off any longer. He looked for a quiet spot where he would be able to hear easily. On second thought, he probably would not need a telephone to hear her volcanic eruption. "Hello," Pete said when Sophie answered.

"What's up?"

"I have decided to go to Paris for a week or two."

"I need you in Santa Barbara, not Paris."

"Nonsense, Toy is there, and there is an army of workmen whirling around executing your every wish. I am as necessary as a third wheel."

"A sidecar needs a wheel," she retorted.

"Listen, I am bored out of my mind. There is nothing for me to do all day long. I am not used to living like that."

"I don't want you going to Paris," she said flatly.

"I am not going to live in a box that you created."

"I need you watching our investment in Santa Barbara."

"Toy is there. You don't need me there, too. They are calling my flight. I've got to run. I'll call you in a few days." With that he hung up.

In the three languages she spoke fluently, she did not know a word that adequately expressed her rage. Damn, she was mad. No one but her husband could make her this mad. Even more frustrating and adding to her rage was her inability to do anything about it.

It took her about five minutes to calm down. Then she picked up the phone and called her secretary. "Who do we know in Paris?" She listened for a few seconds and then said, "Get him on the phone."

6

Pete went through immigration and customs without incident. He had reserved a room in a cheap hotel in the 9th arrondissement that he had found on the Internet. He waited in the taxi line for fifteen minutes. Finally, climbing into the back of a taxi, he gave the hotel's address to the driver. The hotel turned out to be a dump. He understood why it was so cheap, but it really did not matter. He planned to spend his days strolling in the city, not hanging around a hotel. He could do that in Santa Barbara.

After a couple of hours of sleep, he left the hotel and strolled aimlessly toward Saint-Germain.

He wound up on Rue Montorgueil. He picked one of the many restaurants and sat at an outside table. He ordered a Diet Coke and a ham and cheese sandwich. The sandwich was served on a marvelous crusty fresh baguette, as he knew it would be. It was delicious. There was no better bread in the world. They could put anything on it, and it would taste great.

He paid the check and strolled toward the Seine. As he moseyed along, he came across a store selling cell phones. He went in and bought a phone with a hundred prepaid minutes on it. He had the feeling he would need it as soon as he gave Sophie the number. Oh God, this wife business. It wasn't too bad when they were together, but apart she became impossible.

He wandered across the Seine into Saint-Germain. He poked his nose into numerous art galleries and antique shops. Finally, he realized it was getting late, and he realized he was getting hungry. Pete started walking back toward his hotel looking for an appealing restaurant. He crossed the Seine again. Toward the end of Rue Montorgueil he spied a small Italian restaurant. Looking at the menu posted on the outside, he decided veal piccata would hit the spot. There was a chill in the air so he sat at an inside table.

Back at his hotel, he got out his old phone book and called Giselle Renoux. They had worked together in Brussels. He doubted she would still be at the number he had for her. It had been at least a year since he had spoken to her. They had had a brief fling fifteen years ago that had matured into a solid friendship.

"Allo," she said, after answering on the third ring.

"It's Pete Smith."

"Where are you?" she queried.

"I am here in Paris. How would you like to have dinner with me tomorrow night?" he asked.

"I would love to dine with you tomorrow."

They agreed upon a time and place before hanging up.

He spent the next day doing much the same thing as he had the day before. He returned to his hotel about three that afternoon.

In Macau, Sophie read the email describing her husband's activities from his arrival through noon of that day. She smiled to herself. It sounded as if he had had a great day doing exactly what he said he was going to do.

Pete left the hotel for the restaurant a little after seven. He had plenty of time and was just enjoying the world's most enchanting city as he strolled along. He arrived at the restaurant before Giselle. He ordered a bottle of red wine, a St. Émilion. The waiter returned with the wine at the same time that Giselle arrived.

They chatted, ordering a second bottle of wine instead of dinner. As the waiter uncorked the wine, Pete's cell phone rang. "It must be a wrong number. No one has this number except you." But, he was wrong on two counts.

"Hello," he said.

"I don't like you having dinner with other women," Sophie said vehemently.

Pete looked at Giselle and said, "Excuse me," as he left the table.

"Sophie, how did you get this number?"

"That's beside the point. I really do not like this."

"I don't know why not. We have spent most of the evening talking about what a remarkable woman you are. Besides which I am helping you work on your problem with jealousy," he said with a chuckle.

"You are waving a red flag in front of a bull. I want you to know that."

"Sophie, you are making a mountain out of a molehill. I am having dinner with an old friend who happens to be a woman, nothing more, nothing less. Listen, I have to get back to the table, I'll call you in a couple days. Good-bye for now." He hung up.

Sophie was furious. She lit a cigarette and started pacing in the living room. If this went on, she was going to wind up convicted of murder. That thought did not particularly appeal to her. She thought Pete was deliberately antagonizing her, but she could not be sure. Then she thought again about the whole situation. Maybe she had overreacted. She was pretty sure he loved her. She knew that if he was truly in love with her nothing would happen. She continued to pace and smoke. After forty-five minutes she decided to get back in front of things and push his buttons for a change.

Pete's phone rang again just as they were finishing dinner. He excused himself again and walked down the sidewalk ten yards. He answered, resigned to another spat. "Hello?"

"Pete, I may have been wrong. So I want you to move out of that dump where you are staying. There is a suite waiting for you at the Ritz. The Ritz is located on the Place Vendôme. There is also an open charge for you for everything in the hotel. It is prepaid for two weeks. If you want to stay longer let me know and I'll make the arrangements."

"Okay, what has brought about this change?" There was a distinct tone of suspicion in his voice.

"I have decided I have no choice but to trust you."

When she said that, he realized that he had been a bit of an asshole. He should have done things a bit differently, making them easier for her to accept. "Thank you. I will call you in the morning. For now I have a suggestion. Jump in that jet of yours and come to Paris."

"I would love to come. Perhaps I may join you there. I'll know better in the morning if that is even possible." They hung up on the best of terms. Their difficulties were resolved, at least for the moment.

When he went back to the table he still had a somewhat stunned look on his face. "That was my wife and she did a complete about-face. She just advised me there is a prepaid suite reserved for me at the Ritz."

"Well, that was certainly a change from the earlier phone call. What brought it about?" asked Giselle.

"I really don't know."

"What are you going to do?" Giselle asked.

"Go to the Ritz, I guess."

"Your wife must be quite well off."

"My wife is a self-made billionaire."

"What a catch."

"Actually, she caught me. If I told you the whole story, you would never believe it."

"Try," Giselle said.

"I met Sophie in Macau. I guess I was staring at her. After all, she is a very beautiful woman. She invited me to join her so I did. Two months later she found out she was pregnant and sent a couple of guys to bring me back to Macau. After some discussion she persuaded me to marry her."

"I'll bet it did not take much talking, did it?"

"Actually, I thought she worked as an accountant in the hotel until after the wedding. Then it came out she owned the hotel as well as half of Macau."

"That's quite a tale," Giselle said.

"Every word is true."

He paid the bill and they left. Pete put Giselle in a taxi after kissing her on both cheeks as per the French custom. It took some hunting but he found a cab for himself. "Ritz," he told the cabbie. When they arrived in front of the Ritz he told the cab driver to wait. He went up to the reception desk. They treated him like a long-lost son home at last, giving him a key. He went outside, climbed back into the cab, and gave the driver the address of his other hotel. After recovering his clothes, he checked out and went back to the Ritz. The suite Sophie had reserved for him could only be described as opulent. It was beginning to dawn on him exactly what being a billionaire really meant.

When he awoke the following morning, he decided to order room service. Pete had become fond of room service while at Sophie's hotel after the wedding. The service wasn't as fast here, but nevertheless the food was still warm and very appetizing. He had not quite determined which direction to walk today when he entered the lobby. There, seated in the corner, were Toy and Chou. That reminded him that he had not called Sophie as he promised. "Five in the afternoon I think," said Toy, in answer to his question about what time it was in Macau.

"I'll call Sophie later," he said. "What are your orders?"

"We are here to see nothing happens to you."

The only acceptable answer had just rolled off Toy's tongue. And he gained new respect for his wife. She had orchestrated the situation perfectly; there was no way he could complain about her concern for his safety.

"Have either of you ever been to Paris before?" he asked. They both shook their heads indicating no. "Well, let's head toward Saint-Germain."

They walked in the older part of the city for two hours. As lunch time approached, he headed in the direction of a sandwicherie that he knew near the Louvre. They reached the sandwicherie at about twelve thirty. "Have you eaten anything yet today?" he asked. They both shook their heads no. "You know, with me, you guys can speak. Why don't you eat and I'll go back to the hotel and call Sophie."

"We'll go with you," Toy said.

"Your instructions are to stick with me no matter what, is that correct?"

Toy just nodded again. "Let's eat then," he said. They found a small table, ordered sandwiches, and ate. After lunch he led them back to the hotel. "I'm going upstairs and call Sophie," he told them.

He went up to the suite, sat on the couch, and dialed Sophie in Macau. When Sophie answered the phone he said, "Hello."

"Oh, hi," she said, clearly happy to hear from him.

"Listen, I want to apologize to you. I admit I kind of pulled your chain. But I have to tell you something you may not want to hear. I cannot live in a little box that you build. I am a free spirit, and I like to come and go as I please."

"I know that I have become overly possessive. I also know I have to do better in the future. But it is because I love you so much. I have never been in love before, as I keep telling you. This thing has hit me very hard."

"You need to calm down and have a little faith in me, all right?"

"I have complete faith in you; it is other women I have no faith in."

"Are you going to be able to get away for a few days and join me in Paris?"

"I don't think so."

"Why not?"

"I have made a deal to sell the hotel and the land next door, and we are now going over the contracts word by word and line by line. I think it is going to be quite a while longer, unfortunately."

"Well, if you finish in the next week or so jump on British Airways. I think they have a Hong Kong to London nonstop. From there you can catch the high-speed train to Paris. We can spend a few days and nights together."

"It sounds wonderful. I'll try, but don't count on me."

"Have you heard anything about your green card?"

"No, nothing."

"How's the baby? Have you had a checkup lately?"

"The baby is doing well. You only go to the doctor every couple of months at first."

"When will they be able to tell the sex?"

"The next visit, I think," she answered. "Do you want me to bring Toy and Chou back?"

"Send Toy to Santa Barbara and Chou wherever you want. I'll talk to you in a couple of days then," he said.

They hung up. A few minutes later he went downstairs with the intention of resuming his walk. He looked around the lobby, but Toy and Chou were nowhere to be seen. He shrugged and went out the front door. Turning right he continued to Rue Saint Honoré and then turned right again toward the Place de la Concorde. He walked almost to the Arc de Triomphe.

After about an hour, his cell phone rang. It was an old friend, Henri Labonneville. He said he had spoken to Giselle and just found out that Pete was in Paris. He went on to say that they were having a small dinner party and asked if Pete like to attend?

"Yes, of course," he responded.

"Cecile and I are looking forward to seeing you tonight," Henri said.

"Me, too."

That night he went to the party and renewed old acquaintances. Everyone wanted to meet his wife. They were, of course, surprised that he was married and she was not with him. But after listening to his explanation, they were sympathetic. When describing his wife, he didn't mention the great wealth she had acquired.

For the first week of his visit the weather could not have been better in spite of the weatherman's predictions. However, the weatherman justified his existence by finally being right. A cold rain fell for two days, and the predictions claimed it would last for the rest of the week. In spite of the weatherman's dismal track record, Pete decided to leave Paris, knowing full well that this would not be his last visit. Paris had always drawn him like a magnet.

He thought about returning to California via Macau but decided that would be masochistic. He also thought he should talk to Sophie before leaving so she didn't hit the panic button—again.

He called Sophie saying, "Hello," when she answered.

"Oh, hi," she said.

"I just wanted to let you know I am leaving Paris tomorrow."

"Where are you going?" she queried.

"Well, that's a good question. I thought about passing through Macau on my way to California, but I have more or less decided to go directly to California."

"I wish you would come to Macau for a few days, I miss you."

"I miss you, too. But the trip just becomes too grueling going through Macau. Have you heard anything about your green card?"

"Not a word, unfortunately," she said.

"Well, it's been, what, five, six weeks since the interview?"

"Five and a half weeks," she said.

"I am sure you'll hear something soon," he said, and then continued, "I hope so anyway. I don't like the situation we're in right now."

"The Po brothers are here to sign the contracts for the hotel, so I have got to run," she said.

"I'll call you as soon as I get to California," he said hanging up.

7

When he got back to Santa Barbara he felt as if he had spent a day in a washing machine stuck on the spin cycle. He rented a car and went back to the Motel Six. The manager recognized him immediately and asked him if he would like to have his old room back. "Sure," he replied. As an afterthought he asked, "What room is my friend in?"

"He is in the same room, too," the manager said.

The next morning Pete awoke after having slept twelve hours. He felt human again. He rang Toy's room, forgetting to check the time.

"Hello," Toy said sleepily.

"I am sorry, Toy. I did not look at the time. I'm back in my old room. Call when you're running on all eight cylinders."

Half an hour later the phone rang. It was Toy, and they agreed to meet for breakfast before going to the house.

After breakfast they arrived at the house to find an army of workmen. Even from the driveway things seemed pretty well organized. No one was standing around idle, and everyone was doing something that appeared to be constructive. He wondered who the foreman was. Just then Mike came around the corner, shouting orders. He was clearly pissed about something. Pete decided to wait until he cooled off a little before talking to him.

Finally Pete walked over to Mike. "Hi," he said.

"Boy, am I glad to see you! I have a bunch of questions that I can't seem to make your wife understand over the telephone."

"My wife speaks English with no accent but she is not English speaking by birth. Most people think she is American, but occasionally she has problems with vocabulary. She can guess the meaning of most words she doesn't know just from the context of the sentence, but she stumbles on technical vocabulary."

"Well," Mike said, "let me show you the first problem." They went from room to room, and in almost every room there was a question that had to be answered. Pete made decision after decision, occasionally consulting Toy. He knew he was spending Sophie's money like it was water, but she had said to do it so he did. After two and a half hours he and Toy started to head for the car when a man he had never seen before approached them.

"Are you the owner?" the man asked.

"One of them, I guess."

"I am Frank Bertolini," he said.

"Pete Smith," he said, holding out his hand. They shook and Pete said, "This is Toy." Toy and Frank shook.

"I needed to talk to somebody who can make a decision. I've spoken with a Mrs. Smith on the phone a couple of times, but I don't think she understood me or the problem."

"All right, lay it out for me," Pete said.

"Mrs. Smith thinks the garage is too small. She wants four more bays added onto the existing garage and she wants it done in sixty days. The problem is she wants two stories with an apartment above the garage."

"So, how's that a problem?"

"To enlarge the garage is no problem. The apartment, because of the bathrooms, will require a permit. If we're lucky, we'll get the permit in six months."

"Why does it take so long?" Pete asked.

"Because every do-gooder in the area is going to stick their big butinski noses into your business."

"What do you suggest?"

"If your wife does not want to wait, we can bootleg it in."

"Tell me how that works."

"We add things after the inspector has signed off on something. For example, we stub in the waste lines after the foundation inspection is complete. And we finish the building as shown on the plans with the upper floor being a storage area. After the final sign off, we build the apartment.

"Okay, bootleg it in."

"All right, I'll get my men started digging the footings tomorrow. We still don't have a permit but as soon as the city issues it, I'll call for the foundation inspection."

They parted after exchanging good-byes.

"I need to bring Sophie up to speed."

"Maybe it would be better if you do that after lunch," Toy said, subtly implying that he was starving.

They went to the Denny's near the motel. After ordering, Pete asked Toy, "What do you think about this project?"

"In what respect?" Toy asked.

"Let's start with your overall impression," Pete replied.

"Well, basically I like it. I think most of the changes are for the best. But I am afraid that Madame Gin Sling may not like all of the changes. That's why I am so glad you're back. After you left I had to make the decisions you were making today."

He laughed at that. "Don't want the responsibility, eh?"

"Exactly."

"Well, she's not here so frankly I don't intend to listen to a lot complaints."

"You can get away with that, but I cannot," Toy said. "In fact, what you can get away with surprises me. Madame Gin Sling does not like it when she does not get things exactly her way, and you seem to like antagonizing her. That, by the way, is a very dangerous thing to do."

Pete just shrugged and let the subject drop. They paid the bill and left.

Back at the motel, Pete lay down on the bed in his room and dialed Sophie in Macau.

"Hello," she said, answering the phone.

"Hi," said Pete. "I just wanted to let you know what is happening at the house and see how you were doing."

"I am fine. Actually better than fine. The hotel was sold yesterday and the funds are in the bank. The consulate called this morning and said my papers should be ready sometime next week."

"And the baby?"

"Fine, too."

"Oh, there is something I been have meaning to tell you, but it has been slipping my mind. You cannot import ivory into the United States."

"Yes, I know. I already resolved that problem."

"How?"

"You don't want to know."

"Oh, okay. Then let me tell you about the house." He went on to talk about all the improvements and how they were progressing. He did not mention the bootleg portion of the project.

When he finally stopped talking, Sophie asked, "When will it be finished?"

"Optimistically, I would guess six weeks, but realistically eight weeks, possibly ten."

"Tell them to finish the closets in the master bedroom first. We need a place to start storing things, and then the master bedroom."

"I'll do it," Pete said. "Where are you staying," he asked, changing the subject?

"In the apartment. I made that part of the deal. It is strange to be here with no responsibilities and nothing to do all day. I am starting to go slowly crazy."

"It's only been two days," Pete observed.

"I know. At the end of a week I'll probably be ready to shoot myself."

"On that happy note, I'll let you go. Bye-bye."

"I love you and miss you," she said hanging up.

The next morning after breakfast, he and Toy went to the house. As they parked in front of the house, he noticed there was a small backhoe digging the footings for the garage extension. Evidently, Frank Bertolini was not a man to let grass grow under his feet. Pete and Toy went off looking for Mike. When they found him, he and the architect were bent over a set of plans. Mike looked up and saw Pete and Toy. "Mr. Smith, can we borrow you for a minute?"

"Sure, and call me Pete. Mr. Smith is my father," Pete said.

"We were just discussing the ceiling treatment. We think the ceilings would look better if they were all the same but the decorator wants the ceiling treatments different."

"What does the decorator have in mind?"

"She wants an acoustic ceiling in some rooms."

"You mean that stuff they put in track homes?" Pete asked.

"Yeah," Mike answered.

"What do you think would be better, and what is the decorator's reasoning."

"The decorator says it would be faster. She's right about that. But it won't match the rest of the house," the architect said.

"You mean, you want to keep all the ceilings the same as they are now."

"Yes."

"Keep them all the same, I agree with you. It won't look right if the ceilings are different from room to room," Pete said. "Mike, my wife asked if you could finish the closets in the master bedroom first and then the master bedroom itself. She wants a place to store things as she ships them in from Macau."

"We are almost finished with them now, I think. Let's go look." They went upstairs to the second floor and into the master bedroom. "In three or four more days I think we can be done with this. It is going to take two to three days to put the hardwood flooring down in here, and a few days after that sanding and varnishing. The problem is going to be the painting. I don't have all the paint colors yet from the decorator," Mike said. He went on to say, "There is one other problem. And that is the dust from the other rooms getting into the wet paint. But I can figure out something."

"All I can ask is that you do your best," Pete said. He and Toy wandered off, ultimately winding up at the car.

As Pete walked into his motel room, the phone was ringing. He knew exactly who was calling. "Hello, Sophie," he said, picking up the phone.

"Lucky guess," she said.

"No luck involved, I know you are bored."

"I may be bored, but I also need information," Sophie said.

"I will be happy to furnish you with any and all information that I may possess."

"What did you find out about the master bedroom," Sophie wanted to know.

"They think they will be finished with the master bedroom in about ten days to two weeks. The problem, however, is going to be the painting because of the dust being created by the work going on in the rest of the house. Mike doesn't have the paint colors from the decorator yet. Nor does he have a painting crew."

"I'll take care of those problems. Call you tomorrow," she said.

The next morning he and Toy went out to the house to see the previous day's progress. When Mike saw him he made a beeline over to him. "Pete, what did you say to your wife? She read me the riot act yesterday about the painting crew. I haven't been spoken to like that since a thirty-year sergeant in the Marine Corps chewed me a new asshole one day."

"She can be a handful!" Pete said. "Actually, I am sorry about that. I can see I am going to have to be more careful about what I say to her."

"I guess she had a similar conversation with the decorator. The decorator called me about five this morning with paint colors. She is driving up from LA to check on our progress."

"Holy shit!" Pete said. "She must have flown off the handle. Surprising since she was perfectly sane when I spoke to her." Pete glanced over his shoulder and saw Toy grinning. As he and Toy walked back to the car, he asked, "What's so funny?"

"I told you Madame, I mean Mrs. Smith, is someone you need to be careful around."

Shakespeare's *The Taming of the Shrew* flashed through Pete's mind.

8

Three days later, in the early afternoon, Mike called Pete. "There's a guy up here trying to make a delivery, but he says someone has to sign for it," Mike said.

"Just sign my name," said Pete.

"Not on your life," Mike replied.

"All right, tell the guy I'll be there in fifteen minutes," Pete said. "Is there going to be any problem with him waiting?"

"I don't even need to ask, the answer is no."

Fifteen minutes later, Pete pulled into the driveway. Sitting in front of the house was a white Rolls Royce with two young men standing beside it. One was dressed in a gray suit, white button-down shirt, and red tie. The other was dressed far more casually in khakis and a light blue, short-sleeved dress shirt. Parked over by the garage Pete noticed a nondescript blue Chevy. "Holy shit!" Pete said to himself, not yet out of the car.

Pete walked over to the guys. "Are you the gentlemen that need someone to sign for something?" Pete asked.

"Yes, sir," responded the man dressed in the suit. He reached into the car and pulled out a clipboard with a host of papers attached, "Sir, you need to sign here," he said indicating a line on the form. The man flipped to the next page, "and here and here," he said, pointing to two places on the form. Pete signed where indicated. The fellow flipped to the next form down. "Here and here," he said, indicating places on the form. Pete signed again where indicated.

"What am I signing for, by the way?" Pete asked.

"This car, sir," he said, with a shocked expression on his face.

"Where the hell did this thing come from?" Pete asked.

"Someone must have bought it," the young man said, handing him the keys. "Sir, I also am to acquaint you with the operation of the vehicle," he said as he opened the driver's door for Pete to sit down. The young fellow walked around the front of the car and sat in the passenger's seat.

Pete listened to instructions, all the while wondering what he was going to do with the car. Frank Bertolini had already removed one end of the garage, and men and equipment were always coming to the front of the house, so he could not leave it in that section of the driveway either. Furthermore, he could not even drive the thing until he had insurance.

"Do you have any questions," the young man asked, bringing Pete from his thoughts.

"No. Thank you for your time."

"Sir, I'll be back with your new license plates on Monday. You'll be fine with the dealer plates until then."

"Do I need to be here for that?"

"No, sir, but the car does."

The day the purchase of the house was complete, he had bought a homeowners' policy from State Farm. He looked at the contacts in his phone to see if he had been smart enough to enter the insurance agent's number. He had. He got the agent on the phone and after introducing himself said, "I would like you to insure my new car."

"No problem, I can handle that for you right now. What kind of a car is it?"

"Rolls Royce."

'What year is it?"

"It's brand new."

"I am sure you want the maximum coverage available, do you not?"

"Yes."

"And you want collision as well, do you not?"

"Yes, I want the maximum in protection available."

"Okay. . . All right," he said, "you are covered. But I'll need you to get the license plate numbers and VIN number as soon as you can."

"Good," Pete said, "I'll stop by your office and pay the bill in the morning."

At eleven that evening, he telephoned Sophie. Sophie picked up the phone saying, "Hello?"

"Hi," he said brightly. "How are you?"

"Oh, I am fine," she said, "How are you?"

"Just fine," he said. "A Rolls Royce showed up today."

"It arrived! Super!" she said.

"Not super, I have no place to put it," he responded. "The garage is broken open, and the main driveway is being used for the delivery of materials."

"You have a rental car, don't you?"

"A couple actually. How do you think Toy and I get around?"

"Well," she said, "turn one in and drive the Rolls."

"Those things are so expensive I'd be scared to drive it."

"Don't be, it's just a car, and you are worth a lot more to me than any car."

"That's sweet of you to say."

After exchanging news about the baby and the progress of the renovation, they hung up.

The following Monday morning, while Pete and Toy were visiting the house, a huge Mercedes limo drove up the driveway, a Ford trailing behind it. The driver came to the front door. The door was open, and the driver asked one of the workman, "Is there a Mr. Smith here?"

"Yeah, he's around here somewhere. I'll see if I can find him for you."

Pete walked toward the front door, and he saw the limo sitting in the driveway.

As Pete stepped out of the doorway, the driver asked, "Are you Mr. Smith?"

"I am."

"I am here to deliver your new car, sir. If you'll follow me and sign a few papers, sir, we can complete the transaction."

"Sure."

He signed form after form until finally the driver said, "That's it."

"I need to familiarize you with the operation of the vehicle sir."

"Don't tell me, tell him," Pete said nodding toward Toy. "He's going to drive it, not me. Toy, come over here," hollered Pete. "Toy, what the hell are we going to do with this thing?" asked Pete.

"I don't know. I don't think we can leave it here, and it is going to take up half the parking lot at the motel," Toy replied.

"Well, I guess the first thing to do is get some insurance on it, and then see if we can make a deal with the manager of the motel to park this thing."

The insurance agent was delighted to hear from him again. The conversation ended with the agent saying, "You're covered."

Pete drove the Rolls, and Toy followed in the Mercedes. When they arrived at the motel, Pete went inside the office. The manager was there, and Pete asked him, "Can I park that limo here at the motel?"

"Just pull it around back, there's plenty of room back there," the manager said when asked.

"Be happy to pay extra for this," Pete said.

"Nah, that's not necessary," the manager said.

The following afternoon he got another come-up-and-sign-for-a-delivery phone call.

This time it was a freight truck. He went and found Mike and asked, "Can you round up a few men to help carry boxes up to the garage."

"Sure"

The truck was unloaded in no time at all, and everything was carried to the garage. The cargo was all boxes except for a double bed mattress.

That evening he called Sophie. "Hello," Sophie said.

"Why in the hell are you shipping a mattress?" he asked.

"That is the first mattress I ever climaxed on, and I am never parting with it."

Pete couldn't contain his laughter and he couldn't stop. "I married a complete nut," he finally managed to say.

"I am not crazy," she said with complete seriousness. "That was a very important event in my life."

He finally stopped laughing enough to say, "I'll call you tomorrow."

The next day he got another phone call from Mike, "Pete, another delivery for you just arrived."

"Just sign for it will you?"

"Not this one," Mike said.

"Okay, I'll be there in fifteen minutes."

He knocked on Toy's door and asked him if he wanted to see what came this time.

"Sure," Toy said.

When they arrived at the house, they found Sophie's personal maid sitting on a suitcase in front of the door. Toy and she struck up a conversation in Cantonese. Pete went inside to find Mike. When he found Mike, he asked him when the master bedroom would be done.

"Let's go look. I think it should be done pretty soon." When they got up to the master bedroom, the painters were just finishing the last of the trim around one of the doors.

"The floor needs to be sanded and varnished. About three days should do it."

He went downstairs and found Toy still chatting with Sophie's maid.

"I guess we better get you, I am sorry but I don't know your name, a room at the motel."

Toy said, "Her name is Mi Ling, and she does not speak English."

"Great."

They registered Mi Ling at the motel. Pete told Toy he was going to have to take responsibility for Mi Ling, including feeding her. Toy nodded in assent. The next morning, Pete told Toy, "Mi Ling is going to have to wait to start sorting things out at the house. The master bedroom isn't finished yet and won't be for a few more days.

Toy translated for Mi Ling's benefit.

That night he called Sophie. "Hello," she said. "I have some wonderful news."

"What's that," he interrupted.

"I get my green card tomorrow," she bubbled.

"Wonderful! When will you be getting here then?" he asked.

"Tomorrow is Thursday. I will probably leave on Tuesday, arriving on Wednesday. We are going to clear customs and spend the night in Honolulu."

"Sounds like you have everything already planned out."

"As soon as I heard from the consulate today I got the pilots on the phone, and they worked out the flight plan."

"How's the baby doing?"

"He just keeps kicking me. It is becoming difficult to sleep."

"Please be sure to take good care of yourself."

"Don't worry I am very good at that."

In the morning Pete and Toy made their usual trip to the house. Upon seeing Mike, Pete walked over to him. Pete waited while Mike finished talking to a guy installing the electrical panel. "Mike, can we take a short walk?"

Mike knew instinctively that Pete wanted a private conversation. "Sure," Mike replied.

As they walked out to the pool, Pete said, "My wife is arriving Wednesday. I think there are a couple of things you need to know about her. As you already know, she has a volcanic temper. She is a self-made billionaire so she's used to getting her own way. And she does not suffer fools gladly. That means one of the things you do not do is try to bullshit her. If she likes you, she will do anything for you. At times she can be generous to a fault."

"She sounds like quite a lady."

"She is really someone special. She is probably the smartest person I have ever met. In about two weeks she will know more than you do about the building business, she's that bright," Pete said.

"Thanks for the heads-up," said Mike.

"I am going to get out of here. Have a good day."

"Hang on a sec," Mike said. "With your wife arriving next week, do you want to authorize Sunday overtime?"

"I don't think so. See ya."

Riding back to the motel Pete told Toy that Sophie was arriving Wednesday.

"I know," Toy said.

"Do you know how many people are coming with her?" Toy just nodded. "Well, how many?" Pete continued.

"Chou and his wife and four children are coming with her."

An employee (a word he did like for Sophie's people) grapevine surrounded Sophie. Sometimes they knew what she was going to do before Sophie herself knew. But he should have figured that one out himself. Sophie was not going to travel without either Toy or Chou. Chou would not want his wife and family, who spoke no English, traveling alone. Sophie owned a big plane so the solution was to fill it. "We'd better reserve some more motel rooms. Three for Chou and his family, but how many will we need for the flight crew," Pete asked Toy.

"The crew always takes care of themselves. They never stay in the same hotel as Mad …Mrs. Smith. I am sorry but I have a hard time remembering she is now Mrs. Smith, your wife."

"Don't worry about it. I am just getting used to it myself.

9

At six o'clock Wednesday, Sophie's plane taxied slowly from the end of the runway to the private aircraft terminal. The pilot turned into the parking area. He followed the hand signals of the lineman to the parking spot. Once the aircraft stopped, the main cabin door opened and the stairs unfolded. The flight attendant stood in the door preparing to wish everyone good-bye.

Pete walked out on the ramp when the aircraft stopped. Sophie was first to exit. She wore a large brimmed hat that drooped in the front, and she wore her glasses, which he had never seen her wear outside their apartment. Her black hair was hanging long and straight framing her face, a brightly colored scarf was wrapped around her neck, and a tan three-quarter-length leather jacket covered a white blouse. He was surprised that she wore blue jeans, of all things. A tan leather boot was on her right foot, and a light-colored wood for her left leg peeked out from the bottom of her jeans. As far as Pete was concerned she was the world's sexiest woman. When she reached the bottom of the stairs, Pete picked her up, giving her a big hug at the same time. Their passionate kiss lasted so long the others had to wait on the stairs. They both took the kiss as a promise of things to come . . . and in the not too distant future.

As he set Sophie down, he noticed Chou smiling. He heard something behind him. He turned to look and it was Toy in the Mercedes. He had somehow managed to get permission to drive on the ramp.

Toy and Chou were obviously very happy to see one another as well.

"Let's get the luggage and go to the motel," Pete said to Sophie.

"Toy and Chou will take care of it. Let's go."

When they walked into his room at the Motel Six, Sophie took one look and said, "This place is a dump. We're moving."

Pete gave her a leering look and said, "Not now we're not, babe." That brought a large smile to Sophie's face. Sophie had taken off her hat and coat and thrown them over a chair. She looked every bit of five and a half months pregnant. She went over to him and started to undo his belt. Pete, however, started undoing her blouse. As the blouse fell away so did the scarf. Sophie had had rings put around her neck. He felt them, looking for a seam, but there was none. He realized that they were welded into one piece. "Tomorrow morning those are going," he said.

"Let's talk about that tomorrow morning," she replied. In a minute they were both lying on the bed naked. Pete had intended to go very slow, but as they kissed and his hand found her left breast, he knew he couldn't wait. He was about to explode right then.

As he took off her bra he realized she had a new tattoo on her left breast. There were two hearts in her cleavage, one had a P in it and the other an S. Above the hearts were two blue flowers. Below the hearts there was one blue flower.

He managed to regain a modicum of self-control and very slowly slid his hand between her legs. He gently rubbed her clitoris, and she started to move her hips involuntarily. "Are you waiting for something?" she asked coyly. He rolled on top of her and entered as slowly as he could. When he was about halfway in, he backed almost out of her and then started to enter again, this time going a little further. Meanwhile Sophie had grabbed his back and was pulling on it as hard as she could. He finally fully entered her. As he did, she let out a small moan of satisfaction. After twenty minutes, they exploded simultaneously. Pete rolled off Sophie to her right side. They were both covered with perspiration and breathing deeply.

A while later, Pete said, "I'm hungry. Let's go get some dinner,"

"Okay. But can we go to the house first?"

"It's too dark to see anything now," he answered.

"That was the first thing I wanted to do when I got here."

"Didn't seem that way to me about an hour ago."

As she got out of bed he noticed the tattoo on her back had been redone. "When did you have that done?" he asked.

"A few weeks ago," she said. "Do you like it?"

"It looks much better. Wow, what a difference! In fact it looks great."

"How about this one?" she asked pointing to her left breast.

"I love that one, too," he said kissing it.

"Hold that thought," she said, pushing him away.

Pete decided to go to the Chart House. He liked the food there and he had taken to drinking at the bar. As they drove to the restaurant, he asked Sophie, "Why did you buy a Rolls Royce?"

"They're supposed to be the best."

"They are, but it might be difficult to get maintenance done."

"Do you like it? I bought it for you."

"I thought this was going to be your car. It's a little over the top for me," he replied.

"I don't know how to drive," she said.

"You're kidding?"

"No, I've never learned. As soon as I was able to afford a car, I bought a limo. Toy and Chou started to work for me the day I walked out of the whorehouse, and they can both drive. There was no reason for me to learn," she said as Pete pulled into the parking lot.

When they walked in the door, the blonde hostess greeted Pete with a big smile, saying, "How are you tonight, Pete? Are you eating or just drinking?"

"Patty," Pete said, "let me introduce you to my wife, Sophie, and we will be eating."

'It's a pleasure to meet you. Pete talks about you all the time," Patty said. "If you will follow me, I'll show you to a table. Pete, do you want your usual table?"

"Sure," Pete said.

Once seated Pete said to Sophie, "I'm so glad you have learned to contain your jealousy."

"I haven't, and you haven't heard the last of this!"

"Yes, I have."

"If you think I am going to ignore you having been here every night flirting with some teenage blonde Barbie, you're crazy!"

"She's twenty-three," Pete said, regretting it as soon as it popped out of his mouth.

"How do you know that?" Sophie hissed, her rage clearly building.

At this point any further remarks on his part would bring on one of the famous Madame Gin Sling eruptions that, heretofore, he had only heard about and had no desire to experience firsthand. "The New York strip steak is wonderful here. You should try it. American beef is the best," Pete said

"Perhaps I will," she said. She realized she needed to regain her composure. After a couple of minutes of introspection, she started to look around the restaurant. It was elegant in its simplicity. The walls were paneled and had boat models and nautical pictures on them. The table itself had a chart of a harbor fiberglassed onto the top. She looked at Pete and said, "This is really very nice."

"It is, isn't it?" he said. At that point the waiter came up to the table.

"Hi, I am Adam and I will be your server tonight. Would you like to order now or wait a little while?"

Pete looked at Sophie, who nodded silently and said, "Go ahead."

"I'll have the New York strip, medium rare, and a baked potato."

The waiter looked at Sophie who said, "I'll have the same thing."

"Anything to drink?

"Perrier," Sophie said.

"Same for me," Pete added.

"So tell me about the house," Sophie said.

"You really need to see it for yourself."

"How long until we can move in?"

"A month, six weeks, maybe two months. A lot depends on you," Pete answered.

"Me?"

"If you start to order a bunch of changes, you'll lengthen the job."

"Why would I do that?"

"Simple human nature, really. There are bound to be things you do not like that would have been easy to change at first but would be much more time consuming to redo now." Their food arrived so they interrupted their conversation to dig into their meals.

"Are there things you don't like?" she asked after devouring half her steak.

"Well, there are things I'm not wild about. But I've been here for most of the time, and when things came up I gave the builder my input, thinking about what you would like and would please me as well. I have had to make a lot of decisions."

"What are you not wild about?"

"I think I'll let you figure that one out for yourself," Pete said.

"I am sure I will like it," Sophie said.

"We'll go up to the house first thing in the morning."

The next morning they walked hand in hand up to the open front door of the house. After a little looking around they found Mike. "Mike, I'd like to introduce you to my wife, Sophie. Sophie, this is Mike, he's the general contractor."

"It is a pleasure to meet you, ma'am," Mike said.

"And you, too," Sophie said.

"Mike, I'd like you to give Sophie a tour of the house, tell her what has been done, what remains to be done, and when you think things will be complete."

"Sure." They wandered from room to room with Mike giving a running commentary. Most of Sophie's questions had been vocabulary related. Finally, they walked back downstairs. Pete looked at his watch. Mike's tour had taken two and a half hours. He had been extremely thorough. They thanked Mike and walked out the front door.

No sooner had they taken five steps when Sophie spun him toward her, threw her arms around his neck, and gave him a long, hard kiss. "I love it! I love everything about it! It is better than I had hoped it would be." She meant every word of it, too. She knew she had placed her trust in the right man, and if it were possible, she fell deeper in love.

"We need to talk to Frank next," Pete said.

"Who is he?"

"He's the guy you hired to build the extension on the garage."

"Oh yes," she said.

As they walked over to the garage, Pete explained the permit problems to Sophie. "Isn't there someone we can bribe to hasten things along a little?" she asked, dead serious.

"There might be. But if you try and miss, you are going to jail."

"Then get somebody else to do it."

"This is not the Orient," Pete said.

"Greed is greed, and it doesn't matter where you are."

Pete saw Frank and called to him. Frank came over and was introduced to Sophie with the same request. This time the tour lasted ten minutes, there not being much to see.

As they came to the end, Frank asked Sophie, "Do you have any questions?"

"Are there plans for the apartment upstairs?"

"Yes ma'am, but I don't have them here because I don't want anyone seeing them."

"Could you get a copy for me?"

"Of course. I'll bring you the floor plan tomorrow, or do you want the entire set?

"The entire set, I think, would be best."

They thanked Frank and as they were walking over to their car, the limo arrived with Chou and family, Mi Ling, and Toy behind the wheel.

A conversation in Cantonese, or what Pete thought was Cantonese, ensued. After a few minutes, Sophie joined Pete at the Rolls. They went back to the motel. The maid had not cleaned the room. Sophie noticed Pete hanging out the DO NOT DISTURB sign.

"Why are you hanging that out?" she asked, knowing full well.

They made love, and Sophie climaxed again. After she caught her breath, she said, "What's the plan for this afternoon?"

"Check out and find another hotel, as per Madame's request."

Pete loaded the baggage into the car and drove over to the office. He told the manager that he was checking out, but everyone else was staying, and as usual, he would be back on Friday morning to settle up the bill. He asked the manager if there was a Marriot or something comparable nearby. The manager recommended a small boutique hotel near the waterfront with an excellent restaurant.

As they pulled out of the parking lot Sophie asked, "Where are we going?"

"A little boutique hotel recommended by the manager."

When he pulled up in front of the hotel, he said to Sophie, "I'll go check us in."

"I am coming," she said, climbing out of the car. "I had to stay in the last hotel you checked us into!" Pete just shrugged his shoulders as they went into the lobby. It was very tastefully done in neutrals with accents of yellow and orange. Pete looked at Sophie, who nodded subtlety. He asked if they had any double rooms available. They did, and he took one. The receptionist asked him if he would prefer two queen size beds or a king size bed.

He never got the chance to answer because Sophie piped up, "King size bed will be fine."

There was no bellman, but there was a cart. Pete grabbed the cart, took it out to the car, loaded their baggage on it, and pushed it into the lobby. Then he went back outside to park the car. Returning to the lobby he grabbed the cart and pushed it to the elevator. He, Sophie, and the cart took the elevator to the third floor. They found their room and entered. The room was lovely, very clean, and tastefully furnished.

"When are we trying out this beauty?" Sophie asked, patting her hand on the bed.

"Not before lunch, which is where I am going right now."

"Wait for me," Sophie said.

After they had ordered, Pete asked Sophie, "Do you really like the house?"

"I love it, simple as that. Although, I agree with you, it will be at least two months before it is finished. What's the story with the furniture all over the place?"

"The previous owner left it. I don't know what the decorator has in mind for it. That's a question we should ask her the next time we see her."

"Is she around very often?" Sophie asked.

"I think I've only seen her once. But I don't think that matters at this point because the work is not far enough along to really need her services."

"It soon will be," Sophie said.

"Maybe we should give her a call tomorrow then," Pete said.

"This afternoon," said Sophie. "I want to know what colors she has planned and for where."

"You're right. We don't want to waste a bunch of time repainting," Pete said. "Are you sure you really like it?"

"I am telling you, it is better than I could have possibly imagined. When I had the idea of buying a mansion, I really could not visualize what I wanted. When I saw the pictures that you sent, I thought it was really going to be quite nice. But after seeing it, I think this is going to be sensational. I am just thrilled, truly."

"I have been concerned about your reaction. You've spent an enormous amount of money sight unseen and based solely on my taste and my interpretation of your taste. I'm glad you think you got your money's worth."

"Oh, I did, and then some."

Pete signed the bill and they returned to their room. "What's the plan for the rest of the afternoon?" Sophie asked.

"I'm going to a hardware store to buy a hacksaw," answered Pete.

"What for?"

"I am going to saw those rings off your neck."

"No, you are not," Sophie said vehemently.

"Oh yes, I am. I am not going to let you do permanent damage to your body in the name of being sexy, especially based on an off-the-cuff remark I made."

"First of all, it is my body, and I say what is going to happen to it, period."

"Not this time, babe," Pete said.

"This time and every time," Sophie countered in a tone of voice that said she was not changing her mind.

"Well, I got bad news for you. I am bigger than you are, and I am cutting that shit off. Why do you want to keep it anyway?"

"Lots of reasons. I like them for one thing."

"Not good enough," Pete said.

"I like what it does to you."

"What exactly do you think it does to me?"

"They made you bigger," Sophie said pointing to below Pete's belt.

"No, they didn't."

"Trust me, you got bigger," Sophie said.

"Haven't you ever heard the saying 'absence makes the penis grow larger'?"

"The saying is 'absence makes the heart grow fonder.' It was a nice try though. Trust me, you got bigger."

"All right, you can wear the damn things for a week, then they go without any fuss from you. Agreed?"

"Three months."

"One month, my final offer."

"Two and a half months. I'll split the difference with you," Sophie said.

"That's not an even split. When did you have those things put on?"

"Ten days ago," Sophie replied.

"Okay, I guess you won't do any damage in two and a half months. But then they come off with no fuss"

"Agreed, but if you shrink they are going back on and staying on," she laughed.

10

A couple of weeks later, with Christmas coming, Sophie had Toy take her Christmas shopping. She got something for everyone, including Chou's children. Santa Sophie had struck, and Pete was not sure Chou was going to be happy about it, although his kids would be. Pete bought Sophie a pair of Tahitian pearl earrings. She bought him a leather jacket.

The two months before Christmas passed for Sophie and Pete in a haze. Early mornings were devoted to exercise. At six o'clock each morning they went to the house so Sophie could use the workout room. Pete went jogging. After exercising, they returned to the hotel to shower and eat.

They returned to the house every morning about nine o'clock to review the previous day's progress with Mike. For the most part they liked everything that the experts had done. He and Sophie did make changes, but sparingly, knowing that each change they made would delay completion. Afternoons were spent lazing around the hotel or strolling in town. Pete played golf from time to time. At first Sophie had been a little cool to his golfing. She frankly admitted to herself that when he was not with her, she was bored. Her coolness lasted only until she found out that they stopped after every round for a beer at a topless joint on the outskirts of town called the Blue Fox. Then her sangfroid turned to outright hostility.

Her hostility progressed to a declaration of war when Pete showed up late one evening. Sophie, hungry, had gone down to eat dinner in the hotel even though Pete had not returned from playing golf. Pete peered into the dining room when he returned and saw Sophie eating alone. He walked over to her table.

"What are you having?" Pete slurred.

Sophie had suspected he was drunk from his stiff-legged walk, but now she knew it. "Fish," Sophie answered with a definite edge in her voice. "Are you going to join me for dinner?"

"I think I already drank it." With that he turned on his heel and staggered from the dining room.

When she opened the door to their room, she knew that her planned discussion had been put on hold until morning. Pete was lying on the bed fully clothed and snoring like a westbound freight.

Sophie got ready for bed in the bathroom. As she looked at Pete she realized he was lying diagonally across the bed. After some pulling and tugging she had him pretty much on his side of the bed. She removed her leg, turned off the light, and scrambled into bed. There was to be no slipping into a deep slumber that night, however. Pete's snoring was deafening so sleep was impossible. The longer she lay in bed trying to sleep, the madder she got. Finally she fell asleep from sheer exhaustion around four thirty.

When she awoke, he was gone. After showering and dressing, she went downstairs to the dining room. She was still steaming mad, and seeing him fueled her anger. She walked over to his table and sat down as he finished a glass of tomato juice. She did not want to make a public display and doubted she would be able to contain herself. When she felt she had marshaled her thoughts sufficiently and was about to speak, Pete said, "I know you're pissed, but could you wait until about four thirty before you vent your ire," adding, "after my nap?"

Sophie said nothing as the waiter set another glass of tomato juice in front of him and a butter plate beside it with two Bayer aspirin on it. As Pete was finishing his tomato juice, the waiter returned with a menu for Sophie. As soon as the waiter left the table, Pete said, "If you will excuse me, my dear, I am going to go upstairs and die." With that he left the table.

The fact that Sophie had not said a word was not lost on him. In fact, it scared him a little. He knew there was a volcanic eruption coming.

As she sat there, she did a little soul searching. She had every right to be mad, but why was she so mad? Because he went to play golf, and she was bored when he did? She knew that a husband and wife agreed to share their lives. But it was not the husband's job to entertain the wife. She realized equally that he needed to be able to enjoy himself and have friends. If he had gotten drunk at home, would she have been so mad? Of course not! She would have laughed at his hangover. That left the Blue Fox as the source of her irritation.

That place really griped her. She hated the thought of Pete sitting there watching women dance topless. Hated, she decided, was not the word. Detested was better, but still not strong enough. And the thought of him having a lap dance drove her into apoplexy.

She sat back realizing that her jealousy had driven her into a rage that really wasn't warranted. After signing the check, she went back to the room. Pete was lying on his back on his side of the bed with a damp washcloth on his forehead. She had to laugh.

"Let's go to the house. Up and at 'em tiger," Sophie said brightly.

He groaned.

"Come on, let's go."

"I don't suppose we could skip it today, could we?"

"No, let's go."

He considered refusing but being still leery of the coming storm, he forced himself to get up and get ready.

When they arrived at the house, they walked around until they found Mike, who perked up when he saw them. "I think we'll be done in a week." They walked through the house together, Mike pointing out the remaining things to be done. The list had dwindled to almost nothing. They thanked Mike for his time and walked out the front door. Halfway to the car, Sophie grabbed Pete by the arm, stopping, and asked, "Where are we going to get sheets, towels, dishes, pillows, and all those sorts of things?"

"I don't know, there must be a store around here somewhere that sells that sort of thing," Pete said. "I'll call Mary Schumann, she'll know."

"Call the decorator, she'll have more sources."

"Good idea," he said.

After a short conversation with the decorator, he hung up.

"Well?" Sophie asked.

"She recommended an upscale department store in the San Fernando Valley called Nordstrom."

"Let's go," Sophie said, starting to walk toward the car.

Following her, Pete asked, "I don't suppose we can wait until tomorrow to do this, can we?"

"No." She opened the car door and sat down, folding her arms. He resigned himself to a miserable day.

Upon further reflection, he said, "I think we better go get the limo from Toy. We are going to need the space."

"And probably Toy, too," Sophie said. Pete handed the cell phone to Sophie, who speed dialed Toy. A conversation ensued in Cantonese. "He'll be ready when we arrive," she said, hanging up.

When they pulled into the parking lot of the Motel Six, Toy was standing beside the Mercedes, which gleamed. Toy had clearly spent several hours waxing the car. "The car looks great," Pete said, as Toy held the door open for Sophie. Then he asked a beaming Toy, "Where is Chou?"

"Do you need him, sir?"

"No, I just wanted to give him the keys to the Rolls in case he needs a car today," Pete said. Toy silently held out his hand and Pete placed the keys in it. After Pete got in the car, Toy closed the door and ran over to one of the rooms. When Chou came to the door, Toy handed him the keys. Back at the car, he asked, "Where are we going, Boss?"

"Does this thing have a GPS?" Pete asked.

"Yes, sir."

Pete told him to program the Nordstrom department store into the GPS. Toy took a minute to do that, then exited the parking lot heading for the freeway. As Toy drove out of the parking lot, he realized one of the reasons he liked the "Boss" so much was that he thought about the people who worked for him. He asked their opinion and sometimes acted on it. He respected the people who worked for him. In addition, who else would leave a brand new Rolls Royce for an employee and his family to use?

Before they reached the freeway onramp, they passed the Blue Fox. Pete knew Sophie saw it but she said nothing. The calm before the storm, he thought, shutting his eyes and leaning his head back against the leather headrest.

The next thing he knew, Sophie was shaking him in the parking lot of a large store. They walked into Nordstrom and headed to housewares on the second floor. Pete walked them toward the escalator. When Sophie saw it she said, "I am afraid of those things." Pete simply placed his arm around her waist and lifted her up. Three strides later they were on their way up. He set Sophie down. "How am I going to get off this thing?" she asked. She was starting to panic. As the end approached, Pete, who had said nothing, simply picked her up again and stepped off. Three strides later, he set her down.

When they walked into the housewares department, a nice-looking woman of about forty approached them and asked, "May I help you?"

"You work on commission, don't you?" asked Pete. That drew an elbow in the ribs from his wife. But he pressed on when the saleslady nodded. "Today," he proclaimed, "is your lucky day!"

The sales lady looked a little dubious but smiled anyway. The smile gave way to a full-fledged grin when Sophie told her she wanted forty sets of the highest quality white sheets they sold. Then they ordered another two dozen in light blue. That was followed by an order for forty down pillows and forty foam rubber pillows. From there they progressed to bathroom linens. Sophie was ordering so fast, the saleslady had to ask her to repeat several items. After the linens were taken care of, Sophie headed for the fine china section. However, before she got there, her pregnancy took its toll on her bladder. She headed for the ladies room instead.

"Sir, if you don't mind me asking, are you outfitting a hotel?" the saleslady asked.

"We are in the process of moving to the United States and have bought a very large house. We are starting from scratch to furnish it." Sophie returned and picked a pattern for dinnerware. She ordered thirty-two sets of everything: dinner, bread, salad, and butter plates, and salad and soup bowls. Nothing seemed beyond her desires.

When the dust settled and the numbers added up, the saleslady asked, "How do you want to pay for this?" Pete handed her a debit card before Sophie could say anything. She came right up beside him to see precisely what he was doing.

There was no car made that would hold everything Sophie had bought. Additionally, the store did not have everything in stock and would have to get the rest from other stores and the warehouse. It seemed like scores of people were on computers locating everything and having it forwarded. The general manager graciously agreed to deliver everything to Santa Barbara for free.

Sophie wanted to know how the debit card worked. It worked the same as an Asian credit card she decided after a brief explanation. Asian banks did not issue true credit cards the same as an American bank. Then of course, why she did not have a debit card. "How do you think we pay for all those hotel rooms and meals for our employees?"

"I never gave it a thought, to be truthful," Sophie replied. "How do we pay our employees?"

"I hired an accountant who has a payroll service among other things."

"What's that?"

"They figure up all the taxes to be taken from someone's check, the amount of the check, and the amount to be sent to the government every month. Then they write the checks and I go in and sign them." Sophie sat back impressed.

"How did you know to do that?"

Pete shrugged his shoulders, "I just knew."

Approaching Santa Barbara, his cell phone rang. It was Mike. "You have to sign for another delivery."

"Be right there," Pete said hanging up.

"What was that all about?" Sophie wanted to know even before he had told Toy of the change of destinations.

"Toy, change of plans. Go to the house because there is another delivery that needs to be signed for." Sophie sat back mollified.

As they pulled into the driveway, there was a guy cutting the grass on a riding mower. "Who is he?" Sophie asked.

Pete knew he should be on his best behavior, since they had yet to have it out over yesterday, but he couldn't resist, "Juan," he said.

"Who is Juan?"

"The gardener."

"Who does Juan work for?" she asked, realizing she was being baited.

"Us."

"Funny, I don't remember us hiring a gardener."

"You didn't, you sent your seconds."

"Who are they?"

"Me," Pete said. They both started laughing.

When they finally got back to their hotel room, Sophie looked at her watch. "It is now four thirty-two and you have had your nap. I have a few remarks to make about the events of yesterday evening. I realize you know how stupid it is to drive a car in that condition. Just exactly why did you do it?"

"I sure as hell couldn't have walked in that condition."

"That is not funny."

"I know it was stupid, and I should know better," he said contritely.

"In the future, you can call Toy to come get you, or you can have Toy take you to the golf course and wait while you play. He will take you to the bar of your choice and he'll wait until you are ready to come home. Now, I am going to ask you to stay out of the Blue Fox. That place is like waving a red flag in front of a bull... me!"

"I don't particularly like the Blue Fox, to be honest. It smells like stale beer, cheap perfume, and cigarette smoke. I only go there because that's where everyone else likes to go."

"I am telling you right now, if you keep going there I am going to do something."

"Like what?" Pete queried. "Have Toy and Chou burn it down?"

"That is under consideration." The tone of her voice left no doubt she was serious.

Over dinner that night, Sophie said, "Tomorrow we are taking the plane to New York. I want to go to Tiffany's and buy some good silver and china for formal occasions."

"Look on the Internet first. I think there is a Tiffany's in LA."

"By the way," Sophie said, "I think you have done a really good job of organizing things here: the payroll, bills, and accommodations, just everything. I don't understand how you do it, though. I never see you do anything."

"I do it when you are in the bathroom in the morning, and for the most part, over the Internet. Once it's organized, it doesn't take much time."

Sophie got on the Internet when they got back to the room. "My goodness," Sophie said, "there is a Tiffany's in Santa Barbara!"

"You can have Toy take you tomorrow morning. I think I'll take a pass."

"You have to come. You're the only one with a debit card."

"Okay, we'll go there right after we go to the bank."

11

Sophie declared that the house would be sufficiently complete to start their move in seven days. She took the bull by the horns and jumped on poor Mike's back with her spurs on, saying, "I hope it doesn't take me as long to pay you as it did for you to finish this house."

The decorator was not spared her wrath either. She wanted all the furniture for the upper floors delivered one morning, and the downstairs furniture delivered that same afternoon.

Pete knew when to stand back and did.

When the big day came, trucks started arriving early in the morning. They borrowed all of Mike's men he could free up. Sophie and the decorator stood in the foyer directing traffic as things came through the front door and giving instruction on the final placement.

Pete spent the day on the second floor assembling beds and whatever else came along. He was not working alone on the second floor. A plumber was hooking up the sinks, an electrician was installing the faceplates on the junction boxes, and a painter was putting the final touches in one of the closets.

Whenever there was not a truck in the driveway, Sophie would take a quick tour of things. She went from room to room issuing orders. No, Pete thought, orders was not the right word. Edicts correctly expressed her utterances. The ruthless efficiency that had made Madame Gin Sling a success and a legend in Asia was on display and unrestrained. By about two o'clock, everyone had started keeping an eye on the driveway knowing that as long as a truck was unloading,

Sophie would be in the foyer. However, when there wasn't a truck being unloaded people seemed to find hiding spots. The electrician spent twenty minutes in a closet at the far end of the upstairs hallway playing with a faceplate. Pete finally asked him, "What are you doing in there?"

"No offense, sir," the electrician replied, "but your wife is making one of her inspections again." Pete just started laughing.

At five thirty, Pete saw Mike in the living room. Mike looked spent. Pete walked over to him and said, "It's Miller time."

"I'd love to, but I still have a lot to do," Mike said.

"Don't worry, I gotcha covered, and I'm buying."

Smiling, Mike said, "We're outta here."

"Pass the word to your guys. I'm buying at the Blue Fox."

Mike, still smiling said, "You could wind up with a pretty big bill."

"That's all right, they earned it."

Pete went into the foyer and asked Sophie where Toy was. She just waved in the direction of the patio. When he found Toy, he said, "Come on, Toy, you're up as a chauffeur. I am buying beers for the crew." Toy started grinning. He went around the side of the house to get the limo.

As he passed through the foyer, Sophie asked, "Where are you going?"

"I'm buying beers for the crew," and as Toy pulled up in the drive-way with the limo he added, "and taking your advice." Sophie said nothing, turning away so Pete could not see her grinning.

At about quarter of nine, a very pregnant Sophie walked into the Blue Fox. She saw their table immediately. They had pushed about four tables together. She walked over to their extended table and the conversation came to a complete halt, not only at their table, but the surrounding tables as well. "Well, isn't someone going to of-fer me a seat?" Mike was the first to react, scrambling to get her a chair. Just as she was sitting down, a top-heavy waitress wearing a very tiny top and a G-string came over and asked Sophie what she wanted to drink.

"Do you have champagne?" she asked.

"Yes, of course."

"Bring about four bottles, glasses for everyone, and a club soda for me." Sophie looked at Pete and said, "You're right, this place is a dump."

After a couple minutes, one of the guys down at the end of the table, a carpenter, Pete thought, asked Sophie, "Is it true that you're a billionaire?"

"That's true," Sophie said without hesitation.

"I never had a beer with a billionaire before," he said.

"Well you can't say that anymore, can you?" The guy simply hoisted his glass in a toast to her as the rest of the table laughed. She went on and said, "I personally want to thank you all for a great day's work."

Five minutes later Sophie stood, and the conversation ceased again, "I'll send Chou back with the Rolls to help with the transportation. Looks like you guys are going to need it."

The same guy down at the end of the table said, "I've never ridden in a Rolls Royce before, either."

"Well, then I guess tonight is your night for firsts. Good night, everyone." Smiling, she took her leave. A chorus of good nights followed her.

An hour later, Pete walked into their hotel room. "You were magnificent tonight. After you left, no one could talk about anything else. You made yourself a lot of friends tonight. And I especially want to thank you for coming in and showing everyone your human side. It meant so much to those guys." He undressed and crawled into bed. Sophie turned out the light on her side of the bed and snuggled up to him. Pete rolled on to his right side as did Sophie. Pete put his left arm over her. Sophie's last thought, before dropping off to sleep, was how lucky she had been to find Pete.

The next morning, they awoke about seven. She asked him brightly, "How do you feel?"

"Just fine. I took it easy last night."

"Do you have any idea where the car is this morning?"

"No. The last time I saw it, it was headed to Carpentaria. I thought we would have breakfast and then give Toy a call," Pete said. Sophie chuckled at that.

An hour later over breakfast Pete said, "Sophie, you really were sensational last night."

"I had a great deal of reservations about going into that joint. I didn't want to appear to be a pregnant wife in there tracking down her husband, that sort of thing. I also thought you might be embarrassed and lose face in front of the workmen."

"Exactly the opposite happened. Take heart, I doubt you were the first pregnant wife to enter that place."

"Just so there is no misunderstanding in the future, you should not take my appearance there last night as tacit approval of your going there in the future."

"You have to admit it was the perfect place for that group."

"Grudgingly."

They did not get to the house until a few minutes before nine. Sophie and the decorator resumed their traffic direction duties, and Pete wandered off to start assembling patio furniture. About eleven, after checking her clipboard, the decorator declared that there were no more trucks coming.

Shortly thereafter, Pete walked back into the house from the patio. He had never seen such a mess before. All the furniture had come with some sort of protective wrapping, and the wrapping, when stripped off, was starting to overwhelm the house. Pete grabbed a couple of Mike's men and asked them to give him a hand taking all the wrapping outside. Sophie and the decorator borrowed them next. The decorator started having the men position the furniture. The unwanted furniture that the former owner had left behind was taken to the garage.

Sophie went back to the hotel to rest during lunch, not returning until two o'clock. She immediately went upstairs and walked to the far end of the hall. She went up to the first workman she saw and said, "My husband and I have decided to give a barbeque for everyone who worked on this house to show our appreciation. Your wives, girlfriends, and families are invited as well. Come next Saturday at four o'clock, nine days from now. Anyone who wants to can bring their suit and use the pool."

"I'll be sure to be there," he said.

She went through the house repeating the invitation to each man she could find. When she spoke to Mike she asked him, "Would you call everyone who is not here and invite them? About Wednesday or so, give me a rough head count so we can be sure to order enough food."

"You better plan on a lot of people. After last night, these guys would walk across broken glass to attend anything where you are going to be." That brought a large smile to her face.

Sophie had Toy drive her back to the hotel around four o'clock. When Pete entered around six thirty she was just waking up from a nap. "You really need to take it little easier in the future," Pete said to her.

"The last two days just wore me out," she said, reaching for her glasses on the bedside table. Once she had them on, she extended both arms indicating she wanted a kiss. Pete was only too happy to oblige.

"What do you want to do for dinner?"

"Something quick and fast. I've never been to McDonalds. I see the advertisements all the time. Can we go there?" she asked.

"Sure. I think I am going to sneak down to the bar for a quickie while you get ready."

"See you there in five minutes."

When Pete got to the bar, he ordered a Diet Coke and called Toy. "Toy, I want you to bring Mi Ling over to this hotel in the morning about eight forty-five. Have her pack Sophie's things, but tell her not to say anything to my wife."

"Okay, Boss," Toy replied.

As they walked up to the house, Pete said, "We are almost done." As they walked through the various rooms, all the furniture was in place. In the ballroom the chairs were all correctly placed, but the floor was replete with scuff marks and needed cleaning and waxing. There were still workmen there, but they were finishing odds and ends. A couple of guys were installing curtain rods for the draperies. Another was hooking up the washer and dryer. Two more were installing the biggest stove he had ever seen in the kitchen.

"We need a cleaning crew," Sophie said.

"I think I know how to solve that problem," Pete said. He went outside and had walked almost all the way around the house when he finally saw Juan. "Hola, Juan, I need four or five ladies to clean right now. The job pays a hundred dollars a day."

"Let me make a call, Boss," Juan said, reaching for his cell phone. A rapid-fire conversation occurred in Spanish. "Okay if they bring their kids?"

"Sure." More Spanish ensued.

Finally Juan said, "I got five coming but they are not sure how long it will take them to get here."

"Get an address, Juan," Pete said. "I'll have Toy pick them up in the limo. It should hold everybody."

Forty minutes later an army of cleaning ladies was hard at work, and a gang of urchins was racing around outside under the supervision of Mrs. Chou. He sought out Toy again. "Toy, I want you to go down to the delicatessen we found and pick up some sandwiches. Get about ten turkey, ten chicken, six tuna salad, and twenty roast beef," he said, peeling three hundred dollars out of his money clip. Then he added, "Better get a case of cold Coke and a case of cold Diet Coke also, four or five bags of chips, and maybe a couple of bags of cookies for the kids.

Toy nodded, and away he went. Pete found one of the cleaning ladies and took her out on the patio. He tapped the large tables and said, "Primero."

He indicated to her he wanted all the tables and chairs cleaned first. That done, he went in search of Sophie. She was in the master bedroom and had just realized everything she thought was in the hotel was going into the bathroom and bedroom closets. He sensed she was close to erupting. He walked up behind her and put his arms around her. He felt her go limp in his arms, the pent-up tension leaving almost instantly. "I thought we'd eat lunch here, is that okay with you?" Pete asked.

"Sure," Sophie said leaning back into him.

He kissed her on the cheek as he stood upright before going to find Mike. Mike was in the kitchen with the electrical inspector. The electrician had a new circuit breaker panel open and pulled down for inspection.

"Okay," the inspector said, signing a card on his clipboard and handing it to Mike. As the inspector left, Mike said, "That was our final sign-off."

"Great!" Pete said. He then invited Mike and all his men to the "picnic on the patio," as he had come to think of it.

Toy had taken the initiative to stop at a grocery store and buy paper cups, napkins, mustard, and mayonnaise. Sophie organized a buffet table of sorts. Piles of sandwiches were laid out by type. Plates, chips, and napkins were all orderly placed. The patio had two large tables, each would seat ten people. Sophie sat down at one. Pete turned around to get a sandwich, but when he turned back the workmen had taken every seat at Sophie's table. He looked at them, smiling. Sophie was gabbing away with them, and they were all smitten by her charms. When lunch was over, everyone helped with the cleanup.

Sophie caught up with Pete as he was walking back into the house. "I wish you had told me we were moving today."

"Why?"

"So I could have made some plans," Sophie said.

"What would you have done differently?"

"I don't know because I never had a chance to think about it," Sophie replied.

"Well, I have a question for you."

"What is it?" Sophie asked.

"Where did you put your souvenir mattress?"

"It's right across the hall," she said laughing.

When five o'clock came, Pete got Juan to ask the cleaning ladies if they would come back the next day starting at eight o'clock. All agreed to return.

Three days later, the house was finally finished and cleaned, at least to Pete's satisfaction. Sophie made the error of suggesting to Pete they change the mantel in the living room. A resounding, "No!" was all she heard. Her "Why not?" follow-up was met with a diatribe on workmen under foot and something about his privacy. She decided to defer the subject, but only for the moment.

The day of the barbeque came, and the weather cooperated. It was clear, cloudless, and seventy–two degrees—unusual for the end of February. Sophie had had the pool heater turned on to make sure the water was warm enough for the kids to swim in without catching cold.

Mike had estimated one hundred people would attend. Sophie planned for one hundred and forty. Jean Claude, the French chef from the French restaurant in her former hotel, had arrived two days before. Pete had taken him aside and explained that the people coming to the barbeque would be middle-class working men and their families. "No frog legs or escargot," he explained. "Nothing more exotic than spicy chicken wings."

On the day of the barbeque, Jean Claude started cooking at five in the morning. He instinctively knew that this barbeque was very important to Mrs. Smith, and he was not going to let her down. Sophie had also hired a French woman, Veronique, as a sous chef to help Jean Claude with big affairs and prepare breakfast in the morning. When Pete walked into the kitchen, the two of them were chattering away in French and giving instructions to two other women who appeared to be Spanish. He had no idea where the two Spanish women had come from. As he looked around, his jaw hit the floor. There was enough food there to feed the army of Finland for a week, and food was still coming out of the ovens.

When Sophie came out of the house she was wearing one of her many big floppy-brimmed hats. This one happened to be dark brown. Her oversized horn-rimmed glasses and a tan muumuu completed her ensemble. She deliberately dressed down because she did not want to be thought a snob in some designer pregnancy clothes.

At four o'clock people started arriving, and by five o'clock there had to be a hundred and forty people in the backyard. Some kids were running around while other kids swam. At one point Sophie came over to Pete and said, "Look at that, black kids, white kids, Latino kids, and Chinese kids, all playing together."

"The language barrier doesn't seem to be a deterrent to everyone having fun," Pete observed.

"Too bad the whole world is not like our backyard," Sophie said, drifting away. Pete watched her stopping to chat with everyone who said anything to her. Sophie finally ran into the guy who had had his night of firsts in the Blue Fox. He had clearly told the tale to his pregnant wife. "I'm Jack, by the way, and this is Carol, my wife."

Jack was tall and well built, about thirty with brown hair hanging over his collar. Carol was five feet, four inches tall, the same as Sophie. Carol's hair was light brown with blonde highlights, and she had a pretty face with a fresh and natural look. "When is your baby due?" Sophie asked, as Jack drifted off to get another beer.

"I'm due mid-April, how about you?"

"The end of March," Sophie replied. They sat down and continued to gab like long-lost sisters. Somehow the Blue Fox came up in the conversation. "I hate that place," Sophie said.

"Not as much as I do," was Carol's retort. The vehemence in her voice caused them both to start laughing.

At that point Jean Claude started serving. There were stacks of New York strip steaks, racks and racks of barbequed ribs, potato salad, coleslaw, mounds of chicken wings, plates of assorted cheeses, and three different sauces for the steak.

On one corner of a table there was a stack of hamburger patties and hot dogs for the kids. As they got closer to the buffet table Carol said, "We are never going to get a seat."

"Don't worry, we'll go inside," Sophie said. The two of them went into the small dining room and gabbed away as they ate. When they were finished, Sophie asked Carol if she would like to see the rest of the house. Carol jumped at the opportunity. Sophie gave Carol an extensive tour. When they were back where they started, Sophie said, "I have to get back before I am missed, but let me give you my number and if you want to have lunch or something call me." Carol gave Sophie her number as well.

They went back outside. Pete watched Sophie as she passed through the crowd. She should have been a politician the way she worked the crowd. Even though she was smiling, Pete noticed a wan expression on Sophie's face. He went over to her and said, "I think it is time for you to go upstairs and lie down. There is no reason to overdo." For once, she did not argue.

But as she slowly climbed the stairs, she thought about her husband. He always seemed to be taking care of her. And to a large degree, she had put herself in his care. She liked having someone else worry about her, she decided.

As Pete came into the bedroom a couple of hours later, Sophie muted the TV. "I think that was a big success," he said.

"I hope so,"

"There's something else we need to talk about," Pete said seriously.

"Let me guess," she interrupted, "your parents' visit."

"That's it. Just think about it. We don't need to make a decision tonight," he said, undressing. He went into the bathroom and took a quick pass at his teeth and crawled into bed. Sophie turned out the light on her bedside table as Pete rolled onto his right side. Sophie wiggled over to him so that her back was against his chest. He put his left arm over her, and just as he was dropping off, he realized the depth of his love for her.

The next morning, with Sophie hovering over him, Pete dialed his parents' number from memory. "Hello," his mom said, answering the phone.

"Hi, Mom," Pete said.

"Oh Peter, how are you? When can we come see you? When is that house going to be finished?"

"Slow down. That's really why I am calling. The house is done and we'd really like you and Dad to come for a visit. When can you come?"

"If the decision were mine alone to make, I'd come tomorrow. I want to meet my new daughter-in-law."

"Well, talk to Dad, and call me back," Pete said

"He is in the shower right now, so it'll be about fifteen minutes before I can call back."

"There's one other thing, Mom. Sophie is insisting that she make all your travel arrangements."

"I don't want my new daughter-in-law buying me airplane tickets. We're not rich, but we can afford airplane tickets."

"Mom, this is something she really wants to do, and if you don't let her, my life is going to be a living hell."

"I'll call you back."

Twenty minutes later, the phone rang. Pete answered it with Sophie standing by his side. "Hello," he said.

"Can we come tomorrow?"

"Of course," he answered. "How did you get Dad moving so fast?"

"He decided he didn't want to sleep on the back porch," his mom said, adding, "It's cold out there this time of year."

Pete started laughing. "What?" Sophie wanted to know. He waved his hand indicating he would tell her later.

"Okay, Mom," he said trying to control his laughter, "What time would you like to come?"

"I haven't looked at the flights yet."

"You're not listening, Mom. What time do you want to leave your house?"

"Your dad said to let Sophie make the travel arrangements, and we'll pay her back when we get there."

"What time?"

"Is ten o'clock okay?"

Pete, a little frustrated said, "Mom, are you trying to accommodate Sophie or is that when you really want to leave?"

"Peter, you always were an impossible child. That's when we want to leave."

"All right, Mom, pack your bags, and a car will call for you at nine thirty. See you tomorrow. Bye-bye," Pete said, hanging up.

Later that morning, Sophie answered the phone. She didn't say anything for a long time. Then she said, "That will be fine," and hung up.

"What was that about?" Pete wanted to know.

"Oh nothing, it was just some old business."

About an hour later he came into the library. Sophie said, "You never did take me to the bank and Tiffany's," as Pete walked into the room.

"Oh yeah, that's right. I was hoping you'd forget about that."

"Why?"

"You are the deadliest shopper I know. Right now, however, there is some unfinished business I need to resolve."

"What's that?"

Pete pulled an old hacksaw from behind his back.

"You're not using that thing on me!"

"Your two and a half months are up."

"I had hoped you'd forget about that."

"Not hardly," he said. "Now, come over here and lie on top of the coffee table."

"No."

"A deal is a deal."

He had used the magic words. Sophie prided herself on her word, and with a shrug of her shoulders she lay down on top of the coffee table on her side. Twenty minutes later the rings were removed.

"Now, doesn't that feel better?"

"No!" And she stomped out in a huff.

The next morning they left for the bank and Tiffany's, returning an hour and a half later and a hundred grand lighter.

Toy met them in the driveway. Sophie and Toy had a conversation in Cantonese. "Your parents will be arriving in about an hour," Sophie said. After taking about four steps toward the house, she turned and said to Pete, "Come with me. Your wedding present has arrived."

As they approached the garage, the door started opening. Pete looked over his shoulder at a grinning Toy. He knew he'd been set up, but just did not know the outcome. Sitting in the garage there was a perfectly restored 1964 Aston Martin DB IV. But the piece de resistance was an equally perfect 1964 Shelby AC Cobra. Pete went to the cobra absolutely agog. The keys were in it. As Sophie approached the cars she said, "Do you like them?"

"Love is the word, and yes. Let's go for a ride."

"I can't get into that thing."

Pete picked her up and lowered her gently into the passenger's seat. He reached in and fastened her seat belt. He climbed in himself and fired up the car. He went to Old California 1 turning north when he reached it. About five minutes later, he turned off the highway onto a windy two lane road that went into the foothills behind the city. There was no traffic in front of them, so Pete floored it. The Cobra responded with a roar and leapt forward. The tires were squealing as they rounded the first corner. After a minute or so, Pete glanced at Sophie out of the corner of his eye. She had grabbed the bottom rails of the seat and was hanging on for dear life with a terrified look on her face. A couple of minutes later, he glanced at her again, she was still wide eyed but had let go of the seat rails. Pete slowed, and pulled into a convenient driveway to turn around. He started back down the hill at the same speed he had come up. The next time he glanced at Sophie, she was grinning like a Cheshire Cat.

Back at the house with the Cobra safely in the garage, Pete lifted Sophie out of the car. Sophie said, "I never had so much fun in my life! When can do it again?"

"That was probably the last time that this car will ever get driven."

"Why?"

"It's just too valuable and too rare. If something ever happened, you could not replace it."

"Why did you drive it this time?"

"Because, basically, I'm still twelve years old and could not resist."

That brought a grin to her face. Her present was a huge success.

"Boss," Toy said, "we have got to go to the airport."

Sophie turned to go back into the house. They had decided earlier that Pete should go to the airport so he could have a few minutes alone with his parents, whom he hadn't seen for over a year.

"You know," Pete said, "they made about twenty-five of these things with automatic transmissions."

Sophie turned around and just said, "Really?"

"Boss, we have to go," Toy said, holding the rear door to the limo open.

Earlier that day in Mystic

"Sally, I don't understand why we don't just go to the airport," Pete's dad said.

"Pete told me Sophie arranged all this as a surprise. And I had better be prepared for what might be the biggest surprise of my life. Sophie also arranged a car for us."

Joe Smith, Pete's dad, was looking out the window when a limo pulled up in front of their house. "Well, if that don't beat all. Look at that, Sally."

The driver came to the front door and knocked on it. "When Sally opened the door, the driver said, "Good morning. I am Charles, and I am here to take you to the airport. Where is your luggage?"

Pete's mom just pointed to three suitcases by the door. The driver took the suitcases and set them down behind the car. Then he opened the door for the Smiths. She had to admit that a chauffeur-driven limo was a pretty big surprise.

The surprises kept coming. When they passed the small public terminal at the New London airport, Pete's dad leaned forward and tapped on the glass partition. As the driver was rolling it down, Pete's dad asked, "Where are we going?"

"To the aircraft, sir," the driver said as he turned onto the tarmac, stopping in front of a large private jet. The hostess was standing at the bottom of the stairs. She wore a dark blue skirt, a white blouse, and a tan blazer.

She opened the limo door for them as the driver was getting their baggage out of the trunk. When Pete's parents were both standing outside the car, Pete's dad asked, "Are you sure this is for us?"

"Mr. and Mrs. Smith?"

"Yes."

"Then there's no mistake, sir."

They followed the hostess up the stairs as the copilot stored the baggage. "Sit anywhere you like." Then the hostess said, "I need to give you a safety briefing before we take off." She did, concluding by asking if they would like something to drink before takeoff. Both declined. Then she proceeded to acquaint them with the amenities of the aircraft; movies, lavatory, bunk room, shower, and GPS readout.

After they had been in flight for about twenty minutes the hostess returned to ask them if she could bring them anything. They both declined, but Pete's dad asked, "Who owns this airplane?"

"Mrs. Smith, sir."

It was the biggest surprise of their life. Their son had married a woman who owned her own private jet.

Santa Barbara Airport

Pete, with Toy at the wheel of the limo arrived at the airport just as the plane was touching down.

When it stopped in the parking area, Toy pulled out on the ramp stopping in front of the plane. Pete hugged his Mom and Dad. The three of them climbed into the car while Toy and the copilot put the baggage in the trunk.

"Gee, it's really great to see you," Pete said.

"We're very happy to see you, too. I want to meet your wife. Where is she, by the way?"

"Sophie is up at the house. I wanted the chance to tell you a little about her before you meet her."

"We're all ears," Pete's Dad said.

"Sophie was raised in the slums of Saigon. That's where she lost her leg. She managed to get into the gambling business and made a fortune. She is a billionaire."

"How did you manage to marry her son, she sounds like a catch?"

"She got pregnant, tracked me down, and persuaded me to marry her."

"It doesn't sound like that was a tough sell."

"I am going to tell you the truth Dad, when I married Sophie, I thought she worked in the accounting department of the hotel and approved gamblers' credit. That's what she told me, anyway. That was true as far as it went."

At that point, they pulled into the driveway. Looking at the house his Dad said, "Son, I think you may be in over your head."

"I know I am."

Sophie met them in front of the house.

After the introductions, they went inside. They were standing in the foyer when Toy entered with the luggage, "Where should I put the luggage, Mrs. Smith?"

"Check with Mi Ling and ask her which room she has prepared."

"They went into the den and chatted. Toy came and stood silently with his back to the wall. Finally Sophie asked, "What would everyone like for lunch?"

"What are the choices?" Pete's dad asked.

"Dad, just tell Toy what you want, and he will let you know if we don't have it."

They all gave Toy their choices, and twenty minutes later Toy announced, "Luncheon is served." Pete was really kind of shocked by Toy. He knew Toy was a very good bodyguard but had no idea Toy could double as a butler.

The visit went really well until the fourth day. As Pete walked through the front door, his mother came across the foyer with her mascara streaked and tears running down her cheeks. Before he could say anything, she was up the stairs. He found Sophie in the den also in tears. "What the hell happened," he demanded?

"I told your mother the real story of my life, all of it. She got so sad she started crying, and that got me crying, too."

Later that night, his mother got him aside and said, "Peter, you have married an exceptional woman. She has more character in her little finger than I do in my whole body. Frankly, I did not think there was anyone in the world with as strong a character as Sophie. I doubt you know how lucky you are. I would say that even if she didn't have a dime. The only thing I don't understand is why she married a bum like you who never comes to see his parents." With that she spun on her heel and started to go upstairs. But she turned back and approaching Pete she said, "If you ever hurt her, I'll castrate you with a rusty razor." She turned again and went upstairs.

Pete was stunned. A rusty razor?! His mother never spoke like that. The strongest thing he had ever heard her say was "drat!"

The next day, Pete's mother got Sophie aside, "Listen Sophie, you have never had a baby before. There are things you don't know and can't learn from any book or class. When you come home from the hospital, there is no substitute for having someone who loves you to help you. Normally, it's your mother who does it. But in this case, it is going to be me. So the minute you get the first contraction, you call me, and I'll be on my way. You are not coming home alone. I won't have it. I intend to have the same conversation with Pete."

By the time she finished speaking Sophie, normally a take charge lady, was in tears again, saying between sobs, "I will."

The evening after Pete's parents had left, Pete and Sophie were in bed, and Sophie said, "Your parents are the finest people I have ever met. I want to do something for them.

"Sophie, you tend to go over the top at times. If you try to do something for them, there is a very good chance you will offend them. You have to tread lightly. Remember, they have been independent and self-reliant for fifty years."

Macau

At the mahogany conference table in the Po brothers' conference room, Wing said to his brother, "We don't have the money, and I think we can be certain Madame Gin Sling will foreclose forthwith. Once foreclosure starts, the only thing we can do is to pay the entire amount; an additional hundred million."

"What do you suggest we do?"

"I have spoken with our lawyers in California and here. If Madame Gin Sling were to die, the debt would not be extinguished under either Portuguese or California law. But under California law, the court must appoint an executor before any action may be taken on behalf of the estate. Normally that takes about three weeks. Then the executor has to understand all her business dealings. That will take time. This would give us at least a month to raise the money."

"And if this hotel goes into foreclosure, I think we can safely assume Lo Yang will kill us and everyone in our families."

"I don't see that we have any choice."

"Neither do I. Do you have anyone in mind who can do the job with no blowback?"

"Yes, I'll take care of it."

"Good, I never did like that woman."

Santa Barbara

At eleven in the morning, Sophie was scheduled for her appointment with the OB/GYN. Pete decided to go with her. It was a beautiful clear cloudless morning. Toy had pulled the car as close to the front door as possible and left the door open as Pete helped Sophie. Toy slid behind the wheel. Toy knew Pete preferred to help Sophie himself. They were standing beside the open rear door, but just as Sophie bent over to enter the car a supersonic bullet hit the door, passing through the metal rim just above the window, and continued passing between Sophie and Pete.

Pete grabbed Sophie and pushed her over her peg leg, holding on to her as they fell toward the rear wheel. As they were going over, Pete twisted his body so Sophie landed on top of him. The back of her head hit him in the mouth causing his teeth to cut the inside of his lips. His head then hit the concrete, causing a gash on the back of his head. He immediately rolled Sophie toward the car and then pushed her under the car as far as he could. A second shot shattered the window, showering Pete and Sophie with small pieces of safety glass. A third shot passed through the door. Pete got to his knees. Sophie started to turn toward him. "Don't move," Pete shouted vehemently at her. "Toy, throw me a gun." Three seconds later a .40 Sig Sauer landed on the back seat where, only moments before, Sophie had been prepared to sit.

Pete checked to be sure there was one in the throat and the safety was off. Then he got down on his stomach and crawled to the front of the car. He knew roughly where the shooter had to be. There was a canyon on that side of the property with a park beyond it. The shot had to have come from the park. There was only one tree in the park that would permit the angle to give a reasonable chance of hitting the target. The tree was about eight hundred yards away. He figured if he could get a couple of rounds through the leaves of the tree, he might be able to get the shooter moving. The tree was on a hillside, so he did not have worry about hitting anything but the hillside behind the tree. He took a guess on the elevation and wind and popped off three rounds.

Thirty seconds later, just as he was getting ready to take a couple more shots, something which looked like a rifle fell out of the tree. It was followed shortly thereafter by a man who dropped to the ground. He was holding the inside of his right thigh and limping away as fast as he could, the rifle forgotten.

"I think it's all clear now." He got up and walked toward Sophie, saying to her, "Lie still, there is broken glass everywhere. "Toy, call the cops. It's 911 here," thinking Toy probably didn't know the number. Chou came running from the garage. "Don't move," he shouted again at Sophie! "Chou, get a broom."

Chou took off running. Returning about a minute and a half later, Chou handed Pete the broom and Pete started sweeping the glass off Sophie and the ground around her. A siren in the distance grew louder. When Pete finally had the glass swept away, he carefully rolled Sophie away from the car. Then he got down on one knee, slid his hands under her, and carefully picked her up. Just as he was starting to let her stand on her own, the first police car spun into the driveway. The sound of a second siren indicated another car was not far away.

The first policeman took in the bullet holes in the door and the ricochet marks on the concrete and knew there had indeed been a shooting. As the second officer came over, Pete told them about the guy who had fallen out of the tree and that there was possibly a rifle lying on the ground under the tree he was pointing out. The first policeman jumped on his radio, while the second roared off to check under the tree.

Sophie meanwhile was fussing over Pete. He was bleeding from the mouth, the back of his head, and numerous small cuts he had sustained while crawling through the glass to the front of the car. "Please," he said to her, "I'm fine. This is just superficial; nothing to worry about." His pronouncement did nothing to allay his wife's concerns, however.

The first officer took everyone's statement. After about twenty-five minutes a detective arrived and they all gave their statement a second time to this newly arrived detective.

While the detective was still there, his radio squawked. He stepped away to listen. When he came back, he said, "An Asian gentleman just drove into a parked car and killed himself. He had a bullet wound that apparently severed the femoral artery in his right leg."

Pete went over to the detective and asked, "How are your relations with the Hong Kong and Macau police departments?"

"Okay, I guess, but to be honest, I don't ever remember having a case affecting either of those jurisdictions."

"I think you'll get a hit if you run the dead guy's prints through those departments."

"Why would you think that?"

"My wife ran a casino in Macau for many years. This could be somehow related to that."

After a few more questions, the policemen left.

"Toy, get Chou and meet me in the den in five minutes," Pete said.

"Yes, Boss."

"Sophie, I need you in the den in five minutes, as well." She nodded. Pete went directly to the den himself and was pacing back and forth when Sophie arrived with a Perrier in hand. She stood in the doorway with a look of admiration on her face watching him. Deep in thought, he had not noticed her. He looked up as Toy and Chou arrived.

"Before we can insure that this sort of thing is not repeated, we need some good intelligence. Toy and Chou, I want you to go to Macau. Do you both have two passports in phony names?" They nodded. "Good. I want you to make a reservation to get there in those names. Don't travel on the same plane or routing. For example, Toy, if you choose to go through Tokyo, then Chou, you change in Manila or anywhere else. When you change planes, change passports. But watch the entry and exit stamps. Sophie, do you know a forger in LA?"

"No. But I know how to find one."

"Good. Find him and give Toy the name. Toy, when you think out the entry, and exit stamps, you may find you need to buy a couple of entry/exit stamps. Any decent forger will have them. I want you to leave through Vancouver. Take a plane to Seattle. When you get there, buy a car out of the classifieds, something non-descript. Pay cash and don't register it. Drive out to one of the crossings where there is no border patrol. I know you know where there is one." Toy smiled at that.

"Don't leave on the same day. Make your reservations one way. Also, make the reservations from internet cafes in the LA area. If you make the Vancouver to Tokyo reservation in one café, make the reservation to Hong Kong in another.

"This afternoon go to Ventura and buy a nondescript Chevy or Ford. Two Chinese guys your size in a Rolls is unforgettable. Don't forget to bargain with the dealer. When it is time to pay, have the dealer call our bank.

"Sophie, would you call the bank manager and tell him to transfer whatever funds Toy and Chou request? Then I need you to set up four accounts in the names on Chou and Toy's phony passports. Put $25,000 in each account. It will be best to do that through Switzerland. You'll have to get up at two in the morning to call. Get a debit card on each account and have the cards FedExed here.

"While you are taking care of that, I am going to North Carolina," Pete continued.

"Why," Sophie wanted to know?

"I want to speak with the army intelligence people to make sure I was not the target. We know the shooter was Asian, but that's no guarantee that he came from Macau. Additionally, my "back up" passports are there.

"Would you call the pilots and tell them I want a five o'clock departure for Kingston, North Carolina, tomorrow morning?"

Looking at Toy and Chou, he asked, "Any questions?"

"No, Boss," Toy said, as Chou shook his head.

"Good, let's plan on meeting back in this room at 5:00 in the afternoon three days from now."

"Okay, Boss," they both said as they left the room.

"Why would anyone be after you?" Sophie asked her husband.

"I was the mission planner in Afghanistan my last two tours. The Taliban actually put a price on my head."

"Oh," she said. Then she asked, "Why are you doing this?" Sophie wanted to know.

"Nobody takes a shot at my wife and lives to tell about it. Nobody!"

"And, another thing, why did you speak so sharply and harshly to me outside?" Sophie asked somewhat indignant.

"That's because I needed you to do something you are not very good at," he said, with a slight grin.

"What's that?"

"Obey."

Sophie pushed her glasses up her nose, stuck out her tongue at him, spun on her peg leg, and left.

She had heard Toy and Chou call Pete "Boss" before, and after a few moments of thought, she realized everyone called Pete "Boss." She wasn't sure how she felt about what that implied. She had been the unquestioned boss of her world for the last twenty-five years, and she wasn't sure she was willing to forego that. Two strides later, she realized she was on her way to do exactly what he told her to do. A big grin appeared on her face as she realized he really was the boss. How it had happened was something she would spend years pondering.

North Carolina, two days later

Pete walked into the offices of the Special Forces intelligence section about ten in the morning. He saw a major he had worked with for years. "Tom," he called, happy to see him. Tom Henry turned and his face lit up at seeing his old friend. "How's retirement, Colonel?"

"Considerably different than I thought it would be."

"Really, why? Come on into my office and tell me about it," Tom said.

"Well, I got married for one thing."

"Do I know the lucky lady?" Tom asked.

"She is from Macau, so I doubt it," Pete said.

"Where are you living now?"

"Santa Barbara," Pete said.

"What brings you here?"

"Someone took a shot at my wife and me. It is impossible to know which of us was the target because the bullet passed four inches in front of my face and four inches behind her head," the bonhomie left Tom's face upon hearing that.

"Why would anyone want to kill your wife?"

"She ran a gambling joint in Macau for many years; big loser perhaps?"

"How can I help?"

"Do you have any intel on any crazies entering the country who have sworn to kill me?"

"No, nothing. In fact, everything has been very quiet. The only crazies we have any rumors on at all seem to be Syrian or Lebanese."

They chatted for a few more minutes before Pete took his leave. After stopping at his bank and emptying his safety deposit box, he went to the local Bekin's Moving and Storage. He made arrangements to have the contents of his two storage garages shipped to California. That done he noticed that it was approaching five o'clock. He went back on post and went into the NCO club.

He saw a Sargent sitting at the bar that he had known for years. He asked him if he had seen Sargent Jarwarski. "Usually you can find him this time of day at the Pony Club. He's fallen in love with one of the dancers," the Sargent said.

Twenty minutes later Pete found the Pony Club and Mike Jarwarski. The stool next to the Sargent was empty. He sat down, but the Sargent had not yet looked at his new neighbor. "How have you been, Sargent?" Pete asked. Mike Jarwarski was the finest soldier with whom he had ever served. His respect for the Sargent knew no bounds. The feeling was mutual. After the usual catching up, Pete got right to the point. "Mike, someone tried to kill either my wife or me."

"How sure are you about that, Colonel?"

"The bullet passed four inches in front of my nose and four inches behind my wife's head."

Mike said, "That's about as certain as you can get."

"Mike, have you had so much as a sniff of any crazies coming into the country who may have threatened me at some time in the past?"

"No, nothing," he said.

They talked about other things for a while before Pete said he had to leave. In the parking lot, he called the pilot and asked if it was possible to leave now instead of in the morning.

"I think we can get air born in forty-five minutes."

"See you on board," Pete said.

It was ten o'clock at night when Pete came through the front door. The convenience of having access to a private jet was driven home by that single step over the threshold. He went upstairs to their bedroom. Sophie had herself propped up in bed watching TV. Her hair was undone and hanging over her shoulders. She was wearing a t-shirt and the big glasses had slid down her nose. She had never looked so desirable to Pete.

Pushing her glasses up on her nose, Sophie asked, "What did you find out?"

"I am about ninety-eight percent certain I was not the target."

"I've been thinking about this ever since you left," she said. "I really don't want you going to Macau. Toy and Chou are perfectly capable of taking care of anything that needs to be done. Macau can be a very dangerous place. Plus, I am due in less than a month, and I want you here. This is something I don't want to go through by myself."

"Sophie, sweetheart, I have been in a lot of dangerous places in my life, and I am still here. I truly appreciate the sentiment, and I know it is heartfelt. But really, don't worry. I am a very careful man."

"I can't help it."

"Well then, don't worry too much," he said as he undressed.

She took off her glasses, put them on the table, and pulled the t-shirt over her head. As she did so she said, "Why don't you ask me to do something that I can actually do; like jump over the moon?" She snuggled back into him. As she did so she felt him getting hard. "Not tonight, buster, I'm upset," she said. He held her a little tighter than normal, and a few seconds later he was fully erect. Sophie knew exactly what was going on with him. Try as she might to contain herself, his erection was stimulating her, as well. Finally, she reached between her legs and grabbed him. After a minor amount of maneuvering, he was inside her. J…just where he belonged, she thought before pleasure overcame her ability to think rationally.

The next morning, FedEx arrived at exactly eight thirty. Pete signed for the package and took it inside, then resumed his trip to the garage. He decided to take the new little white car that Toy and Chou had bought. He drove to the bank and picked up the cash they would need for their trip to Macau.

Pete stopped next at the local police department. He asked the receptionist for the detective who had investigated the shooting at his house. Five minutes later, the detective came into the reception room to escort Pete back to his desk. The detective sat behind his old gray metal desk while Pete sat to one side. Before the detective could say anything, Pete asked, "What did you hear from Macau?"

"The suspect had a record in Macau. Two arrests for murder, no convictions because the witnesses failed to appear."

"So he was apparently the guy who took a shot at us?"

"The dead guy's prints were on the rifle, so there is no doubt he is good for it. I spoke with the DA this morning and he's not going to file on the shooting. The autopsy report put the cause of death as a broken neck. He thinks a first-year law student would walk you out the front door without any problem," the detective said.

"What about self-defense?" asked Pete.

"Never comes up because the cause of death is a traffic accident."

"Well, I guess that's that. Thanks for the info," Pete said.

"Now I have a question to ask you, if I may. I did a hitch in the navy before becoming a cop, made port in Hong Kong one time. Is your wife Madame Gin Sling?" the detective asked.

"She is indeed Madame Gin Sling." Pete responded, smiling.

"I saw her picture when I was in Hong Kong, but I never thought I would meet a woman so beautiful."

"Yes, she's a lovely lady. Well, thanks again for the info," Pete said, rising to leave.

Sophie knew she was turning herself into one great big ball of worry. Now she knew how soldiers' wives felt when their husbands went off to war. She was staring vacantly out the front window when a funny little white car came roaring up the driveway. She went outside with the intention of telling the driver to slow down since there were children playing. When Pete climbed out of the car, she asked instead, "Where did that thing come from?"

"I think this is the car Toy and Chou bought. I found it, with the keys in it, in the garage so I thought I'd give it a test-drive."

"Well?"

"Actually, it's not bad." They went inside the house together.

An hour later, they were all assembled in the den. They reviewed the travel plans and distributed the cash and credit cards. Pete added a couple of additional instructions. "When you get to Hong Kong or Macau, I want you to get your hands on five pounds, no make that seven pounds, of composition C4, detonators, and a sniper rifle, a Barrett .50 cal., if possible. If not, the Chinese version of it, sighted for five hundred yards."

"No problem, Boss," Chou said, "that stuff is all available."

"When you get there, Toy, I want you to concentrate on seeing what you can find out from the casino employees. Chou, you do the same thing with the underworld."

As he said it, Sophie shuddered involuntarily. A few phone calls later, a flight to Seattle had been arranged. An hour and a half later, Pete drove the little white car back up the driveway. Sophie met Pete at the front, "I'm so worried."

"If it makes you feel any better, so am I."

"Why?" Sophie asked. If he was worried, she was going to be terrified.

"They may try again while I'm gone." Sophie waved away his concerns with a flick of her wrist. "Sophie," Pete continued, "I'm going to take the jet to Honolulu tomorrow and leave it there until I get back, if that's okay with you."

"Of course."

Macau

"What do we know so far?" Pete asked.

"The vice president in charge of the casino told me they had been hit twice last month by two of the whales getting lucky. They apparently lost more than forty-seven million U.S.," Toy said. "I haven't yet been able to speak to anyone in the accounting department, but I should be able to do that tonight."

"Chou, what have you found out?" Pete wanted to know.

"The few people I spoke with know nothing, but they low level. Tonight I should do more," Chou replied smiling, thinking his English had been perfect.

"All right, why don't you guys hit the street again, and we'll meet back in my room again about ten tomorrow morning," Pete said.

"How about noon, Boss?" Toy asked.

"Noon it is, then."

Toy and Chou left his room to resume their prowling of the underbelly of Macau. Pete faced about fifteen hours of boredom.

It was twelve fifteen when Toy joined Pete and Chou in Pete's room. "Chou, why don't you tell us what you found?" Pete said.

"Nothing, really," Chou said.

"How high up were you able to get?" Pete asked.

"I speak with four different guys who, I would say, second level. No one hear anything about Madame Gin Sling. She clean. But Po brother going to have trouble soon. Don't pay bill to triad."

"Toy?"

"Things are very bad at the hotel. I spoke with Wu Pot and he told…"

"Who is he?" Pete interrupted.

"Sorry, Boss, he is the chief accountant. Anyway, he told me the hotel is in a very bad position right now. They have only nine million in the general account and are running with four million cash in the cage. Also, they are more than forty-five days late with about five million dollars of, what he called, trade debt. The casino manager told me what happened; two whales came into town and hit the casino for forty-seven million. That put them in a hole that they are having trouble getting out of."

"When Sophie ran the hotel, do you know what kind of cash balances she maintained?"

"Sophie always kept fifteen million in the cage and twenty-five to thirty million in the general account. The casino manager told me if they have a bad Friday night, they won't be able to pay off all the winners."

"I got it now. Killing Sophie buys them time on the twenty-five-million-dollar payment due next week."

"That's what it looks like, Boss," Toy said, as Chou nodded his agreement.

"Chou, this afternoon I want you to go buy a soldering iron," Pete said.

A conversation in Cantonese then took place between Toy and Chou.

"You exceeded his English, Boss, but he understands now," Toy said. Chou smiled his concurrence with that statement.

"Toy, you get a friend of a friend to buy two cell phones with prepaid minutes on them. Buy an hour's worth of time. Oh, and I want you guys to buy one of those motor scooter–powered rickshaws."

"What do you want with one of those things? They aren't a Cobra," Toy said, with Chou laughing in the background.

"A white guy like me sticks out in Macau everywhere except in the tourist haunts. Well, that's how the tourists get around. It will help keep my presence quiet."

Toy and Chou both nodded knowingly, their respect for the boss growing daily. They left to carry out their assignments.

Chou came back with the soldering iron and advised Pete he had bought the rickshaw.

"Take me for a ride. I want to go around the hotel, but don't get closer than five hundred meters to it."

When they returned to the hotel, Toy was waiting for them and they went to Pete's room. "Well, I don't see any way to take a shot at them when they are in the hotel. There is no building high enough that will give a decent shooting angle, let alone target recognition. Tomorrow I want you, Toy, to go to one of their houses, and Chou, you go to the other one's house. Follow them to work, and then follow them home.

"We'll meet back here tomorrow afternoon," Pete said. "Can one of you guys do me a favor?"

"Sure."

"Go out and get me a pizza? I am trying to stay in the hotel and room service doesn't have pizza."

Late the next afternoon Toy and Chou came into Pete's room. "Well?" Pete said.

"A limo from the hotel picks them up in the morning and then takes them home in the afternoon."

"Oh, isn't that nice? How convenient. Follow them again tomorrow."

The next day they met in Pete's room. "Same routine again today, Boss," Toy said.

"Was it the same car?" Pete asked.

"I didn't look. I am sorry, Boss," Toy said.

"No, it not same," Chou said.

"I wonder how they pick which limo to use on what day? How many limos does the hotel have, anyway?" Pete asked.

"Three," answered Chou.

"Tomorrow morning follow the limo from the hotel to see if you can figure out how they pick which one they are going to use."

The next afternoon they met again in Pete's room. "Well?"

"We think we got it figured out, Boss. The driver comes down the elevator and takes the limo closest to the elevator."

"It's that simple?"

"Appears to be."

"Do the same thing tomorrow morning and then let me know if it's the same routine. Where is the stairway exit in relation to the elevators and the limos?"

"The elevator doors are in the middle of one wall. If you are standing in the garage, the limos are parked to the right, diagonally, because they are too long to fit in a normal parking place. The stairway door is to the right of the parked limos, maybe fifteen feet away from the closest one."

"Do the Po brothers leave the hotel at the same time every day?"

"Yes, five o'clock."

"Okay, as soon as they get to the hotel in the morning, come back and give me a report."

The next morning Toy and Chou came back to Pete's room and reported the same routine had occurred again.

That afternoon at four forty-five, a cab dropped Pete off at the front of the hotel. He was wearing a gray wig, a baseball cap with a large brim, and a pair of large, wraparound sunglasses. The backpack he was carrying contained the seven pounds of composition C4. It was wired to a cell phone trigger. He went directly to the stairwell, descending one flight into the parking garage. He cracked the door and peered into the garage. The attendant was making change for someone leaving the garage. Ducking down, he went to the limo closest to the elevator and crawled under the rear of the car. Pete slid the backpack over the rear axle. Using a little duct tape he insured that the backpack would not move. Then he slid out from under the limo, and ducking down again, he went back to the stairwell.

As he walked through the front door of the hotel, Toy pulled up in the rickshaw. Fifteen minutes later Toy's cell phone rang. Hanging up he said, "They both are in the limo." They watched through his hotel room window, finally seeing the limo climbing the road going up the hill. Pete hit speed dial number one. A mile and a half away Pete and Toy could feel the concussion from the blast.

"Think you used enough dynamite there, Butch?" Toy asked.

Pete laughed, saying, "I'll see you guys in Santa Barbara." With that he took his suitcase and left the hotel.

Santa Barbara

Pete drove the little white car up the driveway. Sophie saw him coming, and as he got out of the car, Sophie ran to him, to the extent she was able. She just leaped on him. "I was so worried! Toy and Chou got back yesterday."

"I had a flight cancellation in Manila."

"I understand there was a nasty explosion in Macau a couple of days ago."

"I don't think all the pieces of the Po brothers have come down yet."

12

The next day when Pete came back from the golf course, Sophie met him at the front door. One look told Pete she was very concerned about something. "Can we go in the den and talk in there?" she asked.

"All right," Pete said, "calmly, tell me the problem."

"Lo Yang wants to come here for a meeting with me."

"Refresh my recollection, who is Lo Yang?" Pete asked.

"Lo Yang controls the heroin and opium trade in northern Laos and most of Thailand."

"What does he want to talk to you about?"

"I don't know," she answered.

"What did you tell him?"

"I said I would call him back when I return from a business trip."

"Call him back and tell him you'll meet with him whenever he wants."

Sophie looked skeptical. "He is really very dangerous. To be honest, he is the only man in this world that scares me."

"Call him back. We need to find out what he wants," Pete said.

An hour later, Sophie found Pete watching TV in their bedroom. "He'll be here two days from now, at ten in the morning." He shrugged and went back to watching his show.

The day before Lo Yang was to arrive, Pete told Sophie, "I won't be home tonight."

"Why not? where are you going?"

"I am going to be outside the house watching to make sure we don't have any uninvited guests who are prepared to participate in tomorrow's meeting."

Sophie didn't sleep well that night. At six o'clock the next morning she was in the kitchen looking for something to eat when Pete came into the house. He wore his "ghillie suit," and his face was covered with camouflage paint. He had a pistol in his hand with a silencer screwed on the barrel.

"What is that getup?" Sophie wanted to know.

"I want you to know that this is one of the finest ghillie suits ever made. These suits are used for camouflage by snipers. It saw me through two wars. We are all clear outside. I am going upstairs to sleep for a couple of hours before these guys get here," he said.

At nine o'clock Pete was back in the kitchen eating a waffle. Sophie came in and said, "I am really nervous about this."

"Don't be."

"Easy for you to say."

"There is nothing to be nervous about until we know what it is he wants."

At ten o'clock, Lo Yang came up to the front door. He was followed by two men whom Pete was sure were nothing more than bodyguards. Toy opened the door and showed them to the den. Pete went into the den and introduced himself to Lo Yang. Lo Yang did not introduce him to either of the other two who had come with him. "Have a seat," Pete said, indicating a chair in front of Sophie's desk. A minute later Sophie came in followed by Toy and Chou. He took one look and knew they were both armed.

Sophie sat at her desk and said in English, "I am Madame Gin Sling. You asked for this meeting, and I am listening."

Pete was really stunned by Sophie's poise. From the moment she walked into the room she was in command and everyone else knew it.

"As I am sure you know," Lo Yang responded in English, "the Po brothers met a tragic end last week. But what you don't know is that I was their silent partner. In a couple of days, a twenty-five-million-dollar payment will be due to you, and a failure to make this payment will give you the right to foreclose." Lo Yang paused and looked at Sophie. She said nothing. Yang continued, "I have the funds, but I need a little time, shall we say, to be able to put them in circulation."

"How much time?" asked Sophie.

"I need thirty days on this payment, and the subsequent payments extended by thirty days as well."

"Done," Pete said.

Yang looked at Sophie, who only nodded in agreement. "I think that concludes our business," Yang said rising. "I am happy we were able to conclude our business so quickly. I came a long way for a short meeting, but with a happy conclusion."

After he left, Sophie said in an outraged tone of voice, "That was my decision."

"Sophie, we are not going to war with him over thirty days."

"The decision belonged to me."

"Yes, that's true. But I am the guy who has to fight the wars."

She knew he was right about that. He made the right decision, too, in retrospect. However, she did not like having her authority usurped.

"Okay, Boss," she said, throwing her hands into the air.

Later that afternoon she found Pete in the bedroom just waking up from a nap he had taken to compensate for his sleepless night. "I am due in ten days," Sophie said.

"I am aware of that fact."

"Your mother wants to come out here to help with the transition from hospital to home. I would like her help, so I would like to send the jet to New London for your mother, Boss."

"Are you going to stop?"

"No, Boss," then adding, "Boss, I'm still pissed"

"Get over it."

"Get over it?"

"Yeah."

"No! But seriously, do you need or have any plans for the jet?" she asked.

"My plans don't go any farther than tomorrow; golf and the Blue Fox." He felt lucky she didn't have anything close at hand to throw at him.

"You are such a rat!"

13

Three months had passed since Lo Yang's visit. Alexis Sally Smith had arrived, weighing in at seven pounds one ounce. Sophie had hit the ceiling over the name, however. She had wanted to name the baby Gisele Suzette Smith. Pete had disagreed. They had never reached a mutual decision on the name and he doubted they ever would. As Sophie was wheeled into the recovery room the nurse had asked Pete the baby's name. So he named her, and when Sophie found out she went ballistic.

She had decided to have a boy, but that had not happened. Things just seemed to be slipping from her control.

Pete's mother was safely ensconced back in Mystic, and the entire house now revolved around the nursery.

It was a lovely June day. Pete had just come out of the front door on his way to play golf when Toy arrived in the limo with Sophie in the backseat. He remembered that this morning Sophie had her final checkup with the OB/GYN after Alexis's birth. He went over to the limo and opened the door for Sophie.

Climbing out of the limo, Sophie looked at Pete and said, "You are not my favorite person right now."

"What did I do this time?"

"You are one mighty potent little devil!"

"Are you pregnant again?" Sophie nodded. He grabbed her and spun her around saying, "That's wonderful! Alexis is going to have a little brother or sister." Sophie was grinning, too.

"I was just starting to get my figure back, too," Sophie lamented.

General John Lane had served with Pete in Delta Force. When he heard that the Po brothers had joined their ancestors, and Pete Smith had married the previous owner of the hotel the Po brothers owned, it wasn't much of a leap to realize Pete Smith was probably involved in the demise of the Po brothers. That meant Pete Smith was still active and prepared to act when necessary. He decided to pay an unannounced call on the former colonel. He had an idea for intelligence gathering that would require the help of Pete's wife.

So two days later he and two other gentlemen rang the door at Pete and Sophie's house. As it happened, Toy was closest to the door, and when he opened the door one of the men asked to see Colonel Smith. "If you will follow me please." Toy showed them into the den that Pete used as his office. "Can I tell the boss who wants to see him?"

"Tell him General Lane would like a word with him."

"General," Pete said, walking into the room. "What brings you to our humble abode?"

"This is hardly humble, Pete. As you may have heard, I joined the CIA after separating from the army. This gentleman to my left is Bernie Holms, and to my right Emilio Morales. Bernie is with the company, and Emilio is with the DEA."

"You have my complete attention, General. But what can I, a simple old soldier, do for the U.S. government?"

"I did not know you were doing a comedy routine since you got out of the army, Colonel." Speaking to his companions, he said, "This gentleman is one of the finest soldiers I ever served with and the finest intel officer ever. Accolades aside, we were wondering if your wife would be willing to help her soon-to-be-adopted country with security?"

"What specifically do you want her to do?"

"Have you heard of Lo Yang?"

"Yes," Pete noncommittally.

"As you may or may not know, Yang is one of the biggest drug dealers in Asia. During his rise to prominence, Yang acquired what is probably one of the largest private arsenals in the world. Recently, he has branched out by selling arms to anyone with cash. Hence, the obvious interest of our respective agencies. We hoped your wife would be willing to help us locate Yang."

"I'll save you the trouble of looking," Pete said. "He is going to be sitting right where you are in about nine months." Surprise evident on their faces, the General recovered first.

"How do you know that?"

"My wife sold her hotel in Macau to the Po brothers. Unbeknownst to my wife, Yang was the hidden partner in the transaction. The deal was five hundred million. Three hundred fifty million at closing, and payments of twenty-five million every three months until the balance was paid. The deal also included an option for some adjacent land that must be exercised two years from the date of closing by paying an additional two hundred million. Yang never mentioned the option, giving us the impression that he did not know the option existed."

"Why was Yang here?"

"Yang needed more time to make the second payment. He came here and asked for an additional thirty days. Sophie gave it to him."

"Did he pay it?" the General asked.

"He must have because I didn't hear Sophie scream."

"Pete, can we get together tomorrow about one o'clock? We need to speak with Washington."

"I'll be here."

The General and the others left.

That night in bed Pete told Sophie about the General's visit.

"I don't think there is anything I can do to help even if I were so inclined," Sophie said.

"Would you help if you could?"

"I don't know," she said thoughtfully. "If Yang ever found out someone had tried to set him up, well, you talk about a war; that would be it."

"I'm sure you're right about that," Pete said. "He doesn't seem like the forgiving type."

"There is something I have wanted to talk to you about all day," Sophie said.

"You have a captive audience now, my dear," Pete responded.

"I want you to get a vasectomy."

"No," Pete said.

"Just like that? We are not even going to discuss it?"

"There is nothing to discuss."

"Well, I think there is."

"Sophie, let me explain something to you. No one, and I mean no one, is going to get near my nuts with a scalpel or any other sharp instrument."

"That seems like an awfully one-way attitude."

"They are my nuts, and I make all the decisions about them. You may consider this decision to be written in stone and handed down from a mountaintop."

"I want you to think about it. I understand it is only one night with a bag of frozen peas, nothing to it."

"I have spoken."

"'I have spoken'? Oh, brother, I hope Alexis does not grow up to be as stubborn as you are," Sophie said. But Pete had dozed off.

Pete went jogging in the morning. After a quick shower, he went in search of food. He was sitting at the table when Sophie came into the small dining room. She was still wearing her workout clothes. "Can I join you?" she asked.

"Of course, would you like to share my waffle when it comes?"

"I think I'll get my own," she said.

"Sophie, those guys from the government are coming back at one o'clock. They're probably going to want to speak to you. I want you dressed the way you used to dress, like you were dressed the night we met; electric blue dress, ivory peg leg, four-inch heels."

"How do you know my ivory leg is here?"

"Oh, please."

"I don't think I can get into those dresses yet. And, I may never be able to again, thanks to you."

"Do your best, will you?"

"Why? Do you have something in mind?"

"Just a feeling really, nothing I can put my finger on exactly."

At one o'clock precisely, the General and his associates returned. Toy showed them into the den, where Pete was waiting for them. After a quick exchange of small talk, the General got right to the point. "Pete, we don't want to wait a year to nail Lo Yang. The damage he is capable of doing in that year is infinite."

"Well, exactly what do you want from me and my wife?"

"The same thing the CIA always wants, information," the General said.

"You probably ought to talk to Sophie about this. Let me see if I can find her. If you'll excuse me for a minute, I'll go look for her." He returned five minutes later with Sophie, dressed again as Madame Gin Sling. Pete and Sophie entered the room. "Gentlemen," Pete said, "may I present my wife, Sophie Smith." Just as when Yo Lang was there, her presence was commanding; beauty, intelligence, and authority all in the same person.

"Mrs. Smith," the General started, "I am John Lane, the assistant deputy director of the CIA. This gentleman is Emilio Morales of the DEA, and to his left is Bernie Holms of the CIA."

But Sophie interrupted him, saying, "It's Sophie."

"Thank you for that," the General said, continuing, "I don't know what your husband has told you so I am just going to start at the beginning. I hope to be able to persuade you to share with us any information you may learn from any of your sources in Asia that might affect the security of the United States."

"Your persuasive talents are not necessary," Sophie said, "I would be happy to do that. But I no longer have access to the kind of information that might be of interest to you."

"Yes, we know that your contacts with Asia have been almost nonexistent since you arrived in this country. However, we think we can change that."

"How would you propose to do that?" asked Sophie.

"You sold your houses to Wu Chang. He died about a month ago, and his widow wants to sell them. We would propose that we buy them, and you take over the management of the operation, letting everyone think that you own them again."

"When I ran the businesses, there were never any cameras or listening devices of any sort anywhere on the premises. We guaranteed discretion, security, and privacy. It was a large part of the reason for our success. My establishments were frequented by a great many very powerful men. If they were to conclude that their secrets were being revealed by my people, you can be assured that they would react, and in a most violent and unpleasant fashion."

"That thought has occurred to us as well. What we propose is that we place a man inside your organization. You train our man to run the business, and as he becomes more capable, you can phase yourself out slowly. He will take responsibility for the information technology."

"How long do you envision this taking?" Sophie wanted to know.

"I am really not certain; a year, perhaps fifteen months."

"I doubt I can evaluate the information that I receive."

"Your husband is the best analyst I have ever met, but the operational details we can work out later," the General said.

"Okay, General," Sophie said, her voice taking on a harder edge. "Get to the bottom line."

That drew a big smile from the General. "You get to keep the profits while you front the operation."

"That used to be about thirty million a year."

"The CIA is very good at hiding assets but not so good at hiding income. Extra money always causes problems for us."

Sophie paused for a minute, finally saying, "I would like to think about this a little more. Can you return for dinner?"

"Of course."

"Shall we say cocktails at seven thirty and dinner eightish?"

"Sounds perfect," the General said, rising to leave. Pete and Sophie walked the men to the door.

As soon as the door closed, Emilio Morales of the DEA said, "She is the most sensational woman I have ever met. Unbelievable! I am going to tell the story of having met Madame Gin Sling for years to come, and no one will believe me."

"I'll bet she is a handful," the General said.

"This dress is so tight, I thought the seams were going to split when I sat down," Sophie said to Pete when they had left. "Well, what did you think?" asked Sophie of her husband.

"I think my wife is seeing dollar signs when she ought to be seeing cribs and diapers. What are you going to do?"

"I don't know. I need to make a few phone calls. I have other concerns that no one else has yet considered."

"Like what?" Pete asked.

"Immigration."

Sophie spent the rest of the afternoon in her office. She started getting ready for their guests at five thirty. She had decided to dress as Madame Gin Sling again, but this time in red.

"If you gentlemen will follow me, please," Toy said, when the guests arrived. "The boss thought you might enjoy cocktails on the patio." Toy led them through the ballroom and opened the door leading to the patio. After stepping aside to permit them to pass, Toy followed them out. Sophie and Pete were standing by the Olympic-size pool. "Good evening, gentlemen. What would you like to drink?" Sophie asked. When Toy had finished serving the drinks, she asked, "What would you like for dinner?"

"Whatever you are serving will be fine."

"General, what would you like to eat? We have almost everything. And if you should order something we don't have, Toy will be right back and let you know."

"I'll have a fillet,' the General said.

"How would you like that cooked, sir?" Toy inquired.

"Medium-rare."

"Any side dishes, sir?"

"Potatoes au gratin and peas."

Toy finished taking the orders from the others and left for the kitchen. They chatted about nothing special until it was time to eat. The conversation continued in the same vein over dinner. When the dinner plates had been cleared, Sophie said, "I took the liberty of ordering the hot chocolate cake for everyone for dessert. Just take a bite, and if you don't like it, don't finish it. I promise not to be offended."

When there was no more hot chocolate cake to be seen, Sophie looked at the General saying, "I have given your proposition considerable thought. But there are some things that are very important to me that were not mentioned earlier today. I'm pregnant, and this baby is going to be born in the United States.

"My immigration lawyer says that if something like this were to come out, it could affect my green card and the application for citizenship, which I intend to make. Don't worry, General, I did not discuss this with the lawyer. I made up a plausible scenario for him."

Bernie Holms, from the CIA, spoke up saying, "Suppose we could get you a presidential grant of citizenship before the start of this, would that do?"

"It would. But it would have to include Toy, Chou, and Chou's family. I couldn't possibly undertake something like this without Toy and Chou. Additionally, I want green cards for everyone on my staff and their families. While I am gone, I will need the peace of mind of knowing that everyone here is secure and being well cared for."

"Done," the CIA guy said.

Sophie had impressed Pete once again; take care of the troops. The military spent hours and hours beating that simple message into the heads of their officer candidates. Sophie knew it instinctively.

Sophie added, "There is one more thing, a couple of things actually. I want the Chinese guy you propose having to work with me spend an afternoon with Toy and Chou."

"Why?" the General asked.

"I want to be certain his Cantonese is perfect. If someone realizes he is a ringer we are all dead, and that probably includes you gentlemen as well."

Bernie Holms, from the CIA, got up and walked out onto the patio to use his cell phone. "Is there anything else?" the General asked.

"Yes. I don't want you to make your move on Lo Yang for at least three weeks."

"Why? His payment is due three days from now."

"Sophie orally gave him a thirty-day extension on all payments," Pete said, finally entering the conversation.

"Lastly, when I reach seven months into my pregnancy, I am coming home and staying until at least eight weeks after the baby is born," Sophie continued.

The CIA man returned and said, "Our man, Steven Chang, arrives in San Francisco tomorrow morning at five minutes past ten. I don't yet know when he will get here."

"Tell him when he arrives to go to the general aviation ramp and ask for Madame Gin Sling's plane." Sophie stood, saying, "Gentlemen, subject to the terms outlined, I think we have an agreement." With that everyone rose to leave.

"I'll show you out," Pete said.

The next morning, a car arrived with "U.S. Immigration" stenciled on the door. Pete was in the den when Toy found him. "Boss, there are some government guys at the front door."

"Sir, we are here to issue permanent residence visas to certain of your employees."

"Is this normal? House calls, I mean," Pete asked, opening the door.

"Unprecedented. In fact, no one in the office can ever remember this being done before. Nor can anyone remember the director calling our office to speak to the senior supervisor."

"Please come in," Pete said.

"Do you have a place where we can set up our equipment?" "Sure, let's go into the big dining room. I'm Pete Smith, by the way."

"Marvin Jenkins," he said, shaking Pete's hand. "And this is my associate, Ken Krensa."

Pete showed them into the dining room and then went looking for everyone who was to receive a green card.

Juan proved to be the most difficult to find. Evidently, he had seen the car with "immigration" written on the door and decided to make himself scarce by pulling the weeds behind the hedge on the far side of the tennis court.

It took a little doing to coax Juan out. Pete assured him nothing bad was going to happen. Juan finally agreed to go get his family. Everyone had forms to fill out and had their photos taken. As the men from immigration were packing up, the doorbell rang. This time it was two guys from the State Department. They had copies of certificates of citizenship signed by the President. "We couldn't leave the office until we had the certificates in hand." The first group around the dining room table left, and a second took its place. Juan's entire family had tears in their eyes, they were so happy.

Toy and Chou had met Steven Chang when he landed in Sophie's plane from San Francisco. They had taken him to lunch and spent the rest of the afternoon with him. The three of them had spoken nothing but Cantonese the entire time. About four o'clock the General and the CIA man arrived to check on Toy and Chou's evaluation of Steven Chang's Cantonese. After Toy and Chou had verified his language skills, an informal meeting ensued.

Sophie, still smiling about her new passport, summed things up saying, "General, as soon as you have acquired the whorehouses, then Toy, Chou, Steven, and I will leave to take a tour of them. Steven, I think the best thing for you to do is get the managers aside out of my hearing and offer them money for information. You only want to do this in certain selected houses because if it is too widespread, the word will spread too widely, and too fast. I know which of the houses you can propose such a thing. Our tour will end in Macau.

"Also, Steven, you should probably sample the wares along the way. You want to create the image of the young rogue who plays it fast and loose."

"Once we are in Macau, Pete and Alexis will join me."

"A very able summation," the General said. "Now, let me bring you up to date. We have been in touch with the widow and we have agreed on a price. The transfer should be complete within two to three days."

"Gentlemen, I have one question," Pete said. "Are you going to put the houses in Sophie's name?"

"No, they never were in her name. The ownership is buried in several corporate layers and crooked lawyers."

14

Sophie and company left four days later in her jet. It took about three hours before he started to miss her. She called every other day. Pete was never certain whether she wanted to speak with him or wanted to check on the baby. He may have been the focal point of her life once, but the number one place in her life and heart was now a little pink bundle weighing ten pounds.

She thought it would take about a month to visit all the houses and that the new owner would want to visit the big money makers to check on them first.

The DEA had grabbed Lo Yang outside the hotel as he arrived to arrange for the payment to Sophie. As a result, the payment was never made, and Sophie initiated foreclosure while still traveling. Although the foreclosure was not complete when she entered her former hotel at ten thirty on her first morning back in Macau, she acted as if she were the owner. She went to the offices and found the former chief accountant was now the general manager. He started working for Sophie before the hotel opened eleven years ago. They shut the office door, and two hours later Sophie had a complete understanding of what was wrong.

Finally, she asked if her suite was available. It was. A secretary got her a key, and she went to lie down. After a month on the road listening to how everything she had built had been run into the ground, she was physically and mentally exhausted. Even more grinding on her mentally had been the absence of Alexis and Pete.

Her apartment was not the same. All her personal touches had been removed. She had, of course, taken the art work with her.

Sophie called Pete. When he answered, they gabbed for a bit before she got to the point. "We are in Macau so you and Alexis can join us now."

"We are leaving the day after tomorrow on the nonstop from San Francisco. Do you have your old suite back?"

"Yes, but it's really not the same."

"Please be sure the front desk knows we are coming. That way we'll be able to get in without disturbing you."

"Please, disturb me." Shortly thereafter, they hung up.

Three days later Pete, Alexis, and Lee An, the amah, arrived. Pete took them directly to Sophie's suite. Toy, who had met them in Hong Kong, looked like a pack mule carrying all of Alexis's paraphernalia. It never ceased to amaze him that something so small needed so much "stuff"!

It took a month for the foreclosure to be complete. The week after it was complete, a man named Chen Wu came into the business office and demanded to see Sophie. She had him wait while Toy and Chou were located. When he entered the office, Toy and Chou followed him. Chen Wu explained he was the successor to Lo Yang's empire and that the hotel now belonged to him.

"I think not. It is my understanding that Lo Yang was arrested three weeks ago. As a result he failed to make a payment," Sophie said. "I was not paid and I have foreclosed. This hotel is legally mine."

"If you think you are going to steal a five-hundred-million-dollar hotel from me and live to enjoy it, you are mistaken."

"I have stolen nothing. This meeting is over. Toy, Chou?" They walked over to Chen Wu, who had risen from his chair. As he turned toward the door to leave he said to Toy and Chou, "Neither of you guys is bulletproof either," he said.

The days passed slowly for Pete. Sophie spent ten to twelve hours a day working. Usually, he stopped to chat with Steven Chang every morning about the information he was receiving from the various whorehouses. One morning Steven sought out Pete's advice. "I got some information from Jakarta and I am not sure what to do about it."

"What is it that has you so perplexed?"

"A girl in one of the houses thought she understood enough of the language that the clients were speaking to think that there is a major plot coming against the United States."

"What language were they speaking?"

"Urdu. This girl apparently grew up in India, so she understands some."

"Well, what's this plot about?"

"She didn't get it all, but apparently someone is buying sarin gas and smuggling it into the United States through Mexico."

"I don't understand your quandary."

"Well, look at what the powers-that-be are going to say about this. 'A whore overhears a conversation in a foreign language between a couple of drunks, and all of a sudden we are supposed to go to defcon five?' See the problem?"

"Make the report. Let the powers-that-be assume the responsibilities. Any idea where they are getting the gas?" Pete inquired.

"None," Steven replied, "You have all the information I have."

"Make the report and don't worry about it."

Sophie and Pete decided to go out to dinner that evening. They wanted a change of atmosphere from the hotel. They came down in the elevator and walked toward the front door, Toy and Chou following them as usual.

Suddenly, a small Asian man, leaning against the slot machines, started to pull a pistol with a silencer attached from his pants at the small of his back. Toy saw him and reacted instantly. He grabbed the man's arm, jerking it backward. A shot fired but the bullet buried itself harmlessly in a wall thirty feet away. The noise of the snapping of the man's arm was almost as loud as the shot had been. Pete spun instantly with the sound of the shot but realized immediately that Toy had the situation under control.

Pete said to Toy, "Take him downstairs and find out who sent him. Motivate him a little before you start questioning him."

"Okay, Boss," Toy said with Chou nodding.

Sophie and Pete decided to eat in the hotel after all. Once seated in the French restaurant, Sophie said, "That really scared me. People have tried to kill me before, but I have never reacted like this. Maybe I feel I have too much to lose now. I don't know."

"Don't let it worry you, he missed."

"Thanks to Toy."

"We'll find out who sent him and see if we can't eliminate the problem," adding, "permanently." He saw Sophie shudder involuntarily.

They had just finished their main course, when Toy came up to the table. "Chen Wu sent him."

"Where is Chen Wu now?"

"According to the man downstairs, he is back in northern Laos at his headquarters."

"How was he supposed to get paid?"

"Evidently, there was a man outside the hotel waiting with the cash. Chou is looking for him now, but I doubt we'll find him. I'm sure he is gone by now."

"Thank you, Toy. Let me know if you do find him."

"Sophie, let's go. I have some phone calls to make," Pete said firmly. She got up immediately, full well knowing that this was not the moment to voice any objections or concerns, and followed Pete out of the restaurant.

Once in the dining room of their suite, he called the General in Washington on the secure satellite phone the General had given him. When the General answered, Pete said, "General, can you locate Mike Jarwarski for me? I need to speak to him."

"I think so. I'm glad you called. If you hadn't I was going to call you."

"What's on your mind, General?"

"Have you talked to Steven Chang about the report he filed today?"

"Are you referring to the one about the hooker who overheard a conversation concerning a plot against the United States?"

"Yes."

"I spoke with him about it, but only briefly."

"You probably have a better feel for these things than Steven does, and I just wanted to get your cut at it," the General said.

Pete replied, "I am not sure that's true. But I think there may well be something to it. You need to put the snatch on one of those guys and squeeze him for more information."

"Congress says we can't do that anymore."

"Do it anyway. Then use the pirate approach."

"What, pray tell, is the pirate approach?" the General asked.

"Dead men tell no tales."

Laughing, the General said, "I would, but everyone around here is more worried about their career than the country's security."

"I may be able to help you out a little, General. Someone tried to kill Sophie tonight. It wasn't even close really. We got the shooter. He told us that Chen Wu sent him. Chen Wu is the guy who took over from Lo Yang. Chen Wu now controls the largest private armory in Asia. If someone were selling the type of weapons we are talking about, logic says it is Chen Wu. I intend to pay Mr. Wu a visit."

"Do you have any information to support your theory?"

"General, it's nothing more than a hunch."

"I'll see if I can find Mike for you."

"Thanks, General," Pete said hanging up.

Next, Pete called Jack, the husband of Sophie's friend Carol. Jack was an ex recon Marine who had kept himself in pretty good shape since separating from the service.

Jack answered the phone. "Jack, it's Pete Smith."

"How are you? I thought you were in Hong Kong."

"Macau, actually, and I am. I called because I have a proposition for you."

"I'm listening," Jack said.

"A week or ten days in Macau, all expenses paid. That includes first-class airfare and ten grand in spending money."

"All right, what's the catch?" Jack asked.

"There is a possible mission into the jungle hunting drug dealers. If the mission goes, it pays an additional hundred grand."

"I'm in, but I have to talk to Carol. Give me a number and I'll call you back."

Pete did. Fifteen minutes later, Jack called back. With no preliminaries Jack said, "Carol says I can't go. She doesn't want to be left alone with the baby."

"Bring her and the baby."

"Call you right back."

Five minutes later, when Pete picked up the telephone, all he heard was, "We're coming."

"Great. Call the number I am about to give you in the morning, and Sophie's secretary will give you all the details on your travel itinerary."

"Okay, see you in Macau."

Twenty minutes later Mike Jarwarski called. It was almost a repeat to the conversation he had just had with Jack, including the multiple calls, but at least he had retired two days before, giving him the benefit of not having to report to the army in the morning. He had also married, which perhaps meant he had to report every morning after all. Mike and his bride would be on their way to Macau as well, an Asian honeymoon.

The next morning the General called from Washington. After the usual chitchat, the General got to the point. "Pete, the analysts here give your scenario of Chen Wu supplying the arms for this attack about a twenty-five to thirty percent chance of being right. The feeling seems to be that the drug dealers would have the pipeline to get the material into the country, which gives your theory credibility."

"That's logical," Pete said. "He may also have the sarin gas that we heard about, and given what we have heard about the size of his armory, it would seem to be more than possible."

"Frankly, the arms are our present concern. It sounds like he has enough arms to destabilize any government in the region."

"I'm not so sure about the armory, General," Pete said.

"It makes perfect sense if you think about it. He buys arms with dirty money, smuggles them to Laos, and then sells a boatload of arms to someone under an invoice for televisions and he gets paid with laundered money. The advantage is, he can launder his cash and make a profit at the same time. It is not a bad setup, really."

"I guess," Pete said.

"Pete," the General said, "Steven said he thinks you are assembling a team to go into Laos to eliminate Mr. Wu."

"I am looking at it," Pete said noncommittally.

"As you know, CIA personnel cannot participate in an action like that in any fashion. It could be considered an invasion of a foreign country, a real no-no. But we would be willing to lend you all the support you need. Deniability is the guiding principle for us in these situations."

Pete said, "I had hoped you would make that offer. I need all the maps and recent satellite photos you are willing to part with of the area where the DEA thinks his compound is located. It's in northern Laos somewhere."

"I'll have them delivered to the hotel as soon as possible," the General said.

The package arrived from Hong Kong late that afternoon.

That evening, as Sophie and Pete dined in the suite, Sophie said, "I have the distinct feeling you are going to go after Chen Wu."

"Do you remember several months ago I said no one takes a shot at my wife and lives to tell about it?" Sophie nodded, and Pete continued, "That is still true today."

"I am really scared this time. I want Toy and Chou to go with you."

"I am not going to take them with me. They don't have the skills for this. They are very good in an urban environment, but they have not been trained for jungle warfare, and that is what this will take. Besides, I am not going to leave you unprotected."

Sophie leaned forward and put her head in her hands. Sitting erect again after she had composed herself, she said, "I really don't want you to do this."

"I have to do it. This guy isn't going to stop. He is going to keep coming until he is successful. And, besides which if another guy turns up behind this one, he will be forewarned of the hazards of going after you."

"I have protection."

"We were lucky last time. He sent some inept fool. I don't think we can count on that in the future."

"I know, but I am just so scared."

"Sophie, there are a couple of guys coming to help me with this little project. They are bringing their wives with them. I don't want you to express your fears in front of the wives. Okay?"

"I guess so."

"How are things going with reorganizing the hotel?" Pete asked, changing the subject.

"Okay, I think I have gotten rid of most of the thieves," Sophie said. She knew he was changing the subject.

"Were there a lot?"

"It seems like everyone started stealing after I left. The accountant just assumed that everyone was honest. He was very naive."

"Sounds like it. What are your plans now for the hotel?"

"I want to sell it, but finding a buyer is not easy." Sophie lit a cigarette.

"You've got to quit that shit! It is really bad for the baby, you know that. And, it stinks, too."

"I know. It is filthy habit, but right now I am under so much pressure that I can't quit."

"Sophie," Pete said, "you have more will power than anyone I know."

After she crushed out her cigarette, Pete grabbed her by the hand. She got out of the chair and hand in hand they headed to the bedroom. Clothes fell along the way.

The next morning, he took out the package the General had sent over from Hong Kong. Pete spent the morning pouring over the maps with a magnifying glass. When he thought he understood the problems to be encountered, he set them aside feeling that a fresh look in the morning would improve his perspective.

He spent the better part of the late afternoon on the floor playing with his daughter. She cooed and he giggled. They were lying on the floor when Sophie came into the suite. She immediately went to a chair and sat down. Then she slid off the chair onto the floor. She joined them in the middle of the living room. When it became obvious that Alexis had tired, Pete sat up, saying, "Alexis, it is your bedtime." He stood as his wife rolled onto her back and extended a hand to him. He put his foot at the tip of her peg leg, took her hands, and pulled her up in one swift motion. His strength always amazed her.

They took Alexis into the nursery where the amah took her from Pete's arms. Sophie and Pete went into their bedroom and lay on the bed fully clothed. Sophie looked so cute that Pete leaned over and kissed her. She kissed him back passionately, and dinner got postponed.

It took two days for everyone to arrive. As it turned out, they had been on the same flight from San Francisco. It was early afternoon when they finally arrived. Sophie had reserved a one-bedroom suite for Mike and his wife. She arranged a two-bedroom suite for Jack, Carol, and their baby as well as an amah. Sophie had also made dinner reservations in the hotel's French restaurant for eight o'clock.

Although the two couples had traveled on the same airplane coming over, they had not met. Dianne was the only person Pete had not met previously. She was an interesting lady, about thirty-two years old, extremely good looking, covered with tattoos, and a strong southern accent.

Dinner turned out to be an excellent way to break the ice. Pete could tell by the questions Mike asked that he was sizing Jack up. Jack for his part had asked a couple of questions as well. But when he heard Mike was a Sargent E9 in Delta Force, he had heard all he needed to hear. At the conclusion of diner Jack, Mike, and Pete agreed to meet in Pete's suite at nine the next morning.

When they were all assembled the next morning, Pete laid out the problem: the attempt on Sophie's life and the probability it would continue. He then went on to explain about the arms cache. Lastly, he shared the information they had about a potential gas attack on the United States and his suppositions.

Concluding, Pete said, "I think this guy needs to be taken out, and I would like your help doing it. The job pays a hundred grand a man."

"If it were up to me," Jack said, "I'm in. But I have to talk to Carol."

"I think I better talk to Dianne as well," Mike said.

"As soon as you guys get an answer, let me know."

At one o'clock, Dianne, Carol, and Sophie got together for lunch. After the usual banter about the children, Carol asked Sophie what she thought about the proposed mission to Laos.

"It scares me to death," Sophie said.

"Are you going to let Pete do it?" Carol asked.

"I don't really have a choice. He is going to do it no matter what I say. I think it is better to be supportive than not in that set of circumstances. But I have to say I saw Pete run an operation of this sort a few months ago. He is very careful, and I take heart from that."

"What do you mean when you say 'careful'?" Dianne asked.

"He won't let anyone take chances."

"Why not?" Carol asked.

"He told me once he knows the name of every soldier he ever lost in five combat tours. And he has dreams about seeing their names carved on a wall. He does not want to add to that list. He told me one night when he woke up with the night sweats."

"I was going to say no," Carol said, "but after listening to you I think I'll let Jack go. I don't really want him to go, but he can if he wants."

"I like your approach," Dianne said. "It never seems to work when you present a block wall. All you do is create resentment that comes home to roost later."

On that note, their luncheon ended.

Later that afternoon in Sophie's suite, Pete, Mike, and Jack started going over the satellite photos with a magnifying glass. "Well?" Pete asked Jack.

"There are some obvious problems with the satellite photos and topo maps. They don't overlay very well. If you look at the two together, it appears that the complex is in a small valley. There's only one road into it, and it appears to be about thirty miles long. I think we can assume there are multiple guards along the road not visible in the photos. In all probability, there are guards on the top of these hills surrounding the valley. All in all, it's a difficult target."

"Can it be done? How do we get to Mr. Chen Wu?" Pete asked Jack.

"Yes, I think it can be done, but if you come from this direction," indicating a path through the jungle, "forget the road. Even if we got down to the road, everyone would be waiting for us when we arrived in the compound. It's my suggestion that we do several days of recon watching for guards on the ridge, then at night slip in and plant explosives in strategic places."

"Mike, what do you think?" asked Pete.

"Pretty much the same thing," Mike said. "I doubt there will be guards on the ridges around the valley, however because the jungle acts as a natural guard. However, Jack is right; plan on the guards being there and be pleasantly surprised if they are not. The trek through the jungle will be a son of a bitch, though. We are going to have to carry a lot of weight, about seventy pounds, and carry it for a minimum of four days. There is one other potential problem, though, that neither one of you is aware of. One of the old timers who fought in Vietnam told me that most of the huts had cobras under them. That means that you just can't sneak under them."

"What are cobras doing under the huts?" Pete asked.

"They apparently come in after the rats, which are looking for food scraps that fall through the cracks in the floorboards," Mike responded.

"I agree with you both, by the way. Let's take a look at the photos and topo maps and see if we can find a good route into the area," Pete said.

They collectively studied the maps and found an alternate route that did not look too difficult. Whether it would work out when they got on the ground was something else again.

"These maps are not sufficiently detailed to give stream and creek locations. Some of those can be in very deep gullies and virtually impossible to cross. When that happens there is only one thing you can do—try to go over it on a rope. So we should take a lot of rope and some mountaineering equipment.

"Mike, why don't you and Jack sit down and make a list of the equipment we will need? I think we will need at least fifty pounds of composition C4 and food, probably MREs for three weeks, but give that some thought," Pete said. After looking at his watch, Pete said, "On second thought, let's do that tomorrow."

"Have the women made any dinner plans for tonight?" Mike asked.

"Haven't got a clue," Pete responded, while Jack just shrugged his shoulders.

As it turned out, the women did not have plans, and the couples ate separately that night.

The next morning, Mike, Jack, and Pete reassembled in Sophie's suite. After considerable discussion they agreed on a list of items. "I hate to rain on everyone's parade but what do you guys think all this stuff is going to weigh?" Jack asked.

"We will probably have to carry about seventy pounds apiece, just as I estimated," Mike said.

Jack said, "We could cut the food back to seventeen days and leave a couple hundred rounds of ammo behind."

"Cutting back on the food is okay, but not the ammo," Mike said.

"Have you guys agreed yet?" Pete asked.

"I think so," Mike said.

"If you give me the final draft, I'll call the General and get him working on it."

He had to wait three hours before he could be assured the General would be in the office. Pete read the list to the General, and when he was done the General said, "It will take me about three days to get all this gear to the embassy in Laos. We'll make arrangements for the pickup in a couple of days."

"Can you get any more recent sat photos while we're waiting?"

"I should think I can. Pete, are you planning to go to Laos on Sophie's jet?"

"I thought we would."

"I wouldn't do it if I were you. You'll only be calling attention to yourselves. What I would suggest is that you deadhead the plane up there a few days before you think you will need to exfiltrate."

"That's a good suggestion. One last thing, General. Can we use the sat phone we have?"

"No. If something happened, that phone could be used to prove direct CIA involvement. Can't you get a commercial one that will suffice?"

"There are two problems with the commercial phones. They weigh a lot, and the battery life is limited. We estimate our packs at seventy pounds apiece right now, and I don't want to add to that weight for only three days of communications. If you come up with any good ideas, let me know. I'm sure we'll speak again before we shove off," Pete said, signing off.

15

Things went as planned, surprisingly. They flew into Laos. A van arranged by the General dropped them at the entry point they had selected. When they entered the jungle, they walked in only twenty feet and waited there for an additional hour to be sure no one was going to try and follow them. They continued on into the jungle, but darkness soon overtook them, and they were forced to stop for the night. The travel time had been much longer than they had expected due to the poor condition of the roads.

The next morning they started toward their goal again. It was not very long before they came to a small stream at the bottom of a gorge. They set their packs down, and while Pete waited, Mike went in one direction along the stream, and Jack went in the other direction. After ten minutes they reported back that they had not found a place to ford the stream.

Pete and Mike sat down while Jack went to work. He dug into his pack and brought out a folding grappling hook. He unfolded the tines and screwed a collar down the shaft to keep the tines in place, and he tied the grappling hook to a length of rope. After four tries he managed to snag a root on the other side of the stream. Tying off the rope to a tree on his side of the river, he crossed hand over hand to the other side.

Once Jack had crossed over, Pete untied the rope on his side of the river. Jack freed the grappling hook and untied it. Then he retied the rope securely to a tree. Pete retied the rope on his side of the river using a knot that could be undone from Jack's side of the river by pulling on his end of the rope. The packs were sent across one at a time on a pulley. Finally, Mike braved crossing and then Pete. Jack jerked on the tail end of the rope and it came loose. Once the rope was coiled and stored with the grappling hook again in Jack's pack, they resumed their journey. They were forced to do the same thing many times in the trek to the camp.

After five days they were finally starting to get close, but it was on the sixth day at noon that they saw the hills that they thought formed the valley containing Chen Wu's encampment. They had closed to within about three miles by four o'clock that afternoon. In a small clearing they rested, waiting for sunset, when they could do reconnaissance on the top of the hills to see if they were guarded.

Shortly after dark that evening, having left their packs behind and wearing ghillie suits, they slowly made their way to the top of the ridge. They had been right; there below them was a small village. Once on top of the ridge they separated. They had agreed that Mike and Jack would each go in opposite directions for two hours along the top of the ridge and then return. Pete was to go down below the ridge-line at an angle, then make an arc, returning in the same four-hour time period. They were not only looking for any guards but indications that guards had been there in the past.

"I think they use the jungle as a guard," Pete said.

Jack nodded as Mike said, "I think that's right. However, I would like to know if there are any guards on the trails we have seen."

"Is Chen Wu here?"

Answering Mike, Pete said, "We didn't see him this afternoon."

"That doesn't mean he's not here, though," Jack said.

"What's the plan for tomorrow?" Mike asked.

"I want us to split up tomorrow and spend the day watching the compound from different angles. Let's see if we can figure out what each of the buildings is used for. Take some food and that way no one will have to come back here. Let's plan on being in position at sunrise and staying there until about five o'clock," Pete said.

They spent the next three days watching the camp.

Finally, when they had all returned to their base camp, Pete started to draw a rough map of Chen Wu's compound in the dirt. When he completed the map, he said, "All right, what do we know about this place?"

"The two long buildings are probably the storage buildings where the arms are stored," Jack said. "Why do you suppose they're on each side of the compound? Think it could be some sort of security or safety arrangement?"

"Lo Yang, the guy who built this place, started it as a processing plant for the opium business. Then he branched out into the arms business. As his stock grew, he probably just added a warehouse where there was space available."

"There did not seem to be any activity to speak of at either one of them today, which is consistent with buildings being used just for storage," Mike added.

"Let's see what we know then. These two large buildings are the arms warehouses. From the comings and goings, this long building must be where they process the poppy paste into opium," said Pete.

Jack added, "I think this building is some sort of a dining hall, and this one," pointing to a building near the road access on the diagram, "is probably some sort of barracks."

Pete said, "I think you're right. This other one has to be the boss's house. It is the only decent structure in the compound. Unfortunately, there didn't seem to be a lot of activity around it today."

"What's the plan for tomorrow, more of the same?" Mike asked.

'Yea, I think so," Pete said, "but I'm open to suggestions. Tomorrow I want you guys to think about how and where to place the explosives to blow this place to smithereens."

The next day there was a flurry of activity in the compound. Around ten o'clock about twenty people arrived in four Land Rovers. The number of people in the camp almost doubled. They didn't place any guards on the ridgeline, however.

That afternoon when they met, Pete said, "It looks like things are about to get interesting."

"I am sure that we saw Chen Wu arrive this morning. This afternoon all those trucks came and were loaded with those green cylinders. Usually green cylinders are used for oxygen, but I don't think those were full of oxygen," Mike said.

"I've been thinking about that, too," Pete said. "I think that may have been Steven Chang's sarin gas. There is no way we can contact the General from here. Now, what about explosive placement, and how do we do it?"

"I think the warehouses are going to take six charges each. You need to come in about twenty feet from each corner and then put two in the center. Those charges should each be two pounds to make sure that everything is leveled," Jack said.

"That's pretty much my impression as well," Pete said. "We are lucky in one respect though. All the important buildings that we have to get are built on stilts.

"We need to do a night recon of this place to find out what they do about guarding this place all night long. I'll take the first watch from now till midnight. Jack, how about midnight to three, and Mike, you take from that point until sunrise."

When both men nodded their assent, Pete said, "I'll grab one of these gourmet repasts," he said, reaching for an MRE, "and be off."

At sunrise the next morning when Mike came down the hill, Jack and Pete were waiting for him. "Well, what did we learn last night?"

"I watched the tail end of the party, which I'm sure, began on your watch," Jack said.

"It got going pretty good about nine and by ten it was in full swing," Pete said. "Do you think they will do the same thing tonight?"

"Probably, since there doesn't seem to be anything else to do here besides watch TV on the satellite," Mike said.

"How long do you think Wu is going to stay here, given what we have seen so far?"

"Given what we have seen so far, I would be lacing up my track shoes to get out of here," Jack said. Then he added, looking at Pete, "So would you."

"I agree. I'm sure a newly elevated drug lord is going to want to see bright lights. I think we have to take this place down tonight if we want to be sure to get Wu. Where, when, and how, do we place the C4?"

Mike laid out a plan to take out the main house, processing factory, drug storage facilities, arms storage buildings, and barracks. He detailed the amounts to be used. He concluded by wishing they had more C4.

"I think you got it just right, but while we watch today, let's think about improving the plan," Pete said. With that they dispersed to their respective surveillance positions.

That afternoon when they reassembled, Pete asked, "Any changes to the basic plan? Then I suggest we start placing the charges at two o'clock with zero hour planned for sunrise. I've been giving the potential cobra problem some thought.

"There's enough light down there so that night-vision goggles will wash out. Thermal imaging isn't going to do us any good either because snakes are cold blooded and won't create a heat signature. What I think we will have to do is cut some bamboo poles and use them to push the charges into position."

Mike concurred, saying, "That's the only solution I see. Jack?"

"The only thing I don't like about it is it leaves us exposed for too long, but I can't think of a better way without siccing a mongoose on them."

"I think that leaves us deciding who plants which charges," Pete said. "I'll take the warehouse by the gate, Wu's house, and the dining hall. Mike, you take the other warehouse and the lab. Jack, you get the storage facilities, the generator shack, and the barracks. I want to be in the tree line just outside the compound at two o'clock."

"Let's get started cutting up the C4 into the correct size charges and attaching the detonators." Back in Macau they had decided to use radio-controlled detonators set to the same frequency. In that way they could detonate every charge at the same time. A premature detonation of one charge using a defective timer could have disastrous consequences.

It was exactly two o'clock when Pete crawled from the trees. He was wearing his ghillie suit. Beside him he dragged a bamboo pole. When he got to the edge of the first warehouse and peered under, he saw nothing of any significance. He worked his backpack around his shoulders and took out the first charge. Using the pole, he pushed it into position. When all the charges were in place, he retreated to the tree line and moved down to a position directly behind Wu's house. The party was still going strong. Crawling over to where he thought

Wu's bedroom would be, he placed a charge under where he guessed the bed would be. The second charge went under the center of the house. He crawled slowly back to the tree line and repeated the process for the dining hall.

When he returned to the base camp it was four forty-five. Mike was there waiting for him. "Any problems?" he asked.

"None, it was almost too easy."

Pete asked Jack the same thing when he returned. "I had to kill one guy when he caught me setting the charge on the generator shack. I think he was just taking a leak before turning in for the night. No one heard anything, and no one seemed to miss him."

"What did you do with the body?"

"I dragged it to the tree line. It should be okay there until morning."

"Let's move up to the ridgeline. If someone stumbles on that body, we may have to blow the thing early. Jack, grab the Barrett. I don't want to leave anyone alive, especially the lieutenants. They'll rebuild this place, and we'll be back doing this again. And frankly, I've had it with jungle living," Pete said.

"You know we may wind up killing innocent people," Jack said.

"There are no innocent people down there. They manufacture and sell drugs or support the ones that do. As far as I'm concerned those people are the modern equivalent of slave traders because they sell the same product: human misery."

When dawn came, Pete flicked the arm switch into the fire position, which enabled the detonate command button. He said, "I think we should probably move to the other side of the ridge."

When they reached a position of safety, Pete hit the detonate button. It was the loudest explosion any of them had ever heard. Jack stood up to have a look at the results, but he was a little premature. The concussion wave knocked him down, taking away his breath. "Jesus," was all he could gasp. With a "whoop, whoop" sound a dented satellite dish sailed over their heads.

When they finally looked over the ridge, they saw the devastation was complete. Nothing was standing, not a single person or building. Even trees had been knocked down by the concussion wave.

"Do you think you used enough dynamite, Butch?" Mike asked. That was the second time Pete had heard that quote recently.

"They must have had a shit pot full of C4 in those warehouses to create a hole that size," Jack said, pointing at a crater thirty feet in diameter and eight feet deep, where one of the warehouses had been.

"Let's get our gear packed up and head down to the road," Pete said.

"Is that how we're getting out of here?" Jack asked.

"Eventually, but for now we're going to wait for a few hours. The guards are going to come down that road to find out what all the noise was about.

After packing their gear, they walked right through the center of the encampment. Debris was everywhere. Pieces of rifles and bent barrels of AK47s littered the entire compound. They went up the road three hundred yards to wait in the jungle for whoever was going to come down the road.

As they sat there, the question naturally arose as to how they were going to get back to Macau. "Sophie is supposed to have the jet in Vientiane for us. All we have to do is get to the airport. I have a number for the pilots so we can give them a heads up," Pete said.

An hour later, two guards came down the road. Jack shot one and Pete shot the other. "Let's go," said Pete, and with that they started down the road. They didn't get to the end of the road before sunset, so they ended up having another cold MRE as they talked about their wives. Pete had told Sophie he thought they would be gone only about a week. It had now been eleven days, and they were at least two days away from getting back to Macau. They had no way to call.

About eleven the next morning they came upon the guard shack at the beginning of the road to the compound. The guards were gone. They had hoped that the guards would have a car, but none was in sight. They looked at their maps and decided the best direction was to the right toward the east. The road, if you could call it that, was hard-packed dirt, replete with deep ruts, which made the footing uneven. They abandoned their ghillie suits in favor of the local-style clothing, hoping the locals would think them drug buyers.

Late in the afternoon, they heard a vehicle coming. They threw their rifles in the ditch that ran alongside the road. If the vehicle stopped they would abandon them; if it didn't stop they would retrieve them. The noise they heard turned out to be a truck. The driver stopped and indicated they could ride in the back of his truck. It took three hours to reach a small town.

The town had a small hotel, of sorts. The clerk spoke English. They rented three rooms. After dinner, they went to bed early and slept on mattresses for the first time in twelve days. The next morning, after some difficulties with the language barrier, they got directions to the bus station. After another fourteen hours, various buses, and an hour spent in customs, they arrived in Vientiane. Even though it was almost midnight, Pete called the pilots. They agreed to a nine o'clock departure. "Please don't call my wife," Pete requested. He wanted no conversations regarding them or their mission made on unsecure phones.

"No problem," said the pilot.

16

They called no one, but nevertheless, Sophie was waiting at the entrance to the hotel along with Carol and Dianne. Pete walked toward his wife with a big smile trying to defuse Sophie's obvious ire. As he walked up to her she kicked him as hard as she could in the shin with her peg leg. That drew a howl from Pete just as a second blow landed. "Damn, that hurt!" he yelled. He dodged a third attempt. Mike and Jack were laughing so hard they were doubled up.

"You can consider yourself lucky I don't have a gun! Do you know how worried I was about you? We were getting ready to hold a memorial service. I have never been so mad! You do this again and I am going to ring your neck! Don't ever do this to me again! I have been tearing myself up inside." Then she ran to him and hugged him. "Come on, let's go upstairs." As Sophie's tirade played out, Mike and Jack, whose laughter had died down, were facing their own wives, whose relief had turned to anger as well.

A celebratory dinner was hastily arranged on the way to the elevator for seven thirty.

Sophie and Pete went into the suite, and Pete said, "I want to take a shower and shave." He entered the bathroom and took off his shirt. Like the others Pete was covered with welts from bug bites. His skin had ulcerated in several places. Sophie took one look and rushed from the bedroom. "Toy!" she hollered. Toy came running from the other end of the suite. When she saw him, Sophie said, "Go get Dr. Da Silva, then find Chou and send him to me."

When Chou appeared, she said, "Go tell the other men to come to the suit. I have sent for Dr. Da Silva." As soon as

Toy turned to leave the phone rang. Sophie answered it saying, "Hello?"

"Sophie, it's Carol. Jack needs a doctor. His skin is chewed to shreds."

"Pete is the same way. I have already sent for a doctor, so bring Jack up here."

"We'll be right up," Carol said, hanging up. The receiver had not been in its cradle two seconds when it rang again.

Sophie answered it thinking it had to be Dianne and queried "Dianne?"

Without preliminaries, Dianne said, "Mike needs a doctor."

"One is on the way, bring Mike up here," Sophie said.

Before everyone arrived, Pete called the General from the bedroom. After the General answered, Pete said, "You don't have to worry about that arms dealer or his cache anymore. There's a hole in the ground where it used to be. The cylinders, however, got away. We were there when they left in three trucks. They are green and about the size of the large oxygen cylinders welders use."

"Colonel, I want to thank you for the information and the good work."

They chatted about the ongoing operation for a couple of minutes before hanging up.

When Pete went into the living room, everyone had arrived. Carol was still pissed and said, sarcastically, "Well there he is, Mr. Macho himself. What the hell is the matter with you guys going into the jungle for eleven days and then coming out looking like this?"

Then Sophie jumped on the bandwagon. "Do you he-men know how scared we were? Do you have any idea of what you did to us? You were six days late getting back. We thought you were dead. And now that you're back, the hardship that you endured is all over you. It is clear that you almost died!"

"Ladies, ladies," Pete said in his calmest voice, "the jungle always takes a toll on your body, and while it looks awful it is really only superficial. I am sorry we were late returning, but there was no way to contact you. It took us longer to get in and out than we thought it would. Then we spent a couple of extra days on recon to be sure we could pull it off with no one getting killed. We needed the extra time. And right now we need a little understanding."

"You're still a rat," Sophie said, trying to kick him again. Everyone started laughing.

At that point the doctor came into the suite. "Madame Gin Sling, what is so important I had to leave my patients in the office or face the wrath of Toy?"

Sophie pointed at Pete. "Look at my husband," she said with tears welling up in her eyes behind the big glasses.

The doctor came over to Pete. He took a magnifying glass from his case and looked very carefully at the sores on Pete's arms and torso. "This is really no big deal," Pete said. The doctor made a non-committal grunt. "Let me see your legs. You others strip to your underwear," he said. "Ladies perhaps you would like to give these gentlemen a little privacy while I finish the examination." Reluctantly, Sophie and the others left. He examined every inch of all three men with his magnifying glass. He found an infection on Jack's shoulder blade and another on Mike's calf. Those he cleaned out and drenched with disinfectant. Jack and Mike got prescriptions for antibiotics. All three got prescriptions for an antibiotic cream that was to be applied twice a day for seven days.

Sophie sent Toy to get the prescriptions filled, telling the others Toy would bring it to their rooms when he returned.

The other two couples left together. As they were walking toward the elevator, Dianne said to Carol, "Sophie doesn't act like a billionaire does she?"

"Sophie and I have become good friends. She is a really nice person who genuinely loves her husband."

"Maybe that came out wrong," Dianne said. "I never thought that a billionaire would be such a regular person, so down to earth."

The dinner was a huge success. The passage of time had calmed the ladies down. Success was celebrated and minor wounds forgotten. After some discussion, it was decided that they would leave in two days on Sophie's jet, all having agreed that they should let the men heal a little before leaving.

Back in the suite, Sophie told Pete she had sold the hotel again to a group of businessmen from Hong Kong in an all-cash deal.

"Did you get seven hundred million again?" Pete asked.

"No, only six hundred million. I am getting soft in my old age."

"Soft, my ass! How much does that give you in the bank right now? One point seven billion I think, unless my math has gotten rusty," said Pete.

"A little less," she said with her little girl smile. "Do you think the General will care that I am going home before I reach my seventh month?"

"I'll call him tomorrow and see if I can't smooth that potential problem over."

The next morning Pete said to Sophie, "I spoke with the General. Evidently the CIA is very pleased with the job you have done for them in setting up Steven Chang. He sees no problem with going home early. I also explained that we might have a problem with customs because of the equipment we're bringing back. He said he'll make arrangements for us to clear customs at a military facility in Hawaii. Apparently the fix will be in, and we can sail through customs."

Sometime during the course of the day, Sophie proposed a stop in Hawaii for five days to Carol and Dianne.

"But suppose the guys object?" Dianne had asked during the discussion.

"After being six days late getting back and scaring us to death, they have nothing to say. If we want to spend a few days at the spa in the Royal Hawaiian, we will. They will just suffer the agony of waiting," Sophie said. It was obvious that while she may have let the subject drop, she was still pissed, and as she looked at the others, she knew they had the same feelings. Luckily, the amah Sophie had arranged for Carol when she arrived agreed to accompany them to Hawaii. After the women had decided on a plan, they informed their respective husbands.

Before leaving Macau, Pete took John Chen, the hotel's IT guy, aside. "I want you to let it be known that the disappearance of Chen Wu can be attributed to Madame Gin Sling."

"I will, of course, if that is what you want. But why would you want that?" John asked.

"I want her reputation for being dangerous to grow. Hopefully, it will act as a deterrent to others in the future."

"That's a very good idea," John said.

Two days later, when they landed in Hawaii, a customs inspector came out to the airplane even before the door opened. He looked up at the captain and said, "Just bring the passports into the office." After collecting everyone's passport, the captain walked into the customs office. The customs agent took the passports and stamped them all with entry stamps. When he completed stamping the passports, he said, "Have a nice day."

The captain was stunned but returned to the aircraft. They departed shortly thereafter for Honolulu International. Sophie had arranged two limos to take everyone to the hotel.

Their visit was a smashing success. The breakfast buffet at the hotel could not be beaten, and they usually ate together, with the various members of their group coming and going the rest of the morning. The five days passed all too quickly. When they arrived in Santa Barbara, Sophie had arranged a limo to take Jack and Carol home. There was another to take everyone else to Sophie and Pete's.

As they walked to the front door, Sophie said, "There's no place like home."

"Be it ever so humble," Pete mumbled under his breath.

Sophie showed Mike and Dianne to the guesthouse, thinking they would like the additional privacy it afforded. "Toy will be by later to see what you would like for dinner," Sophie said as she left to go back to the main house.

"I really never thought I would see this side of life," Dianne said to Mike after Sophie left.

"The ole colonel really fell into it, didn't he?"

"It's really hard to believe Sophie made all that money herself. She is so nice. I thought you had to be mean as a rattlesnake to get that far ahead. I really can't get over her, she is just so…"

"I'm sure she has her moments," Mike responded.

Later that evening, after they finished making love, Sophie asked Pete, "What do you think of Dianne?"

"She seems nice enough, I guess. Why do you ask?"

"Do you think she is bright?"

"I haven't spoken with her enough to have an opinion. But I will tell you this. If Mike Jarwarski married her, she has to have something going for her. He's an excellent judge of men and I would assume of women, too."

"What do you think about all those tattoos?" Sophie asked.

"If that's the way she wants to look, more power to her. It really doesn't make much difference now that you can remove them without a scar."

"You mean you can get a tattoo off without a scar?"

"Yeah, they use a laser," Pete answered.

"You mean I could get rid of my tattoo if I wanted."

"Apparently it doesn't work on red tattoo ink. Your dragon is basically all red so it won't work on yours. Beside I'd miss having it against my chest every night. Dragons bring good luck, you know."

"I'm thinking of offering Dianne a job. What do you think?" Sophie wanted to know.

"Doing what?"

"Working in the hotel I bought."

"What hotel, and when did you buy it?"

"Do you remember the hotel we stayed in when we left that dreadful Motel Six? Well, I bought it while you were lost in the jungle."

"On the phone, just like that, huh?"

"I decided I needed something to do. I am no good at just sitting around."

"What's the matter with being a wife and mother?" Pete asked. "But if you want to offer Dianne a job, go ahead. I'm sure she'll talk it over with Mike. They'll make the right decision," Pete said.

"What do you consider the right decision?" Sophie wanted to know.

"Whatever is best for them."

"Oh, I made an appointment to see the OB/GYN for tomorrow morning. I don't feel the same as I did last time."

"I am not sure I would worry about that. Every pregnancy is different, even in the same woman."

The next day when Sophie came back from the doctor, Pete was standing out by the pool. "How did everything go at the doctor?" he asked.

"You are not my favorite person right now," she said, trying to kick him with her peg leg.

"Hey, don't do that. It hurts when you connect. What did I do this time?"

"It is supposed to hurt," she said, taking another try at connecting with his shin.

"What the hell did I do?"

"You are too potent."

"What the hell does that mean? I don't understand why you are so mad," Pete said.

"Twins! I am going to have twins! I'll never get my figure back. You know that don't you? And it may extend or shorten my due date by as much as a month. I am not happy about this."

"I am," Pete said, grabbing her and giving her a big hug. "Are they boys or girls?"

"Boys."

"That is great! Alexis is going to have two little brothers. Let's see, what will I name them?"

"We! What will we name them! I'm still pissed about Alexis, by the way." With that she pushed Pete in the pool and turned her back on him, walking into the dining room.

Mike and Dianne were just coming out of the guesthouse as Pete took his plunge. Mike was laughing so hard he had to sit down on one of the patio chairs. The laughter did nothing to assuage Pete's anger at his dunking. As Pete was hoisting himself out of the pool, Mike said, "I think you said the wrong thing there, partner."

"Ya think?"

Dianne came over and asked, "What started that?"

"Sophie is going to have twins, and this was the beginning of the discussion on their names."

"What did you do, suggest Fauntleroy or Prufrock?" Dianne asked. She was laughing now, too.

Sophie stopped upon hearing the conversation behind her and looked over her shoulder. She couldn't help laughing either, he looked so mad. Pete came into the dining room where Sophie was standing. He was dripping water all over the floor. The closer he got the harder Sophie laughed. When Pete was about ten feet away, Sophie realized what he had in mind. She started to back up. Pete grabbed her seconds later, picked her up, and carried her through the dining room and across the terrace. As he reached the edge of the pool, he just kept walking. Not being able to swim, Sophie let out a howl and hung on tight. Pete went under the surface, taking Sophie under with him. He surfaced with Sophie still in his arms. He had walked into the shallow end of the pool, so he merely stood up with a sputtering, irate Sophie.

Now Pete was laughing as Sophie's rage erupted. "You asshole!" she screamed. He had the good sense to get away from her. Sophie heard Mike and Dianne roaring with laughter. After a minute, Sophie was laughing, too, realizing how ridiculous the situation was.

When they were upstairs changing Sophie asked, "Are you really happy about twins?"

"Delighted! I couldn't be happier."

"This seems like a big shift in attitude for a guy who had to be . . . ah . . . coerced into marriage."

"Alexis's birth changed my life. That was the greatest day of my life. There is no other day that even comes close." Sophie, who had taken off her leg and had been in the process of drying it, got off the bed. She hopped over to Pete, threw her arms around his neck and kissed him long and hard. He had never seen Sophie hop anywhere. In the past when she had taken off her leg, she used crutches, as much as she disliked them. Pete picked her up gently and took her back to the bed.

When Pete went back downstairs, he saw Mike and Dianne sitting on the patio. He went out to chat, but before he could open his mouth Mike asked, "Can we borrow a car?"

"Sure, let's go down to the garage and see what's there." They walked through the house and down the driveway to the garage. Pete hit the button to open the first four doors. When they opened all the cars were there. "Why don't you take the Rolls," Pete said?

"No way, I'm afraid to drive it. Can we use the white car over there?"

Pete glanced over toward the white car and thought he noticed a new addition in the garage. He went to the door opener and punched the button that opened the rest of the garage doors.

"Jesus," Mike said, "you have two cobras!"

"Tell me, does that one have an automatic transmission?" he said pointing at the red one.

Mike glanced in and said, "Yeah."

"Madame Gin Sling has struck again," said Pete. In response to the quizzical look on Mike's face Pete added, "It's a long story. I'll tell you one day."

"Take the Rolls, and don't worry about it. It's just a car and fully insured, at that.

It didn't take much more convincing before Dianne and Mike departed in the Rolls.

Sophie was just coming down the stairs when Pete walked through the front door from the garage. "I see Madame Gin Sling struck again. A red cobra! Do you have any idea what kind of a cop magnet you are going to be in that car?" Pete asked.

"I guess I'll just have to learn how to charm them, won't I," Sophie said, going on her way.

Two weeks later Sophie's purchase of the hotel had closed. She had offered Dianne a job, and Dianne had asked for a week to consider it. She and Mike had several lengthy discussions, but finally, Dianne realized Sophie was offering her a career. She knew she was coming to the end of her days on the pole. She just wished that the job paid a little more.

Sophie told her she was going to learn the hotel business from A to Z. Sophie's training plan started with a couple of weeks working with the handyman, then she would work a couple of weeks as a maid, etc. Essentially, she would know how to do every job in the hotel when her training was complete.

Mike and Dianne moved out of the guest house and into their own apartment after ten days. Sophie had offered them a free room, but Dianne did not want to live where she worked. Mike was looking for a job, too, although not very hard. Mike spent most of the day in the garage helping Pete restore an Austin HealeyAustin-Healey he had had shipped to California from North Carolina.

Pete had also shipped an old MGA from North Carolina, but space requirements forced him to push the ratty old MGA outside. It took only two days before the unsightly, rusting old wreck started to irritate Sophie.

"We live in a beautiful mansion, not a trailer park! Get rid of that thing," she said to Pete one evening over dinner.

"That car is going to be beautiful one of these days, and I am going to sell it for a lot of money," Pete had responded.

A derisive snort was all he heard from her as she let the discussion drop.

The next day, Mike and Pete pushed the car around behind the garage where it could not be seen from the house or the driveway. Apparently, that was not sufficient for Sophie. When and how she found out the car was back there, Pete never did find out. But find out she did, and then she started complaining. Pete discussed the problem with Mike. He suggested a storage garage until they were able to finish the Austin-Healey. They climbed into the little white car, heading for a set of storage garages Mike had found. Approaching the edge of town, they saw an old long-ago abandoned auto dealership. It looked perfect for the mission. There was plenty of garage space inside and plenty of storage outside. There was also a "For Rent" sign in the window. Pete called the number on the sign.

An older woman answered. She advised Pete that it was still available, but a two-year lease would be required.

That evening over dinner, Pete brought up the subject of moving his little restoration operation to the old garage. Sophie was happy to get rid of the ratty MGA and readily agreed. A decision she would later come to rue.

After three days, everything Sophie thought of as Pete's junk, and that dreadful old MGA, had been moved to the garage. One day Sophie dropped in for a visit. She was horrified when she saw Pete sitting on the greasy, cracked old floor. It was obvious the building had been abandoned for many years. "This place is awful," she said.

"It's perfect for the mission at hand," Pete said. "It's dry and has a door that can be locked. That's all I need."

"I am worried it is going to fall down on you," Sophie said. As she was leaving, she muttered, "Worse than Hong Kong."

The next morning Frank Bertolini wandered in through the open garage door. "Hi, Pete," he said.

"Hi, Frank. What brings you here of all places?"

"Your wife wanted to meet me here. She didn't say about what, though."

"This is the first I've heard of it," Pete responded, confused. At that point, the Mercedes limo arrived with Toy driving. Sophie climbed out of the back. "Hello, Frank. It is good to see you again."

"What is the project you have in mind that's so urgent?"

"This," Sophie said, waving her arm at the building. "I want this place remodeled. I don't want it brought back to like-new condition, but I want it livable. Right now, when I come in here, I have the feeling that I have a pretty good chance of catching something, do you know what I mean?"

"Whoa, Sophie, I only have a two-year lease on this place."

"Not anymore," Sophie said. When she saw the look of surprise on his face, she said, "I bought the building." Pete threw his hands in the air and walked away.

A month and a half later, Frank had completed the remodel, and Pete had to admit that it really was a big improvement. The garage had become a sort of clubhouse for old British car enthusiasts. Almost every Friday afternoon at least a couple of guys, sometimes as many as six or seven car buffs, would arrive bringing a six-pack each. Pete usually arrived home mildly tanked up, a fact that irritated Sophie no end. But after thinking about it for a while, she decided it beat the Blue Fox.

17

Sophie was almost eight months pregnant. She was so big with the twins that she was starting to have trouble getting around. The doctor had told her that she could possibly go past her due date by a week or two. She was tired of being pregnant. The thought sent chills down her spine.

The phone rang one morning as Sophie was reviewing the previous day's receipts at the hotel. "Hello, Sophie, it's General Lane."

"Hello, General," she responded cautiously.

"Sophie, can I speak with Pete?"

Sophie had a very strong feeling the General wanted Pete to do something again. She made an instant decision. "No," she said emphatically.

"Sophie, please, this is important."

"The last time he got involved with you he came back a mess; skin ulcers, bug bites, and parasites, you name it. It took almost a month before he was right again. So, no!" and with that she hung up!

The General called back again immediately. Sophie answered his call for the second time. "Sophie, the country needs him," the General said without preliminaries.

"The country can find someone else. He's done enough," Sophie said. Then she added, "Thank you for calling." She hung up again.

Sophie went around the house and told everyone who answered the phone to say Pete was not there and to take a message. The messages were then to be given to her, not Pete. They were further informed that they were not to mention this new arrangement to Pete.

Two days later, the General walked into the garage. "What brings you here, General?" Pete asked.

"I couldn't get you on the phone."

"Really? I wonder if it's out of service."

"Evidently, your wife decided that I should not talk to you. She said the last time you did something for me, it took you a month to recover."

"She can be pretty determined when she wants to be." Mike walked around the corner holding a carburetor he had just cleaned.

"Hi, Mike, I'm glad to see you. I want to talk to you both."

"What's on your mind, General? I know you didn't come all the way out here just to shoot the breeze."

"You remember the gas cylinders you saw leaving Chen Wu's compound?"

"Yeah, what about them?" Mike asked.

"We have turned up a little more information on them. They're apparently full of Russian nerve gas. The stuff is really toxic. The experts estimate that the potential is one million deaths if the crazies open the valves in a major city. We know part of the routing into the United States; it's going to Ensenada just south of the border and after that we have no idea where or how it's going to enter the United States."

"So what's the problem? All you have to do is flood Ensenada with agents."

"We did that. Or rather the FBI did, but they turned up nothing. They're about to pull out and leave it to customs. There are a couple of possibilities that need to be considered. It is possible that the cylinders have not yet reached the United States. Or, they entered through a different port.

"The potential disaster is not abated in either case," the General said.

"Well, what can we do? We're only two guys."

"The problem for the CIA is that we are prevented by law from operating inside the United States. The FBI is pulling the large part of its men from the hunt for the cylinders and relying on customs and the border patrol to interdict them.

"We at the CIA have serious doubts about their ability to do so, but the people at customs have convinced the powers that be in Washington that they can get the job done."

"I gather you don't think so," Mike said.

"Given the fact that the crazies bought the stuff from drug dealers, I think we can assume that the deal included delivery in the United States. The southern border is as porous as a strainer. Yes, we have serious doubts."

"What about the DEA, are they in the hunt?" Pete asked.

"Yes, but they are spread very thin."

"What can two guys do?" Pete repeated.

"Let's brainstorm a bit before I answer that question," the General said. "It is logical to assume that a shipment from Asia would go to the west coast. The odds of it getting through customs at a U.S. port are good, but if it went through Mexico there is no chance of it being found. Steven Chang has developed a little more intel. According to Steve, it is definitely going through Mexico. That leads us to the question of where it will cross the border. If we knew that, I wouldn't be here.

"Our best guess is that they are probably going to 'mule' it across."

"I don't think so," Pete said. "The stuff we saw being loaded looked to be pretty heavy." Mike nodded his concurrence. "They are going to need a truck or something for that stuff," Pete added.

"How do think it's going to come in?" the General asked.

"I really don't know. Is customs giving every truck coming through a good going over?"

"Yes."

"You can be assured the bad guys know that, and so it won't come through a checkpoint," Pete said.

"Then how do you think it's coming in?" the General asked.

"Plane maybe, tunnel, or a tank at a time with six mules carrying it over forty-five days," Pete said.

"All possible, but what is your best guess?" asked the General.

"Tunnel," Pete and Mike said at the same time.

"Why?"

"Well," Mike said, "they can bring it in a tank at a time, store it, and then easily ship it in bulk to its final destination."

"That's what our analysts think as well."

"Well, what is the FBI doing?" Mike asked.

"They're looking in the Mexican ports. Complete waste of time, if you ask me. Their customs officials are bought and paid for," the General said.

"That brings us back to the original question; how can we help you?" Pete asked.

"The CIA has contracted with several independent contractors whose personnel can keep their mouths shut. We are looking for the tunnel exits, and we are going to put considerable effort and resources into it. We would like you to put your team back together again, pick a city, and do the same thing."

"Aren't you limited to working outside the United States?"

"As a general rule, yes, but we can pursue anything where the original information was generated outside the country.

"You can submit a nice fat bill, and we will pay it into whatever accounts Sophie set up the last time for your people."

"Why don't you come by the house tonight at about eight thirty?"

"I'll see you then," the General said, turning to leave.

"Pete, I think we need to have a little powwow with our wives before the General shows up," Mike said.

"Without a doubt," said Pete. "I'll call Jack."

Pete went home so he could have a little preliminary conversation with Sophie before everyone arrived. As soon as he mentioned the General and the new mission for them, Sophie went ballistic.

"No!" she screamed. "You are not going anywhere or doing anything for that man ever again, do you understand?"

"Now, Sophie, just a minute…"

"The hell with just a minute! I said, 'never again,' and I meant it! That man comes around here and I'll see that he disappears! I mean it! The last time you came back six days late all chewed up. No! Never again! It scared me to death!"

Pete walked over to Sophie as she was turning to leave. He put his arms around her—the right arm below her tummy and the left arm above it. He gently pulled her to him until her back was touching his torso. He kissed her on the left shoulder and moved to the lower side of her neck. He gave her a series of kisses going up her neck, and as he did, he felt the tension leaving her body. "Would you listen to me calmly for a minute?" he said, continuing to kiss her slowly on the cheek.

"All right, I'll listen, but the answer is still no."

"All we are going to do is look for a drug smuggling tunnel," Pete said.

"What happens when you find it?"

"We call in the cavalry and go home."

"I'll think about it," Sophie said grudgingly.

Later that evening they all met around the dining room table. Toy and Chou were asked to join the group as well. Jean Claude had been asked to make some light hors d'oeuvres and as usual, he outdid himself. There was enough food on the table for twenty. Finally, Pete tapped on the table and said, "The reason we are all here tonight is to discuss whether we should get involved with the conclusion/completion of the mission we started in Laos.

"The General dropped in to talk to Mike and me this afternoon. He believes that the cylinders are going to be brought into the country across the Mexican border, probably using a tunnel. Mike, jump in any time you want to add something to what I am saying." He then went on to detail his conversation with the General.

The women had a host of questions about why the government wasn't doing anything. Finally, Pete said, "Before any of us undertake this search, we wanted you ladies to know what was involved. Your support will be vital to our success. In my own personal case, if Sophie doesn't agree that I should go, I will be staying home."

"You haven't mentioned the money yet," Jack said.

"Ten thousand a man."

"Okay, Pete, you've told us what the mission is, but you haven't said how you are going to accomplish it," Carol said, perceptively.

"Well, let me give my rough outline of a plan. Please remember, it is by no means final, and I'm sure it will be modified many times before becoming operational.

"We know that drug dealer tunnels go either to warehouses in a busy commercial area or to an isolated house. In either case, the coming and going of a small truck will not attract attention. So we'll have to plant surveillance cameras and monitor them. Once we have the location of the cylinders, we call the FBI and go home."

"That sounds almost too easy," Carol said doubtfully.

"I think there is a remote possibility of danger in this, and I don't really want to minimize it. We are going to be looking for drug dealers, and as you know, they are very violent."

Pete looked at Sophie. She just nodded yes.

Jack looked at Carol who nodded slightly. "I'm in," Jack said.

Pete looked at Mike, but before Mike could respond Dianne said, "If he's going, I'm going."

"Dianne," Pete said, "I don't think that's the best idea I've heard tonight."

"Look, once all the cameras are in place, you're going to need someone to monitor them. I see that as something I can do as well as any of you."

"Once we get the cameras set up and start monitoring them, I am willing to have you join us at that point. That's the best I'll do," Pete replied. "The second thing you have to remember is that you are a member of a team. Wifely concerns and input will get you sent home immediately. Orders are to be obeyed without question. If you think you can live with those conditions, you're in."

"I can live with that, we're in," Dianne said, answering for both of them.

"Toy, Chou?" Pete said, looking at them.

"You going, Boss, we going," Toy said, answering for both of them.

Shortly thereafter the doorbell rang. The General had arrived. After taking a seat at the table, the General said, "I am sure you have rehashed the conversation I had earlier today with you and Mike. I see no reason to repeat what you already know. So why don't you ask me to clarify anything you don't understand."

"Actually, General, I do have one request to make; I would like the Calexico, California sector," Pete said.

"That shouldn't be a problem. But do you mind if I ask why Calexico?"

"Not at all. I think that's where the cylinders are going to cross the border, and the three of us saw the cylinders," answered Pete. The meeting broke up shortly thereafter with the understanding that they would meet again in the morning to work out the equipment list.

Before leaving, Dianne asked Sophie for the time off to go on the mission. Sophie readily agreed, thinking that a woman along would help diminish all the testosterone and maybe keep them from doing something stupid. She looked at Pete, hoping against hope that his presence would keep anyone from being hurt—or worse.

18

*F*or a mission that they had pitched to their wives as basically sur-veillance, the General thought the list a bit broad. Seven MP5 automatic rifles, two dozen flash-bang grenades, two dozen antiper-sonnel grenades, three Barret .50 caliber sniper rifles, fifty pounds of composition C4 plastic explosive, and electronic detonators. But when he asked Pete if he was planning on starting World War III, Pete stated it would be better to have it than to need it. Pete also put forth a re-quest to borrow a technician to show them how to install all the latest surveillance gear.

Two days later they headed for El Centro in Sophie's jet. Pete was not certain how it happened, but somehow Dianne had wrangled her way on the airplane. While flying to El Centro, the airport closest to Calexico, Pete gave everyone a short brief on the town itself. It was an unusual town in that the buildings and streets ran right up to the border fence. It was a town in which all of the buildings were in need of serious maintenance. It was also difficult to find people who spoke English.

They rented three nondescript cars from Hertz. On arriving in Calexico they found a small motel apparently built to handle tourists who wanted to visit Mexico for the day. The manager was delighted to rent five rooms.

They spent the next day doing general scouting, looking for pos-sible tunnel exits.

After dinner with the group, Pete told them he was going to his room to check in with Sophie. He simply told her he had ar-rived and had spent the day doing recon. She accepted all his news calmly but said before hanging up, "I have a very bad feeling about this."

"Please don't sit there and worry. This is a nothing mission," Pete said before hanging up.

The next morning, after buying maps at the local stationary store, they scattered to do additional reconnoitering.

The group had agreed to meet at the Denny's in El Centro for breakfast. Pete and Chou were the first to arrive. Within ten minutes everyone else had arrived. Pete looked at Mike and asked, "How did you make out?"

"Fine," Mike said, "what's the plan for this afternoon?"

"More of the same," Pete answered.

They met later that afternoon to review their findings. They identified several potential sites for tunnel exits and decided to hone in on them in the morning.

"Well, I suggest that everyone is on their own for dinner," Pete said.

Pete had seen a McDonald's down the road and decided a couple of Big Macs would hit the spot.

Toy and Chou had seen a Chinese restaurant in town, and they headed off for some home cooking. It turned out that the restaurant was owned by a Chinese man who spoke Cantonese. The three traded gossip late into the night. The owner had also heard of Madame Gin Sling and was impressed to learn Toy and Chou worked for her.

The next morning Toy and Chou recounted their conversation of the previous evening to Pete.

"Go back there tonight and tell him Madame Gin Sling sent you here because she is looking for a way to get ivory across the border. Tell him she needs to have some new legs made. You can also tell him Madame Gin Sling will owe him a favor."

Toy smiled, saying, "That's a pretty good marker to have. Everyone knows Madame Gin Sling's word is good and that she repays favors generously."

"Maybe you guys found a way to make this whole thing simple," Pete said grinning.

They had decided to eat breakfast at the El Centro Denny's again. As they were finishing breakfast, Pete's cell phone rang. It was the General. "In two hours a C-130 with all your equipment aboard is going to land at NAS El Centro. Also aboard will be the technician you requested. You're going to need a van," he said, not wasting any words.

"No problem, General, we'll be there with a van," Pete said hanging up.

A phone call to Hertz proved fruitless. Pete could see a Ford sign rotating a block down the street. "Jack, come with me. The rest of you stay here. Our gear is going to be here in two hours, and we need a van. I'm going to go buy one. Be right back."

"Right back" turned into an hour and a half. "Let's go everyone. We have to be at NAS El Centro in thirty minutes." On the way to the navy base he said to Mike, who was sitting in the front passenger seat, "I can't believe what a pain in the ass car dealers can be."

"There's always something to take the joy out of living," Mike responded.

The C-130 landed ten minutes after they arrived at base operations. The flight line personnel allowed them to drive the van out onto the ramp. The rear door opened, and the crew chief drove a dark blue van down the ramp, which had deployed automatically with the opening door.

A short, thin guy about thirty years old, wearing thick glasses and an afro hairstyle came down the ramp behind the van. He walked over to Pete and said, "Hi, you must be Pete Smith. I'm Marvin Applebaum. The General sent me to help you with setting up this equipment. The General said you can keep me as long as you need me."

Pete stuck out his hand, saying, "Pleasure to meet you. This is Mike, Toy, Dianne, Chou, and Jack. Is everything in the van?"

"Hell, no! All that stuff in there is for you, too," he said, pointing to the cargo bay.

"Let's get all this stuff loaded up and head for the motel. Then you can give us an overview of how everything works," Pete said. Unloading the plane almost filled the new van.

Marvin followed Pete to the hotel. Once he saw which rooms were theirs, he backed into a parking place in front of their rooms.

As Pete was walking over to the blue van, Marv said to him, "Let's get the white van unloaded, and I'll give you a thumbnail sketch of how all this works. Do you have a room for me yet?"

"Yes, it's a couple of doors down. I'll show you after we finish here."

When everything from the white van had been brought into Pete's room, Marv started pointing out crates, saying, "This is the hardware the General sent for you." Then he reached into his briefcase saying, "The General also sent these for you. He thought you might need them." He handed Jack credential packs. They were from Homeland Security. Pete looked at them. There was even one for Dianne with what appeared to be a recent picture. He idly wondered how the General had managed that.

Marv opened one of the boxes. He took out a small camera about half the size of a cigarette pack. "This is the basic camera. It has an off/on switch here," he said, indicating a small button on the side of the camera. "It's wireless, all weather, and works no matter what the temperature."

"What's the range on this thing?" asked Pete examining the camera.

"Well, the manufacturer says five miles, but in my experience once you pass about two miles, it doesn't work as well,' Marv answered.

"How do you mount the camera?"

"There are several different methods. Where do you want to mount it?" Marv asked.

"What I would like to do is place two cameras outside at each location, one watching the front, the other watching the back."

"That's no problem," Marv said. "We can set a different frequency for each camera. Come outside for a second." When they were outside Marv opened the rear doors of the blue van. In the cargo compartment there was an array of about thirty monitors, each six inches by six inches square running down the left side of the van. "Each camera can be set up to be monitored on one of these small screens. If we see something interesting, we can transfer to the larger one over here. All the camera images are being recorded whenever they're on. If you need, I can add more monitors. We also have GPS tracking available, thermal imaging, and eavesdropping capacity. In addition, I have some mini cameras for inside the building, quite small, actually."

"How long before we can start installing the cameras?" Pete asked.

"The first one can be ready in five minutes," Marv answered.

"Okay guys, let's open up the other boxes of equipment and allocate it all to the various cars," Jack said.

Each of the rental cars was apportioned two MP5s, a ghillie suite, two of the silenced pistols, and some of the grenades. They decided to keep the C4 and detonators in Pete's room.

That evening Toy and Chou went back to the Chinese restaurant. After the owner was done with his kitchen duties, he joined them at their table. He enjoyed being able to speak his native language again. After a few minutes Toy got to the point. Madame Gin Sling needed a little help smuggling ivory into the country for some new legs she wanted to have made.

"I don't know anyone who has declared himself to be smuggler, but I think I know where there are some, a lot of comings and goings late at night, usually involving a truck."

"How do you know that?" asked Chou.

"I live about a mile down the road. Because of the restaurant, I don't get home until late and I see all the activity going on down the road," he replied.

"Where is this activity going on?" Chou asked.

"If anyone finds out I told you this, I will be dead."

"Don't worry, we understand this. Madame Gin Sling will owe you a favor for helping us find someone for her."

This promise of a favor made his decision for him. He went on to describe where the house was and the activity taking place there.

"You will have to be very careful how you approach them. All the smugglers are dangerous men."

Both Toy and Chou recognized the description as being one of the houses they had targeted for surveillance.

Back at the motel, Toy and Chou reported to Pete what they had learned.

At midnight they left the hotel, and Pete and Chou approached to within three-quarters of a mile of the first house they had targeted. They had removed the passenger compartment overhead lightbulb. Pete opened the door and started to put on his ghillie suit. "Would you rather I did that?"" Chou asked.

"No, but thanks for the offer. I've spent years doing this."

"Be careful, Boss," Chou said. With those simple words he knew Toy and Chou had special instructions from Sophie to keep him safe, probably at all costs. He walked erect for the first four hundred yards. Then he got down on his stomach and crawled the last half mile. He put one camera in position to see the back door and another in position to cover the front door and the garage door. He succeeded in placing enough cameras to cover the other two suspect houses before returning to the motel.

When Pete and Chou returned to the motel, they opened the rear door and looked into the back of the blue van. Dianne and Marv were inside perched on stools. All the cameras seemed to be working. "Everything okay?" Pete asked.

"Couldn't be better," Marv responded.

After two days of surveillance, they were fairly sure all three houses probably contained tunnel exits. The problem was that a truck would back into the garage and the garage door would close. When the garage door opened again a fully loaded truck left, but it was impossible to tell what was in the truck when it left.

The next afternoon when they were all together, Pete asked "Marv, didn't you say that you had cameras that could go inside a building?"

"Of course," Marv said.

"How big are they?" Jack wanted to know.

Marv went over to a small box and pulled out something the size of a postage stamp and a sixteenth of an inch thick. "Is this small enough for you?"

"Yea, that's perfect," Jack said.

"There's only one drawback," Marv said. "The battery only lasts for about two days."

"Is the battery rechargeable?" asked Jack.

"No, you just change it out, takes twenty seconds."

"We need to plant these tonight," Pete said. "We'll wait until all the activity is finished at those houses and then do it." Then as an afterthought he asked, "Can we put a listening bug in there as well?"

"Sure!"

"All those garages have exterior doors," Pete said. "Does anyone know how pick a lock?" Pete asked.

Toy and Chou both proudly raised their hands. That evening Toy and Chou planted cameras and bugs in the three garages. The next evening, when the truck came to the first house, they watched as bales of marijuana were loaded in a van. After another week had passed everyone was thoroughly bored. Pete finally called the General. "How much longer do you want us to stick around here?" Pete asked.

"Call me again in a week," the General answered.

"Ugh," was Pete's response.

Pete had problems on the home front as well. Sophie's due date was three days away and she'd made it clear in no uncertain terms she wanted him home NOW. She had also sent the jet to New London to pick up Sally so she would be able to help her with the transition to home again. With every passing day she got angrier. Pete had to confess that he wanted to be there with her as well.

It was three days later when they saw the first cylinder loaded into a truck. Then eleven more were loaded into the truck. Everyone was hovering over the monitor watching the drama play out. "Watch the back door of the van carefully. We need to know if they lock it," Pete said. "Marv, you and Dianne get ready to follow the truck. As soon as you are able, put a GPS bug on the truck. Mike, those guys have to pass one traffic light on the way to the highway. I want you to be there and be ready to cross the street as the truck slows down to make the turn. If you can, without being too obvious, stick a GPS tracker on it," Pete said. "Dianne, you drive and let Marv monitor the tracker. When you bring up the tracker on the truck, follow about five miles back. If we aren't able to stick the GPS on the truck, then maybe you'll get lucky when they stop for gas or the bathroom. If you can't follow a signal, keep the truck in sight. For god's sake, don't lose it!

"Toy, Chou, you follow them and if they don't get a bug on the truck, you'll have to tag team it. If they do get a bug on the truck, you guys come back here. Keep in touch with us by cell phone.

"Marv, I want you to check the tape from the bug in that house and tell me what was being said."

Mike got lucky. He was able to place the tracker in the wheel well of the truck as he walked across the street. When Dianne and Marv came by he gave the sign that the tracker was in place. Behind them Mike saw Toy and Chou and gave them the sign. Mike called Marv's cell phone.

"Is it working?" he asked.

"It appears to be," Marv answered.

"Call me back when you're sure," Mike said before hanging up.

Five miles later Toy's cell phone rang. "It's working," Marv said, hanging up immediately.

Toy made a left into a side street, made a U-turn, and headed to the motel. When Toy and Chou entered the room, the others were in the middle of discussing the best course of action. The rest of the gas was probably still in Mexico, and no department of the United States government could go get it without it looking like an invasion of a foreign country. If the government tried to get permission from the Mexican government, the stuff would be gone before they could get there.

"Hello," Pete said when his cell phone rang.

"I don't know what they said. I think they were speaking Arabic, but I can't be sure.

"Mike speaks Arabic. Play the tape into the cell phone and I'll let him listen." Mike listened and said, "It is Arabic but the tape is so grabbled I could only get a few words."

Taking the cell phone from Mike, Pete said, "Thanks, Marv. Keep in touch."

"There's only one solution," Jack said, "and you guys know what it is. All we're doing is talking around it."

"You're right," Pete said.

"Okay Jack, what's the plan?" Pete asked.

"Well, I think the way to do this is for two of us to go in from the Mexican side, and the rest take the house and go down the tunnel from this side. We'll go at four this morning and hope the night shift has gone home and the day shift hasn't arrived yet. Take no prisoners.

Then we move the gas to our side of the border and call the Feds to come and get it."

"Mike," asked Pete, "what do you think?"

"I like the basics, but I would suggest that we need to be really careful about that tunnel. We don't want to get caught in that thing."

Pete made a gesture with his hand for Mike to continue.

"The first thing we have to have before anyone goes into the tunnel is control of both ends. If we were in there and someone cut lose with an AK47 indiscriminately down the tunnel, anyone in there would be dead. That means the coordination has to be perfect. We can use cells phones for this. I suggest we take the American end before the Mexican end. If something goes wrong on this side of the border, we can fade into the woodwork."

"Let me offer a few more refinements," Pete said. "I think we should all take down the house on this side. We are going to have to use that to give us the direction to the building on the other side. Secondly, as soon as we get in the tunnel we start placing C4 charges every forty yards. We use just enough C4 to bring the roof down. That should stop Mike's nightmare scenario. But if all goes well we will blow the tunnel as soon as we have all the gas on this side of the border," Pete said.

"How do we get the guns through the border? Going in doesn't appear to be a problem but coming out might be."

"The first thing we do is put stolen plates on the van before we enter Mexico. The hardware goes back to the United States through the tunnel. We change the plates back before leaving Mexico. That will make it harder for someone to figure out when the van entered Mexico."

"I think that leaves only one question. What time do we go?" Jack wanted to know.

"We leave here at three forty with the idea that we hit the house at four," Pete said. "We still have a couple of hours so let's see if we can get some sleep."

Just before four, Pete grabbed the knob for the garage door. Surprisingly, it was not locked. "Get the garage camera," he said to no one in particular. Moving quietly to the door leading into the house, he grabbed the knob in his right hand and twisted it. As he opened the door, he shifted the silenced .22 pistol from his left to his right hand. The door opened into the kitchen, which was empty. He proceeded to the door leading to the living room, which was also empty. A hallway led off from the living room. He and Mike went slowly down the hall trying not to make any noise. There were two bedrooms off the hallway. Mike took one and Pete the other. Both doors squeaked at the same time. Two men were reaching for their guns when Pete got the door fully open. He shot them both in the head, then walked over to the bodies and calmly put another bullet in each man's head just to be sure they were dead.

Toy had proceeded down the hallway past the bedrooms and cleared the bathroom at the end of the hall.

The tunnel exit was in the middle of the living room. "Mike, I want you to guard this end. For the moment everything is secure here, but be really careful about who you shoot coming out of the tunnel. They have to have lights in there, so watch for them to come on. When one of us comes through, we'll give a holler first."

Toy said, "Come in here and take a look."

Mike, Pete, and Jack walked into the bedroom. Lying on the floor were fifteen of the gas cylinders. "That's going to make our lives a little easier," Jack observed.

"Let's take a compass into the tunnel and get the direction. Pete descended into the tunnel. When he reemerged he said, "The bearing is about 175 degrees." He looked at his compass and held his arm in the direction the tunnel was going, looking for the probable building where the tunnel exit was. Everyone concurred the tunnel exit was probably a tan building about five hundred feet from the fence.

"Mike, heads up! Let's go guys," Pete said.

Chou had just finished changing the license plates on the van when everyone came out of the house. At that hour of the morning the border checkpoint turned out to be no more than a speed bump.

They found the building they had identified as the outlet of the tunnel on the Mexican side. They drove by once and noted only two cars in front of the building. They drove a block after passing the building before parking. Moving quietly they went back to the building, and this time the door was locked. It took Toy only a minute to pick the lock. As usual Pete entered first. The door opened into a large open room. The tunnel entrance was to his immediate right. In the back corner of the room an office protruded into the room. The top half of the office wall was glass and the bottom half wood. Pete went toward the office as quietly as he could and looked through the glass window. He saw three guys sleeping on cots. As he entered the room he hollered, "Rise and shine!" Two of the guys woke up immediately and a third was coming around groggily. "Hands up," he said, thinking he could silence them with duct tape for several hours. The guys on the left and in the center complied. The guy on the right, however, decided to go for a gun. He got a bullet in the ear before his hand touched it. That gave the one on the left an opening and he went for his gun. He took a bullet in the left eye. Pete shot the third guy in the forehead on the theory that dead men tell no tales.

They found another twelve of the gas cylinders lying near the tunnel entrance. Toy and Chou were strong enough that each could carry a tank. Pete and Mike passed the tanks into the tunnel. The tunnel was six feet in height so both Toy and Chou had to stoop while carrying a cylinder.

While Toy and Chou carried the cylinders through the tunnel to the other side of the border, Pete and Mike stood guard at the tunnel entrance. Toy and Chou had just come back to get the last two cylinders when the rear door to the building opened. Two men armed with AK47s walked in the door. As soon as they realized what was happening, the two started to raise their AKs. The barrels of their weapons never reached waist high. Mike and Pete fired first with deadly effect, and both of the drug smugglers were dead before they hit the floor. Mike climbed down into the tunnel, and Pete passed him their arms and the explosive charges they had prepared. He kept one of the silenced .22 caliber pistols for himself.

Pete went out the front door as the other three disappeared into the tunnel. Crossing the international border proved to be a nonevent once the border patrol agent looked in the back of the van and saw it was empty. Pete drove directly to the house containing the tunnel exit. When he got there he backed the van into the driveway. He hopped out of the van to open the garage door but Jack was in the process of opening it. Pete returned to the van and backed it into the garage.

"Let's get the cylinders loaded into the van."

Pete went down the tunnel shaft just as Mike was finishing placing the last charge. "Hurry up," Pete said, "we're about to have company!"

As Chou shut the rear door of the van, Mike climbed in and drove off. When everyone was outside the house, Pete followed. As he reached the driveway, he armed the detonator. A second later he pushed the detonate button, and four explosions went off simultaneously, destroying the tunnel. "Let's get out of here," Pete said.

They went directly back to the motel.

When they reached the motel, Pete said, "Take the gas cylinders and distribute them equally among the three rental cars."

The first thing he did when he was back in his room was to call Marv. He answered on the second ring. Before Marv could even say hello, Pete said, "I want you to go to wherever they have that gas stored and get eyes on the site. If they move it follow, and call me as soon as you can."

"You got it. We're moving now," Marv said.

The next phone call Pete made was to the General. When the General answered it was apparent that Pete had woken him. "Hello," the General said groggily.

"General, Pete. We found the gas last night and seized approximately two-thirds of it. It will be delivered to base ops NAS El Centro in about forty minutes in three rental cars. I would appreciate it if you could see that the cars are returned to Hertz."

"Holy shit," the General exclaimed, raising his normally calm voice. "You were not supposed to seize the stuff, just locate it. What the fuck are you doing?" he said, becoming more and more animated.

"A good portion of it was in Mexico," Pete said.

"Oh," the General said, somewhat mollified. Then he asked, "Where's the rest of it?"

"It's in a small house outside Lake Elsinore," said Pete. He then gave the General the address, adding, "Marv and Dianne should have eyes on the house now. The rest of the team will be en route in forty-five minutes. I am guessing two hours of travel time."

"Keep me posted," the General said, hanging up.

Pete went back outside. "Pack up guys. As soon as you can the cars are going to base ops. Toy, you, Chou, and I are driving the cars. Jack and Mike, take the van," Pete said.

Thirty-eight minutes later, they left the parking lot at base ops with Jack behind the wheel of the new van. "Where to, Boss?" Jack asked.

"Lake Elsinore, the address is loaded in the GPS on my phone, and step on it." Pete added, "Don't forget, you're the man."

19

An hour and thirty-eight minutes later, Jack pulled over to the side of the road behind the blue van. Everyone piled out of both vans. "I don't think there's anyone in there," Marv said.

"We've been watching this place for two hours and haven't seen a sign of life," Dianne added. "They must have moved while we were parked around the corner," Dianne added.

"Let me call the General and see what he says. While I'm doing that, Mike I want you to warn the neighbors in the two houses to the right that there may be terrorists next door and they should leave for a couple of hours. Jack, do the same with the two houses over there," Pete said, pointing to the houses to the left of the suspect house. "Oh, and use your creds, that should make things easier."

With that said, Pete reached into the van and grabbed his cell phone. The General answered on the first ring, "Pete?"

"General, where's the team that's supposed to be here?"

"Standby," was all the General said. Two minutes later he was back on the line. "They are at Santa Monica Airport and should be leaving in five minutes. The ETA is thirty-five minutes en route to your position."

"General, we don't think there is anyone in there. Dianne and Marv have been watching the place for more than two hours and have seen absolutely no sign of life. I am thinking we should do a little re-con, thermal image the place at least. Marv has the equipment, and I can't see any reason not to do it."

"Okay, that's approved," the General said.

"I'll let you know what we find out," Pete said, hanging up. He turned toward the group as Jack and Mike were returning.

"Marv, get the van as close as you need to get good thermal imaging results. The General has approved a little recon," Pete said

"What's a 'little recon' mean?" Mike asked.

"We're going to find out," Pete answered Mike, who was now smiling.

Marv got as close as he needed. As he moved the van, three pairs of binoculars were trained on the house. No one saw the slightest indication that the house might be occupied. Pete opened the front door of the van. "Anything?" he asked.

"I think it's empty," Marv answered.

"I think I'll get a little closer. Mike, get one of the Barretts and watch my back, will you? Now that I think about it, Jack, will you do the same thing? Get some distance between you for a little more coverage," Pete said.

Pete walked over to the neighbor's house on the garage side of the terrorists' hideout. Then he crossed the neighbor's front yard and went to the side of the terrorists' garage and peered through the window. The garage was empty. He slid around to the front of the house and looked in the first window he came upon. It looked like the living room, and no one was there. He continued on to the next window. The curtains had been pulled, but there was a thin slit between them, and he peaked in. It contained two unoccupied, unmade cots.

With that, Pete walked across the street. "There's no one home," Pete reported to the others.

"What are we going to do?" Jack asked.

"I think we need to go in through the back and confirm that. I don't think we'll find anyone, but we might as well go in and see what we can find. Toy, would you come with me? I may need your lock picking skills."

"Sure, Boss," Toy said.

Together they walked around to the back of the house and looked in each window. They still saw no one. When they got to the back door Pete tried the knob. It twisted in his hand, which surprised him. They stepped into the kitchen. It was like everything else they had seen, empty. Nevertheless, with his gun held in front of him in a shooting position, Pete cautiously entered every room. He found no one.

He went out the front door and waved the others to come in as well. Mike was the first person to enter. He told them not to touch anything. As Pete looked around at the depth of the trash left over from takeout food still lying on the floor, he knew whoever had stayed here had been there for quite some time. The trash was everywhere in the bedrooms, living room, and kitchen. The only furniture consisted of folding chairs in front of a twenty-four-inch flat-screen TV in the living room and three cots in the bedrooms. This place had not been intended for long-term residence.

Marv came into the living room at that point and said, "The GPS bug is laying on the floor in the garage. We probably tipped our hand some way, and they decided to check the van."

"Hey, look at this," Dianne said.

Mike came over, looked down, and said, "Looks like an old ash tray to me."

"No, look at the matchbook next to it, silly. It's from a San Francisco go-go joint. Slightly out of place, wouldn't you say?"

"Let's go, everybody. I want to get out of here before the FBI shows up, and we don't have much time right now. Let's go! Let's go!" Pete said, clapping his hands. Everyone jogged across the street. Dianne got in the blue van with Marvin, and everyone else piled in the white van. They had left the doors open for the FBI so they wouldn't have warrant problems or trouble clearing an empty house.

Marv followed Pete since he had no idea where they were going. They had gone about three blocks when the FBI task force passed them going in the opposite direction. "Dodged that bullet," Pete said.

"Why do you say that?" asked Jack.

"Do you have any idea how many hours we would spend being debriefed by the FBI?"

"Hadn't thought of that," Jack said. "Where are we going, by the way?"

"San Francisco," Pete answered.

"Why San Francisco?" Jack wanted to know.

"The matchbook is the only clue we have about where they may have gone. I suppose you could call it a hunch. Mike, use my phone and call the General. Get him to use his contacts to find out the names and addresses of the radical mosques in San Francisco. His number is in contacts under G," Pete said.

"General, it's Mike Jarwarski. Pete asked me to call you and ask you to prevail on your contacts to get us the names and addresses of the radical mosques in San Francisco."

"Let me speak to the good Colonel," the General replied.

"Pete, he wants to speak to you," Mike said. "General, he says he can't talk right now, he's driving."

"Is he pulling my tit or what? I've got dead bodies all over the place, guys buried alive in a tunnel cave-in apparently started with military grade C4, and a compromised crime scene. And he is driving? Is he fucking kidding me, or what?" the General screeched into the phone.

"Pete, I think you better talk to him." Mike passed him the phone.

Taking the phone from Mike, Pete said, "General, how are you?"

Ignoring Pete's question, the General asked one of his own, "What the hell are you doing?"

"General, we lost some of the gas and we're going to get it back. Dianne found a matchbook from a bar in San Francisco in the house in Lake Elsinore. Frankly, it's the only lead we have. We also know that these guys speak Arabic. I'm playing a hunch."

"Pete, let the FBI follow that up. They are more than capable of putting two and two together," the General said.

"General, we're the only ones who have actually seen anyone connected to this thing," Pete said.

"If you find anything, you are going to call us immediately and not try to take the crazies on yourself, right?" asked the General.

"Absolutely!"

After a moment's reflection, the General decided it wouldn't hurt to have extra eyes on the scene. "I'll send an encrypted email to Marv with the information that you want."

"Thanks, General. We are about five hours from San Francisco."

Jack had just climbed behind the wheel after they made a pit stop for fuel, gas, and a bathroom break. Pete was getting in the side door as Marv ran up.

"I got the email from the General with the names and addresses of the radical mosques in San Francisco. The good news is that there are only three," Marv said to Pete.

"Okay, you and Dianne take the lead. Let Dianne drive. Find us a decent hotel on the Internet just as close to all three mosques as possible, and book us five rooms. We also need four rental cars. Book them at different places, and see if you can get them delivered to the hotel."

"You got it, Boss," Marv said.

Four hours later, both vans pulled into the underground parking for the hotel Marv had found on the Internet. After checking in, they met in Pete's room. "Here's the plan; Mike, you take one mosque, Jack you take another, and I'll take the last one. You guys choose. I don't care who goes where. Set up your surveillance so you can see the back and front door, if possible.

"Toy, I want you and Dianne to go to the bar named on the matchbook and look for any of the guys we saw on the surveillance cameras in Calexico. We may get lucky. Play it anyway you want in that bar. Chou, you stay with Marvin and help wherever you can."

"Marv, I want you to hang out with your equipment and be ready. We may need to listen in on someone's conversation. You do have that equipment with you, I assume?"

"Yea, I got everything we could possibly need," Marv said.

"We'll meet back here tomorrow morning at nine o'clock to assess our plan."

The next morning, when they had gathered in Pete's room, he said, "I went to each of the three mosques yesterday and saw one glaring problem. If we find one of those guys how do we figure out where their lair is? Even with a car you may not be able to get it turned around in time to follow."

"I think the best way to deal with the problem is for Chou to get in the fourth car and position himself in a central location," he continued. "As soon as someone sees something, call him on his cell, and he'll get in position to help tail any crazy we may encounter. Does anyone have any other ideas on how to deal with the problem?"

When no one answered, Pete asked, "Chou, how did you and Dianne make out yesterday?"

"We found the bar, it's a topless joint. A 'help wanted' sign was in the window. Dianne is now on the payroll. She starts this afternoon at four o'clock. It's perfect because if she sees someone, she can go in the break room and call immediately."

Pete said, "All right, let's go find the rental the cars and be prepared to be in position by noon to continue the surveillance on the mosques. Dianne should go to work as scheduled."

"Boss," Toy asked, "do you think they might be storing that stuff in one of those mosques?"

Toy, as well as Chou, was normally silent at meetings like this, but when they did speak, they usually had something important to add, Pete thought. This morning was no exception. "That's a damn good question. I think we should have a look inside at least one or two of those mosques tonight. Tomorrow we'll finish searching them. The Feds treat those things as inviolate. We, however, are not bound by such constraints.

"Let's plan on meeting back here tomorrow morning if nothing breaks today."

The next morning when they reassembled in Pete's room, he said, "I guess we pretty much had a zero day yesterday and can probably look forward to another mind-numbing day of boredom, but anyone see anything interesting?"

"The Feds came into the bar yesterday but got nowhere with the manager. I was on the dance floor when they showed up. They didn't seem interested in me, which is good news. They don't seem to have any leads on the Calexico shooters," Dianne said.

"That is good news; they haven't got a handle on who we are yet, but they will. When they do find us, you can plan on an unpleasant day or two," Pete said.

Later that night Pete was watching the news when his cell phone rang. "Pete," Mike said.

"What's up?" Pete asked.

"I came to see how Dianne was doing. I think one of them just showed up, or rather I think it's one of the guys who drove the van out of Calexico."

"For god's sake, don't lose him! I'll get everyone moving, and we'll be there as soon as we can," Pete said.

After dressing hurriedly, Pete got out his list of room numbers and started down the hall. As the various members of the team answered his knock on their doors, he told them all to dress as fast as possible and meet at the white van, except Marv, whom he told to be prepared to follow in the communication van.

Four minutes later with everyone in the garage, Pete brought everyone up to date. Jack said, "I think we should take one car in case we need additional mobility."

"You're right. Jack, you and Chou go together and follow us in one of the cars," Pete said.

As they were pulling out of the garage, Pete's cell phone rang again. "He's moving," Mike said, without any preliminaries.

"Keep the line open, and for God's sake don't lose him."

"He's turning on the 101 freeway southbound toward San Jose," Dianne said. She had apparently abandoned her job, and Mike had passed the phone to her as he drove. Mike ought to have had more sense than to let Dianne come along at a time like this, Pete thought. Then he wondered what she was wearing, besides her tattoos and high heels

Chou, having heard the conversation on the speaker, used his cell phone to pass the information along to Jack and Marv without instructions from Pete.

"He's getting off the freeway and appears to be heading into a neighborhood." A minute later Dianne reported, "He parked. Mike is going to follow on foot."

Pete held out his hand for the cell phone. Chou gave it to him. "Dianne, keep this line open and keep up the running commentary." Turning to Toy he said, "See if you can figure out how to put this thing in speaker phone mode.

"It looks like he went into a house. Mike will be back in just a few seconds."

Thirty seconds later, Mike gave Pete the house address. Chou punched the address into the GPS and called the others, passing the address along. Pete said into the phone, "Mike, the GPS says we are eleven minutes out."

"We'll be here," Mike said.

Pete called the General and gave him an update. "I'll set things in motion, and you sit tight until the FBI gets there."

"Okay, General," Pete said.

Pete pulled in behind Mike and Dianne. Jack and Marv were able to find parking places easily as well. They were in an older neighborhood probably built right after the Second World War. The house was small and nondescript, probably two bedrooms. The architect had been uninspired. It had a detached garage forty feet from the house itself.

Marv came over to the white van. Pete looked at Marv and said, "Can you get us a thermal image with a body count, Marv?"

"No problem, I'll get right on it." Marv went back to the blue van and climbed behind the wheel to reposition the van. As he was getting behind the wheel, Dianne climbed in the back. When Marv had the van properly positioned, he slid around the driver's seat into the back, but Dianne had already brought up the thermal image of the house. Pete walked over to the van. "Well?" he asked.

Marv looked over Dianne's shoulder and said, "Looks like at least ten, and maybe twelve or fourteen. It is tough to tell," Marv said.

"They look like they're on the floor praying," Dianne added.

"Marv, have you got anything in your bag of tricks to listen to what's being said in there?" Pete asked.

"Sure," Marv said, reaching into a drawer just to the left of Dianne. He pulled out a pair of button-like things. "All you have to do is stick these on the windows, and I'll put you in the room with them," Marv said.

"I'll be right back," Pete said, holding out his hand.

Pete casually walked down the sidewalk until he reached the hedge separating the suspect house from the neighboring house. Then he ducked down and moved quickly to the front of the house. Taking one of the buttons, he stuck it to what he assumed to be the living room window. He continued down the side of the house to the next window of a lighted room and stuck the second button on that window. Then he headed back to the van. When he reached it, Mike was listening to the conversation on the speaker Marv had activated.

"They're praying," Mike said

"I didn't know you spoke Arabic," Dianne said.

"The army sent me to language school a few years ago; comes in handy from time to time. They're just finishing their prayers. The leader is speaking now. He's saying, 'Ali, Mohamed, you have the furthest to go, so back your cars into the driveway one at a time, and we will load you up.'"

"Looks like we're out of time. General or no General, we can't let that gas get away again," Pete said and then added, "Ah, shit," as a cop car turned down the street, dispatched probably in response to some neighbor's phone call.

"Jack, get around behind him and stick a gun in his back. I'll take it from there. We don't have the time to fool around with this guy."

As the police car stopped parallel to the white van, Jack slipped down the side of the van to be behind the cop. "Good evening, gentlemen," the officer said, walking toward the sidewalk. Once on the sidewalk he glanced into the white van. All the arms that were in the process of being laid out caught his attention. "What's going on here?"

At that point, Jack stuck the barrel of a twenty-two into the back of the officer's neck. "Don't move," Jack said.

"Listen, officer," Pete said, "We are from Homeland Security, and we are about to take down a house containing some very bad guys. You can either help us or I am going to chain you to the van and thoroughly tape you up."

"You have any ID with you?" the officer asked. Pete threw him his credentials. The officer took out his flashlight and carefully inspected them.

"I'm in," the cop said.

"Good, we may need the firepower. Take your car around the block then get back here as fast as you can. Do you know how to handle a MP5?" The shocked officer could only nod. "Jack, rip the mic out of the radio. If any more police show up, they may tip off the terrorists. Leave the shoulder radio in the car," he said to the officer.

The officer suddenly realized the seriousness of the situation.

Less than a minute later the officer came crashing through the hedge behind them and ran down the driveway. When he reached them, Pete handed him an MP5 and said, "The safety is on, the magazine is full, and the throat is clear."

"All right, here's the plan: Jack, take one of the Barretts and get lined up on the center line of the driveway. If anyone tries to drive anything out of the driveway stop them, but don't hit one of those tanks. Chou, you take the right side of the house from the front. Officer, you take the left side of the house from the front. Get behind the parked cars."

"Toy, you cover the left side of house from the rear. Mike, you get the center, and I'll get the right side, but I'll be up by the corner of the garage.

"Dianne, you and Marv monitor the thermal imaging and the voices on the off chance they start to use English.

"It would sure be nice if we had some radio communications between us," Pete said, finishing his brief.

"Does anyone have any questions?" Pete asked.

Marv ducked into the blue van and came out with six communication units. "Ask and you shall receive," Marv said.

As Marv distributed the communications equipment, Pete said to the officer, "Those cylinders contain sarin gas. So, for god's sake, don't hit one."

They tested the radios and were ready to go. As they were working their way into position, the first of the terrorists' cars backed into the driveway. Two men came out of the back door of the house and opened the garage. After circling behind the house through the neighbor's yard, Pete crawled beside the garage to the front wall. The garage door was of the old style and swung outward, forcing Pete away from the wall. Pete heard the car start as the men walked back toward the house. They had just entered the house, and the car was about halfway down the driveway when the sound of a Barrett .50 broke the stillness of the night. There was no doubt about who had fired and that the driver was dead. The car slowed and veered slowly into the side of the house and stopped.

"There's a flurry of activity inside the house," Dianne's voice came over the radio. "They may be passing out weapons."

A minute later two men, armed with AK47s, ran from the front door and two more from the rear door simultaneously. As Toy and Mike took down the two running from the rear, Chou and the officer did the same thing in front.

The lights went out inside the house. Two minutes later, the radio in Pete's ear crackled with Dianne's voice, "There's at least one guy by each of the side windows."

Thirty seconds later a terrorist jumped from each side of the house at the same time. Pete stood and took a shot at the one on the right. He was dead before he hit the ground, but at the same moment two more came out the back door, spreading out as they ran. Toy shot the terrorist who had come out of the left window, and Mike took the one who had come out the back door angling to his right. The last guy out the door got off a burst with his AK47 at Pete. One bullet nicked his right side and a second hit him just below the rib cage on the left side of his torso. Pete managed to get off a burst himself, and the terrorist went down dead.

Mike realized what had happened immediately. "Pete is down! Marv, get an ambulance! Dianne, how many more are left inside?"

"Looks like two, but I can't be sure," she answered.

"Jack, are you up?" Mike asked.

"Yeah."

"We're going to have to do this the hard way. We've got to clear this place fast so we can get medical help to Pete. Use your pistol and go through the front door. The rest of you guys watch the side windows. Dianne, keep us posted the best you can. You ready? Let's go! Jack, call the door." Jack moved to the side of the house.

"There's one guy right behind the front door," Dianne said over the radio. The officer picked up one of the Barretts and put three rounds through the door, spacing them about six inches apart. "Looks like he's down. I don't see any others. The last guy is probably in the back of the house somewhere," Dianne said. Sirens were growing louder in the background.

Toy saw a movement in one of the windows and cut loose with a three-round burst. "I think I got the last one," Toy said.

"I'm at the door," Jack said.

"Let's go," Mike said.

They worked slowly and methodically, clearing every room. They went out the back door to administer first aid to Pete, but Toy was already in the process. Toy had taken off his shirt and stuffed it into Pete's stomach wound. Two minutes later the ambulance arrived, and the EMTs went to work on Pete. Five minutes later they loaded Pete into the rear of the ambulance. Toy and Chou never left Pete's side.

Mike had everyone else packing up the equipment. They had everything in the vans as the ambulance left with Pete, Toy, and Chou.

Mike went over to the officer and said, "The tanks in the garage are full of one of the deadliest gases ever manufactured. Stand guard over them. The FBI is on its way and should be arriving soon. I think I hear some of your compatriots coming as well. Be careful they don't shoot you. We're going to the hospital to see how our friend is making out. I want to thank you for all your help. You're a standup guy, and you stood tall tonight."

On the way to the hospital, Mike called the General and explained that the crazies had started to move the stuff.

"We made the decision that it wasn't going to happen, and Pete got hit in the firefight. The rest of us are on the way to the hospital to see how he's doing. There's a local cop. guarding the site. He helped us out, by the way, and is a very good man when the chips are down."

"Does Sophie know yet?" the General wanted to know.

"I don't know, sir, but I doubt it."

"She is due any day now, isn't she?" the General asked.

"She's overdue."

"Sophie is going to go ballistic," the General said.

"I don't think there's much we can do, sir, except stand clear."

"I'll see you some time tomorrow. I'd better get out there."

"See you then, General," Mike said, hanging up.

Entering the hospital through the emergency room entrance, they immediately saw Toy and Chou standing guard outside a cubical with a curtain pulled across. "What's going on?" Mike asked.

"They're making arrangements to transfer him to San Francisco General."

"How come?" Mike asked.

"He needs a specialist that's not available here," Toy answered.

"Does Sophie know yet?"

"No, and I'm afraid to tell her," Toy said.

"The longer you put it off, the worse it's going to be," Mike said.

"I am thinking about moving back to China!"

"Call her," Mike said.

The ambulance attendants arrived with the gurney for the transfer. After a few minutes they came out again with Pete. Pete was loaded into an ambulance. Toy and Chou started to climb in with him when one of the EMTs said, "There isn't enough room for you."

"Then you take a taxi," Toy said, pushing the guy aside. Somehow, room in the ambulance was found for everyone.

Mike and the others followed the ambulance up the 101 freeway. The hospital was ready for Pete, and he was whisked into the operating room. The hospital personnel would not let Toy and Chou into the operating room so they stood guard at the door.

Mike realized the call to Sophie had fallen on him.

Santa Barbara

Sophie answered the phone on her bedside table with some difficulty. Her vision was bad enough that she had trouble finding the phone. Finally picking up the receiver with an ominous foreboding, she said, "Hello?"

"Sophie, this is Mike. There's no easy way to say this but straight out. Pete's been shot."

"How bad is it?" Sophie wanted to know.

"I don't think it's too serious," Mike said, "but he's in surgery at San Francisco General. We'll know better when he comes out."

"Shit," Sophie said. "I am on my way. I'll be there as soon as I can."

She put on her leg and called the pilots. Then she went into the closet and found a robe. She raced across the hall and woke up Pete's mother.

"Pete's been shot. He is in surgery in San Francisco, and I am going there now."

"Sophie, you shouldn't travel. The babies are late. It's really a bad idea!"

"Right now my husband is on an operating table. I'm going to him no matter what. Besides, it's only a forty-minute flight. I have already called the pilots. The captain promised me he would put the hammer down, whatever that means."

"I'm coming, too."

Sophie went back in her room and put on a dress, then went back into Sally's room. She was dressed and starting to fill a suitcase.

"Forget that, we'll buy what we need when we get there. Let's go." Sally stood erect for a second and then turned and walked out behind Sophie. Sally had to drive the little white car to the airport with Sophie stuffed into the passenger seat, her belly almost touching the dashboard. When they arrived, the pilot was in his seat with the right engine running, and the copilot was standing by the door. As soon as Sally and Sophie entered, he closed the door. The captain started the other engine as the copilot took his seat. Since the tower was closed at that hour, they spun onto the runway and the pilot cobbed the power to it.

San Francisco

Less than an hour after receiving the phone call from Mike, Sophie and Sally walked into the hospital. "I'm Sophie Smith. I would like to see my husband. He came in earlier with a gunshot wound."

The receptionist looked in her computer. "He is still in surgery, ma'am. The waiting room is down this hall to the right."

Sophie started to say something but Sally put her hand on her arm saying, "Let's see if the others are in the waiting room." They found the waiting room with Mike, Dianne, Jack, and Marv there. Mike stood and started to speak when Dianne rushed around and hugged Sophie. Both Dianne and Sophie had tears coming down their cheeks.

"Sophie, I am so sorry," Dianne said. "We don't know anything yet. He's been in surgery for the last hour and a half."

"Where are Toy and Chou?" Sophie asked.

"They're standing guard in front of the operating room."

Forty agonizing minutes later, a surgeon came into the waiting room. "Mrs. Smith?" he said, looking around. When Sophie stood, he came over to her. "The operation went as well as I could have hoped. I went in and closed two holes in his intestine and stitched up the entry and exit wounds. I put a small piece of mesh inside the abdominal cavity under each wound point. He's doing fine. He's in the recovery room now."

"Can I see him?" Sophie asked.

"You can, but I would rather you didn't. At the moment, he looks worse than he is. He should be in his room by nine in the morning."

"How long will he be in the hospital?" Sophie asked.

"At least five days, but he cannot leave until his intestines begin working again; passing gas, etc. We need to know the holes in his intestines have sealed themselves and begun to heal. There is also the possibility of infection inside the abdominal cavity. We want to monitor him to be sure that doesn't happen."

"How do I get him a private room?"

"You need to talk to Nancy, the charge nurse. She'll take care of you."

"Thank you, doctor, I am sure you want to go back to bed," Sophie said. With that Sophie went looking for Nancy the charge nurse, and the doctor headed back to leave instructions for the nurses. Nancy turned out to be really sweet and said she would get Pete the best room she could and promised to keep an eye on him personally.

As they were walking out of the waiting room, Sophie said, "We need to get rooms at the nearest decent hotel or motel."

"Marv," Mike said, "You're up."

When they went to the parking lot they all walked to the blue van. Marv opened the side door and Sophie looked inside. She was impressed by the array of electronic gear. Marv went to work. "There's a Marriott a couple of miles from here and they have rooms available."

"Where did we get this thing?" Sophie asked.

"The CIA sent it to us. It came with Marv. Oh, sorry, Sophie, meet Marvin Applebaum," Mike said.

The next morning Sophie and Sally were back at the hospital. When they walked into Pete's room they found Toy and Chou. Sophie took one look at Pete and her heart broke. His color was pale, he had IVs in both arms, and he was hooked up to a couple of machines. She whirled on Toy and Chou and said in Cantonese, "I want whoever did this to Pete dead no later than tomorrow! Do you understand me? Dead!" she screamed, forgetting where she was for the moment.

"He is already dead," Toy said.

"Who shot him?"

"The boss shot him," Chou said.

A Chinese cleaning lady came out of the bathroom. She had heard and understood the entire conversation. She had also heard of Madame Gin Sling. Given what had just been said, the cleaning lady was sure she was looking at Madame Gin Sling, and her reputation was justified.

The fact that Madame Gin Sling's husband was a patient went around the hospital like wildfire. In an hour, it was common knowledge everywhere in Chinatown.

Around noon, Sophie sent Toy and Chou to the hotel for some rest. She had registered them when she had checked in, and she simply gave them the keys.

"Toy, give me a gun before you leave."

Sally was shocked when Toy handed Sophie a gun, and Sophie causally put it in her purse. Seeing the surprise on Sally's face, Sophie said, "I want to be sure no one tries to finish what they started. But don't worry, by tomorrow we will have enough bodyguards here." This started Sally worrying.

Sophie and Sally spent the day chatting lightly and watching Pete as a succession of nurses came and went. At six thirty, Toy came back looking much better.

"Chou will be here later."

In Cantonese Sophie said, "Get a hold of the head of the local triad and get some of his best shooters. I want twenty-four-hour coverage here until Pete leaves."

Toy nodded and left.

A short time later Sophie sent Sally back to the hotel. Sophie spent the night in the chair next to Pete's bed. The nurse had offered to bring Sophie a cot but she had declined. She wanted to know immediately if there was any change in Pete's condition. Toy stayed until one o'clock, when Chou arrived. By six o'clock in the morning, there were two local Chinese guys outside Pete's room. They checked the ID of anyone that wanted to get into Pete's room, which was driving the staff nuts, but they were undeterred.

The White House, Washington, D.C.

The President set aside his newspaper and picked up the phone. When his secretary answered he asked her if she would call the national security advisor to join him in the Oval Office.

When the national security advisor walked into his office, the President looked up calmly. He tossed the newspaper at his feet. "Apparently, two days ago there was a shootout in San Francisco that left a dozen terrorists dead, and I am just finding out about it by reading the newspaper. Now, I want know what happened, who did it, and who authorized it. And, I want to know now, GOD DAMM IT!"

"I'll see what I can find out."

A half hour later, impatient, the President picked up the phone and asked his secretary to get the national security advisor on the phone. When he came on the line, the President asked very calmly, "Well, what have you learned?"

"This operation has CIA roots, Mr. President. We think a retired general was running it. He is now in the Bay Area somewhere. We're trying to contact him as we speak, sir."

"If you haven't found him in fifteen minutes, turn the FBI lose." With that the President hung up.

The General had ignored the last six calls, but he finally decided something must be very important. "Hello," he answered groggily.

"General, this is the national security advisor. The President would like to speak with you. Please stand by while I conference him in.

The national security advisor came back on the line and said, "General, the President and the director of the CIA are now on the line. Go ahead, Mr. President."

"General, I understand you are aware of the events that gave rise to the Bay Area shootout. I would like a complete report of that event, if you will please."

"Mr. President, I don't yet have all the facts, but I will tell you what I know. About two and a half months ago, the CIA developed information that the largest drug dealer in Asia had been stockpiling arms for years. Apparently, forty cylinders of sarin gas made their way into his cache, and he agreed to sell a great deal of that extremely toxic gas to some crazies.

"Digressing a bit, if I may, this drug dealer was also in a dispute over the ownership of a hotel with a Mrs. Sophie Smith. He tried unsuccessfully to have her assassinated. Her husband is Col. Peter Smith, retired. Col. Smith spent the greater part of his career in Delta Force, and if I may say so, is a man to be reckoned with. He decided that the only way to eliminate the threat was to eliminate the drug lord. He and two associates spent thirteen days in the jungle tracking down the arms dealer's compound. The result was the total destruction of the arms cache, drug manufacturing capability, drug inventory, and the drug dealer himself.

"Unfortunately, the day they arrived they saw gas tanks being loaded on trucks and taken away before they could stop them.

"Subsequently, the CIA developed further information that the gas tanks were being smuggled through Ensenada, Mexico. The information was passed on to the FBI and Homeland Security. After two months, those agencies abandoned the active hunt.

"The CIA then hired several private security operators to look for a tunnel capable of smuggling the gas cylinders in to the States."

"One of those operatives was Col. Smith. He found the tunnel and the gas cylinders. The terrorists had started bringing them across the border at Calexico and storing them in a house on the U.S. side of the border before sending them on. Col. Smith made the decision to go into Mexico and seize the rest of the cylinders. He did so, destroying the tunnel as he left. The first shipment of cylinders got away from them, but they successfully tracked them down again. They called me, and I alerted the FBI, but it was clear the cylinders were in the process of being distributed for use among the general population. Col. Smith wanted to stop that. As they formulated their plans they waited for the FBI to arrive. They did not attack until they saw the terrorists loading the first tank into a car and it was pulling out of the driveway. The FBI hadn't arrived yet.

"During the ensuing action, the Colonel was wounded. His team accompanied him to the hospital, which is why they were not on the scene when the FBI finally arrived."

"That is an incredible tale, General," the President said.

"As I said earlier, I haven't been able to speak with the Colonel yet," the General said.

"Hire a stenographer and have her standing by so when the Colonel is ready to speak he can make a statement. I want a complete written report as soon as possible," the President said.

San Francisco

That same morning Pete awoke feeling like he'd been run over by a bus! He found Sophie sleeping in a chair next to his bed. Half an hour later the doctor came in making his rounds. Seeing him awake the doctor said, "How are you feeling?"

"Okay, I guess, considering," Pete said. Their short conversation woke Sophie. The doctor reviewed his chart.

"How is he doing, doctor?" Sophie asked.

"He's just fine. I see no problem. He should make a complete recovery."

"When do you think he will be able to come home?" Sophie wanted to know.

"He has to be passing wind before he can leave," the doctor reiterated. With that the doctor turned and left.

"How do you really feel?" Sophie asked.

"Not too bad really. How are you doing, Sophiapotamus?" Pete asked.

"I have been so worried," Sophie said.

"Well, right now I want you to go to a hotel somewhere and get some sleep. Okay?"

"I'll call Chou and get a ride back to our hotel," Sophie reluctantly agreed.

Just as Sophie was leaving, the General arrived. At first the guards would not let him into the room. Sophie waved at the guards to let the General pass. As he walked into the room, Sophie said, "When I have calmed down a little, General, we are going to have words. I am really pissed about this, do you understand me?"

The General felt a cold chill go up his spine, but he managed to say, "Sophie, I cannot tell you how upset I am about this."

Going through the door Sophie said over her shoulder, "Not as upset as you are going to be."

"Pete, she's not going to start a war with the CIA is she?"

"She's calmed down a lot since yesterday now that she knows I'm going to be all right. She'll probably keep cooling down, General. Toy told me that she walked into the room yesterday, took one look, and told him to kill the shooter. Toy told her the shooter was already dead, which is the only thing that stopped her."

"Good god!" the General said.

"She is a very formidable woman," Pete said.

"Well, you guys have really started a shit storm. I was on the phone with the President this morning. He wants a complete report, soon. I have a court reporter outside. Can I bring her in?" the General asked.

"Bring her in. Let's get this over with."

Two hours later, the General left. Pete had started to doze off again when Sophie and his mother came into the room. They both stayed until Pete fell asleep in the middle of their conversation.

Two days later Sophie and his mom were in his room before Pete's breakfast arrived. Sophie was standing by Pete's bed with his hand in hers when suddenly she said, "Damn!"

Pete's mother looked up sharply. Sophie explained, "My water just broke and filled up my leg again." Pete started laughing, and Pete's mom started grinning.

"Excuse me," Sophie said, "I have to go clean myself up a bit, I'm afraid."

Two hours later, the President's plane was on approach to San Francisco International. The election being only a year away, fund-raising season had started. Across the aisle from the President sat the national security advisor. The President said to him, "I just finished reading the entire report on the events that culminated here four days ago. It seems to me that this Colonel Smith consistently called the shots just perfectly, and he saved millions of lives in doing so. Further-more this guy is a private citizen."

When the President's plane had stopped in the private airplane parking area and the stairs had been moved into position, he stood up and asked, "Is the General meeting us?"

"Yes, sir, I thought you might have some questions for him," the national security advisor said.

At the bottom of the stairs, the President was introduced to Gen-eral Lane. The President said, "General, I want you to ride in my car."

"Yes, sir."

As they pulled out of the airport, the President asked the General if Colonel Smith was still in the hospital. He told the President he was, but that he thought he would be released the next day.

"General, tell the driver to take us to the hospital. You probably ought to give him the address, too." Radios started crackling as the agent in the front seat of the presidential limo advised everyone of the change of plans.

The motorcade stopped in front of the hospital, and the President and the General, accompanied by the Secret Service detail, walked directly through the lobby to the elevators. As they waited for the el-evator, the General noticed that the initial shock had worn off. People where running everywhere and phone lines were lighting up. The el-evator doors opened, and they boarded the elevator. On the way up the General asked the President, "You were in the navy, sir, weren't you?"

Somewhat surprised the President answered, "Yes."

"Did you ever make port in Hong Kong?"

"Yes. Where is this going, General?" The tone in his voice clearly indicated his patience was running thin.

"Did you ever hear of Madame Gin Sling, sir?"

"Everybody in the navy has heard of Madame Gin Sling."

"Well, sir, you are about to meet her. Mrs. Smith and Madame Gin Sling are one and the same."

"That will make this visit a double pleasure then," the President said, laughing.

They turned to the right coming out of the elevator. Toy and Chou were in front of the door to Pete's room. Toy said, "General, Mrs. Smith says you are not allowed to come in."

"Do you know who I am?" the President asked Toy.

Toy nodded. "I think it will be okay just this once," the President said, and they proceeded into the room as Toy stepped aside.

Entering Pete's room the President said, "Colonel Smith, I came by to thank you on behalf of a grateful nation," holding out his hand.

Pete shook his hand and said, "Mr. President, I would like to introduce you to my wife and my mother, sir."

He turned to Sophie and Sally, who had both stood up when the President entered the room. The President shook hands with each of them. To Sally he said, "You must be awfully proud of your son." And to Sophie he asked, "When is your baby due?"

"Babies, and they are overdue," Sophie replied.

"Twins," the President said, "that's wonderful." Turning to Pete he said, "If you are able, I would like you to recount the takedown for me."

As Pete started to speak to the President, Sophie indicated by twisting her head that she wanted the General to follow her. He did. They went into the bathroom. "General," Sophie said, "if you ever have any contact with any member of my family again, I will kill you." With that she walked past a slack-jawed General and back into the room just as Pete finished his description of the takedown for the President.

"Mrs. Smith, your husband is a very brave man." Seeing Sophie wince, he asked her, "What's wrong?"

"First contraction," she replied.

The President spun on the Secret Service agent saying, "Get a nurse with a wheelchair and have Mrs. Smith taken to the maternity ward." His tone left no room for argument, and the agent was off and running.

"Let me help you sit down," the President said to Sophie. Turning to Pete, he said, "Congratulations to you both on the imminent arrival of the newest members of your family. And Pete, I would like to thank you again for your service to the country."

"Mr. President, I just happened to be in the right place at the right time. I did what any other American would have done."

"That statement I do not agree with. When you are feeling better I want you both to come to the White House so I can pin a medal on you." Sophie was just beaming. The nurse arrived with the wheelchair and whisked her away. The President turned to Pete and said, "I have several thousand people waiting for me so I've got to run. Thank you again."

"Thank you for stopping by, Mr. President."

When Toy returned, Pete said, "Get me a wheelchair, will you?"

When Toy returned, Pete climbed into the wheelchair and held onto the IV pole. Toy pushed him to the labor room where Sophie lay waiting for her next contraction. This time it was his turn to hold her hand.

"I told you I would be here for you," he said

"You just forgot to mention the bullet holes and wheelchair."

Ten hours later, James Brian Smith entered the world. He was followed a half hour later by Philip Robert Smith. Mother and children were doing fine when Toy pushed Pete back to his room.

The next day the General called and passed Sophie's threat along to Pete.

"I'll let you know how serious she was about that in a couple of days," Pete told the General.

That afternoon Pete asked Sophie about it, finishing by repeating that she could not go to war with the CIA.

"Not going to have a war. Just a one-shot battle if he comes near us, and they going to lose their general," Sophie said, reverting to her Chinese-accented English.

Later that day, Pete spoke to the General saying, "It would probably be better, General, if you lay low for a while. Sophie is still pretty upset, but she will cool down."

"Understood. Thanks Pete."

*****

Three days later they all left for Santa Barbara, expecting tranquility to accompany them.

Once Sophie and Pete were ensconced in their bed Sophie turned to Pete and said, "You still never told me that you love me. Now, I want to know! I need to hear those words."

"My dear, I did but you weren't paying attention, as usual."

"When?"

"Look inside your wedding ring."

"I never take my wedding ring off," Sophie said.

"Well, slide it down your finger and read the inscription inside."

She did. After wiggling her glasses a bit to try and bring the small engraving into focus she gave up. So she opened the drawer in the bedside table and pulled out a magnifying glass. The engraving inside read,

"I will love you forever."

The End

About the Author

Jay Alt grew up in Connecticut. He graduated from United States International University with a Bachelor's degree in English Literature in June of 1971. He attended Western State University, College of law, graduating in June of 1975. Jay was admitted to the California bar Association shortly thereafter.

After practicing law for five years, Jay decided to pursue a career in aviation. He worked as a flight engineer for UPS, and then subsequently moved to a major airline in May of 1987.

Jay and his wife of forty-five years divide their time between Virginia and the island of Bequia in the southern Caribbean.

Easy the Cat

𝒥 found Easy when he was five weeks old. He stayed with me for a year and was always nearby.

Most of the time when I was writing, Easy was either dozing in my lap or he was busy keeping the gecko population in check.

The moment I finished Gin Sling, Easy disappeared. I like to think he left to chase "painted ladies". Perhaps he was a muse, sent to me for a brief stay.

www.ingramcontent.com/pod-product-compliance
Lightning Source LLC
Chambersburg PA
CBHW070626170726
48291CB00003B/901